PRAISE FOR AN UNSUITABLE JOB

Award Recognition
Gold Book Award (2026) — Literary Titan
Honored for excellence in historical fiction, storytelling craft, and character development.
American Writing Award (2025) — *Winner*
Recognizing outstanding achievement in historical mystery.

Editorial Praise
"*An Unsuitable Job* drops readers straight into Josie MacFarland's world and wastes no time showing the grit behind the glamour. The pages move fast, the dialogue stays crisp, and the world of 1930 New Mexico feels alive and loud."

"Hardy hits a sweet spot—simple, direct, no fluff. The mystery unfolds piece by piece, with just enough clues to keep readers leaning forward. Josie is easy to root for, especially when she pushes back against those who underestimate her."

— **Literary Titan**

"*An Unsuitable Job* completely swept me off my feet. Josie is witty, determined, and unafraid to break the rules in 1930s New Mexico. A gripping mystery, vivid setting, and a perfectly timed touch of romance make this a must-read."

"Bonnie Hardy has created a heroine whose inner strength rings true on every page. The tension between what's expected of Josie and what she demands of herself gives the story depth far beyond the crime."

"The ambiance of 1930s New Mexico—the hotel's charm, the era's hardships, and the quiet conflicts—comes vividly to life. I finished the book hoping Josie's journey continues, because she's a character worth following."

— **Jules Whitcomb, Dear Author Book Reviews / Speak Up Talk Radio**

A Celebrated Historical Mystery

Set in 1929 New Mexico at the elegant Castañeda Hotel, *An Unsuitable Job* introduces Josie MacFarland, a former Harvey Girl turned investigator—solving crimes in a world that insists she shouldn't. Praised for its authenticity, sharp dialogue, and quietly defiant heroine, this award-winning novel launches A **Harvey Girl Detective Mystery.**

AN UNSUITABLE JOB

AN UNSUITABLE JOB

BONNIE HARDY

ON THE OTHER HAND BOOKS

Copyright

2026 On the Other Hand Books

By Bonnie Hardy

All right reserved.

This is a work of fiction. Names, characters, places, and incidents either are the product of the author's imagination or are used fictitiously, and any resemblance of fictional characters to actual persons living or dead, business establishments, events, or locales is entirely coincidental.

AI has not been used in any aspect of this story.

All rights reserved. No part of this book may be used or reproduced in any manner without written permission from the author and publisher except in the case of brief quotations embodied in critical articles or reviews.

Ebook ISBN: 978-1-954995-46-8

Paperback ISBN: 978-1-954995-48-2

Hardcover ISBN: 978-1-954995-49-9

Cover Design by Ebook Launch

Editing by Proof Positive

ALSO BY BONNIE HARDY

For a full list please go to

bonniehardywrites.com/Books

Welcome to Lily Rock Holiday Mystery Novellas

'Tis the Season *

All Aboard for Murder *

Wrap it Up! *

Lily Rock Mystery Series

Getaway Death *

Influenced to Death *

Deadly Admission *

A Thymely Death *

Deadbeat Dad *

A Very Tidy Death *

Sit. Stay. Play Dead. *

An Avery Denning Mystery

Dead Drop in Lily Rock

Redondo and Rose Neighbors in Crime

A Doula to Die For *

Between the Sheets *

Sight Unseen *

An Unsuitable Job *

* Available for listening on Audible

CHAPTER ONE

*"A Harvey Girl must be neat, courteous, and reliable.
Above all, she must avoid entanglements.
Unless, of course, those entanglements are criminal in
nature."*

Harvey House Handbook for Western Division Employees

She was the last to step down from the train, her valise clutched tightly in one hand. Enveloped in the engine's exhale, a cloud of steam rose around her, ghostly and warm, momentarily veiling the bright blue sky.

Her nerves fluttered. The crowd surged past, jostling her elbow; the strap of her pocketbook slipped down her shoulder. She hitched it back up and straightened her spine.

Beneath the wide eaves of the station, a row of Indigenous vendors arranged their wares. Silver bracelets, leather concho belts, and polished stone fetishes glimmered against the indigo-and-ochre-colored hand-woven blankets. Native

American symbols had been etched into silver. There were cuff links, belt buckles, and slides for bolo ties. *Probably special orders*, Josie thought. *Tourists will pick up their item tomorrow, on the way to the next train station.*

This wasn't Josie's first time rolling into Las Vegas, New Mexico by train. She'd been here before, over a year ago, wearing the Harvey Girl uniform like it meant something. For a while, she made it work. Smiles on cue, coffee poured to the rim. Then came the mistake, and the long ride home in disgrace.

Now she was back. Not as some wide-eyed waitress hoping for tips and adventure, but as the Harvey Company's first official detective. Older, a little bruised, and no longer buying the silver-screen version of the Wild West. It had taken time to shake off those old ideas.

Back in Boston, she thought she knew what the West was, having been captivated by Saturday afternoon matinees. There were men with six-shooters, women in fringed skirts, and Native people painted in the same brushstrokes every time: braids, feathers, war cries. Hollywood had sold the myth. She'd bought it. But that was before. Now she knew the real West had shadows of its own. She'd learned the hard way.

One last glance at the crowd before her and she sighed. Leave it to Fred Harvey. Turning a train depot into an opportunity to make a buck. The Harvey Company hired the local Natives to meet the trains in full tribal dress, usually reserved for their sacred ceremonies.

A dash of the "exotic," right as the tourist stepped off the train. Just sanitized enough for everyone to feel safe. Josie wasn't sure who was benefitting more, the artisans or the company cashing in on their authenticity.

Everything had been orchestrated for tourists to have

just enough time to buy trinkets, grab a quick meal, and head for a night to the Castañeda Hotel. Some even picked up a side trip called an Indian Detour.

I'm not one of them, Josie reminded herself. *I'm here for my second shot.* Whatever waited in Las Vegas, it wouldn't catch her off guard this time.

Beyond the thinning crowd and the clattering of boots on wooden walkways, Josie spotted the familiar exterior of the Castañeda Hotel. Fred Harvey, the founder of the Harvey House Company, strived to make his accommodations and restaurants convenient, at least within sight from the rails. *Enough looking*, she reminded herself.

"Step this way to the Harvey House dining room," a man shouted in a penetrating baritone. "If you've reserved your meal, go this way. If you haven't, on the other side." He pointed with a gloved finger. He wore a well-tailored black jacket with a Harvey House emblem displayed over the breast pocket along with matching slacks. The white dress shirt underneath appeared unwrinkled.

Josie brushed under her chin, remembering the days when she wore a big Harvey Girl bow at the collar of her blouse. It distinguished the girls from everyone else. Some had compared the Harvey Girls' sparse black and white outfits to a nun's habit. Easily recognizable to harried travelers, Harvey employees announced the Harvey House ideal: dependable and efficient, with a touch of class.

"Will the food come quickly? I don't want to miss my connection," an anxious traveler asked.

"Yes. You'll have plenty of time to finish your meal and get back on the train. Mr. Harvey aims to please. You are our valued customer." He smiled, showing a row of crooked teeth.

Josie cinched the belt of her tan coat to her slim waist. She adjusted the hat box off her arm. "Why do you need that?" her mother asked when she'd first packed. "Your cloche will do. No need for an extra. You'll be home soon enough." She'd sniffed.

For me to know and you to never find out, Josie thought.

No one was more shocked than Josie when she'd gotten the call. The Harvey Company had offered her a new position. "Let bygones be bygones," the head of hiring assured her. "Mr. Harvey really needs the help of a woman such as yourself. Our reputation must be protected at all costs. He thought you might want another chance to make up for your mistakes."

With an opportunity for redemption laid at her feet, Josie couldn't refuse. She explained to her mother right afterward. "I'll be the first woman detective hired by the Harvey Company. That has to mean something. They noticed my worth."

"Perhaps," her mother admitted. Then with characteristic deflection she added, "I'll help plan your wardrobe." As if that was all that mattered, how her daughter looked.

Shoving a strand of red hair under her cloche, she tugged on the brim to cover her eyes. She knew she stood out in a crowd. She was very tall for a woman. And then a second glance would reveal her enigmatic green eyes.

"Miss MacFarland." A man dressed in the Harvey House porter's uniform tipped his cap.

She nodded curtly. "I'm Josephine MacFarland." She did her best to sound official, conveying her new job status by using her full name.

""I apologize for being late. You're expected." He took

the valise and the hat box from her hand. "You're a tall one, aren't you?" He gave her a once-over before elbowing his way into the crowd.

"Six feet without heels," she responded matter-of-factly. She sized him up. "What are you? Five five or so?"

"Five eight," he huffed, obviously offended.

Accustomed to men exaggerating their height, she withheld a grin. She'd felt his observation as a come-on, a danger sign. She vowed to keep silent until they reached the hotel. *No use talking back. He'll think I'm flirting.*

The Castañeda, a magnificent and imposing sight, stood ahead. Built against the arid backdrop of the Southwest desert landscape, it had a presence. Not East-Coast-fancy-hotel kind of presence, but distinctive in its own right. The Mission Revival architecture exuded rugged charm, with its sweeping red-tiled roof, stucco walls, and arched colonnades that framed the entrance. Richly stained wood outlined a row of large windows, which softened the baked stucco appearance.

Box planters had been arranged along the courtyard, filled with geraniums, hollyhocks, and desert flora. A scattering of cottonwood trees provided patches of shade. Well-dressed guests strolled leisurely along the gravel pathways, their laughter mingling with the sound of water trickling in the nearby fountain.

The porter tapped her elbow, directing her toward the lobby entrance. Handmade tile floors, patterned in a Spanish design, contrasted with the adobe walls and the high beam ceiling. The arched doorways also echoed the Mission-Revival style.

Dominating the room was a massive fireplace with a wide hearth. Wrought iron chandeliers with candles would be lit later, to cast a gentle glow over the oversized leather chairs arranged in conversational clusters. All in all Josie felt quite at home in the understated Southwestern elegance of the Castañeda. The porter dropped her bag in front of the wooden reception desk. "Here she is," he announced abruptly.

"Miss MacFarland, I presume?" The man behind the desk barely looked up, his voice flat.

"At your service." She tapped the brim of her cloche with one gloved finger, letting the words hang between them. Too breezy for the moment, but if she didn't pretend to be calm, she might start to shake.

He didn't smile. Didn't blink. Just reached for the counter bell with a heavy hand. "Your room is ready," he said.

Before he could ring, she caught his wrist. "Not my room," she said. "I'm here for the dead body."

He stared, his mouth slightly open.

She fished the telegram from her bag and slid it across the polished wood. He read in silence. When he looked up, his brow pinched.

"Is there some confusion?" she asked. "More than one corpse upstairs?"

The man pulled back his shoulders, his full height shadowing her. "No need for sarcasm, Miss MacFarland," he said. "We moved the gentleman to storage." He paused, eyes narrowing. "You know the way."

CHAPTER TWO

The hotel storage room smelled of damp earth and wooden crates. Shelves lined two walls with stacks of canned goods and cleaning supplies. A single light bulb hung from the ceiling. Muffled voices and footsteps filtered down from overhead.

Josie's nerves tingled; her mind raced. The Castañeda Hotel was a first for Fred Harvey. He'd worked with the Aitchison, Topeka, and Santa Fe railroad executives to realize his vision. A series of luxury hotels with restaurants for travelers along the expansive line, redefining the American Southwest. A cornerstone of hospitality, the Castañeda was an example for the rest.

But now, almost 1930, Josie was here for a different reason. Not hired as a Harvey Girl but to help her former company avoid a possible scandal. The Harvey Company's business reputation needed tending, especially since the stock market fall.

The man who'd called to hire her back made it quite clear. It was her job to keep the Harvey name out of the headlines. "No snooping reporters," he'd insisted. "Bad for business. Our revenue is down due to fewer travelers."

Josie drew her thoughts back to the present. The sight of a body lying on a table, shrouded under a sheet made her wince. *I'd better have a look*, Josie realized.

Folded napkins were stacked and placed under a pair of polished boots sticking out from under the sheet. Her stomach twisted in anticipation. She swallowed the lump in the back of her throat, delaying the inevitable.

But the sight of a pencil and a small pad of paper caught her eye. *Someone must have left it near the basin. Maybe they were in a hurry.*

She picked up the notepad and dropped it in her handbag.

Steeling herself once again, she peeked under the sheet. *My first dead body. He looks peaceful enough.* His eyelids were closed, his lips slightly open. His hands folded over his chest as if in prayer. Despite the coolness of the room, her forehead broke out in perspiration.

She dropped the sheet right as the door behind her opened. Josie turned quickly to find a young woman wearing a Harvey Girl uniform. Her starched white apron fell over the black dress. *Neat as a pin*, Josie thought, her heart beating rapidly. Lily was always the most immaculate of all the girls in their class.

"As I live and breathe. It's Lily Davenport." Josie was the first to speak.

Lily smiled but looked away quickly. She was a compact young woman, a foot shorter than Josie. She held her arms across her chest, a protective gesture Josie knew well.

Lily returned her gaze, a look of distrust on her face.

Tempted to reach over and straighten the bow at her

collar, Josie stopped herself. *That's what a friend would do. I have no idea where I stand now.*

Lily looked her up and then down. "So you weren't abducted. I heard the rumor, but it sounded fantastic even for you. What's this, a drop-in visit?"

"I'm a Harvey House detective. The first female, as it happens." Then sensing more disapproval, she added hastily, "An unsuitable job for a woman. I know."

Lily shrugged and then glanced down at her polished shoes. At the same time her hand reached to straighten the bow at her neck. "You never were like the rest of us," she admitted.

Josie wondered if the gesture was an attempt to cover up her nerves. This situation wasn't easy for either of them. "Let's have a look at you." Lily stepped closer and kept talking. "Who wears a coat like that in New Mexico?" Her eyes narrowed.

"It's great to see you," Josie offered. "Mother's idea, the coat. But as to my reason for being here..." She stepped aside to reveal the corpse.

Lily's brown eyes grew wide. "I was the one to discover him. That's why Matron sent me as soon as you got here. Just this morning, I knocked on the door for his usual wake-up reminder. When he didn't answer, I opened the door. And there he was with his pants down, spread on the floor. A big gash on the side of his head, blood everywhere." She looked away.

"I screamed. The porter arrived. Matron—you remember Delores Delgado? She stuck her nose in. Then Sheriff Cortez with two men. I was rushed away, but not before I saw them wrap the body in a rug."

"They probably wanted to remove him quickly, before

one of the guests figured out something was amiss," Josie explained.

"That would be the Harvey way," Lily admitted.

Josie detected the sound of exhaustion in her voice. But all the Harvey Girls sounded the same after a few days on the job. Run off their feet, the young women barely had a moment for themselves.

Josie lifted the sheet for the second time to ask Lily, "Is this the man, the same one you found?"

Lily shuddered. "That's him. Robert Trask. People called him Bobby. He was a frequent guest. A salesman. A real bounder. Had a different woman in his room every night. Sometimes more than one," she added quietly.

Lily hesitated. "I don't suppose I should've told you that though. It's against company policy to discuss the guests with outsiders."

"I'm hired by the company!" Josie insisted, though she knew she sounded defensive. The Harvey House rules of propriety had always rubbed her the wrong way, and she resented the constraints.

What she wanted was to fling her arms around Lily and say she was sorry for the way she'd run away without an explanation. But now was obviously not the time.

"Bobby's most frequent visitor was the rancher's daughter, Adelle DiWitt," Lily admitted. Forthcoming to a fault, she flushed. Lily did enjoy a bit of gossip now and then.

Josie knew about Adelle. She'd been the topic of much speculation in the past. The Harvey Girls had spent hours contemplating the debutante's lifestyle. Her beautiful clothing, how men swarmed around her wherever she went. Adelle wore the latest fashions and had been educated in England. Rich. Privileged. Beautiful. Every man's dream.

"You said a lot of women visited Bobby's room at night..." Josie wanted to hear more.

"Not just Adelle," Lily admitted. "But I won't name names. Not that I associate with women like that.'

"What brought Mr. Trask to the Castañeda so frequently?"

"We were on his usual sales route. He sold lots of expensive jewelry, most of it Native. He'd commission American Indians to make special items and then sell them to tourists. Even some locals."

Josie made note of that information for later. But before she could ask another question, Lily turned to leave.

"Good luck with your new job. See you around." Her old friend left without a backward glance.

CHAPTER THREE

Sheriff Mateo Cortez leaned his elbows on his desk in front of him. Josie's heart skipped a beat. His chiseled chin and open gaze made her feel unsettled. *He's a real looker, even for an older man.*

Openly appraising her from his side of the desk, he spoke in a smooth voice. "Buenos días, señorita," he said. Then he slipped into flawless English. "So you're the new Harvey House detective. I was informed by the company office that you'd be arriving today."

"Josephine MacFarland. But people call me Josie." She felt her face burn under his scrutiny.

"Most unsuitable," he said quietly. "To employ such a young woman for such a difficult job." When he refused to drop his appraising gaze, her discomfort increased. Her leg under the table began to jiggle.

Those dark eyes and that deep russet skin. His thick straight hair combed back. The way the smile lurked at the corner of his mouth. She felt his charm keenly. She suspected he knew full well his effect on women.

She gulped and stared at him with an unabashed defiance. He was her main source of information about Bobby Trask. This was no time to get all flustered.

Josie reached for her handbag and pulled out the notebook. "I assume this is yours?"

When he scowled she explained further. "You left this next to the body." She slid it across the expanse of desk. He caught it in one outstretched hand.

"I was a bit in a hurry," he explained. "It was necessary for me to interview the upstairs maid, Lily Davenport. Her shift was ending, and I wanted to get her account before she forgot any details." He took the notebook and slid it into a drawer.

"I didn't read your notes," she assured him. "I thought you might want to tell me in your own words." She hoped her discretion would impress him. Reaching back into her bag, she removed her own leather-bound notebook. She opened to the first page, licked the tip of her pencil, and waited for him to speak.

"The victim's name is Robert Trask. People called him Bobby," the sheriff began.

She looked up with a glare. "I already know that."

His eyes flashed. "Did you hear he's a frequent visitor to Las Vegas?"

She made a note in her notebook, not admitting that this too, was old news.

"That's it, señorita," the sheriff finished. His smile felt like a goodbye. *Or an adios*, Josie thought. Leaving now would admit defeat. He'd not shared any new information, so she tried another tactic. One she'd used to distract her father growing up. Stating the facts outright often made him uncomfortable. Maybe because he couldn't pretend she'd not heard him the first time.

"Let me summarize. We've got Robert 'Bobby' Trask

dead in the Castañeda Hotel storage room. He's a frequent visitor to Las Vegas; always stays in the same room. He sells Native jewelry, with individual designs, that's made to order.

"You've never had any actual reason to arrest him before, though you've heard rumors about his behavior with women." She tapped her pencil on her chin. "Did I get everything?" She used her most engaging smile, which he would certainly know was meant to mock the little he gave her.

"He's been seen around town with several young women in the community," Cortez hastily added. "Though not respectable ones. I did hear that he's made a nuisance of himself with a few of the Harvey Girls. Of course those are rumors spread by locals. Las Vegas was labeled years ago as, can I say, less than decent. I'm afraid that's all I have for now." He didn't sound afraid or one bit apologetic. When Josie made notes in her book, he didn't say more.

"Who could blame us? Young women. On their own. No family around. An unwelcome addition to our way of life." Josie wanted to defend herself and her old friends. But she feared her past would rear its ugly head. And no matter how big a hat, it wouldn't cover her mistake.

"So the one woman I interviewed..." Josie didn't use Lily's name. "She told me about Mr. Trask, his frequent visits to the Castañeda. But what I want to know is the cause of death."

Sheriff Cortez frowned. "Dr. Christy will have that in her report. From what I could see, the victim was struck on the side of his head. Right here." He pointed to his temple.

"Dr. Christy?"

"A qualified Las Vegas physician. She runs a small

clinic. She mostly treats locals, travelers, and railroad workers. And women. They have specific needs." He sniffed.

"Was Trask a frequent patient?"

"I don't know." He'd let his impatience get the better of him. "I doubt if Dr. Christy will give you any information about her patients, since you aren't from here."

"Dr. Christy is a female..." Josie was surprised.

"She's a Black doctor, quite unusual. Unacceptable job for a woman, of course. But she refuses to leave."

Josie made another note in her book. "Thank you for this information. I'll report to my employers. That should be all for now." She slipped her pencil and notebook back into her purse and stood.

The sheriff came around the desk to open the office door. He cautioned, "Don't forget it's siesta time in Las Vegas. Things slow down in the heat of the day."

"I thought the midday siesta was a thing of the past," Josie said.

"Sí, señorita. But some of us live by the old ways. Many of the prominent Las Vegas families, like my own, go back three generations and more. So understandably, we take a break, which is our custom."

Again he'd told her what she already knew, as she anticipated, but she had gained information.

"Adios," she said, adapting a jaunty tone.

As soon as she arrived back at the Castañeda, Josie stopped at the reception counter.

"Your bag is in your room," the employee explained.

She made her way toward the stairs, wanting nothing more than to freshen up and unpack.

On first glance, the single bed looked inviting. The

spread was carefully tucked over the pillow, most likely by a Harvey Girl on early rounds. Her valise had been placed on the bed. A tall wooden wardrobe and a small dresser provided plenty of storage.

She shook out a navy-blue day dress with piping. Reaching back into the bag, she lifted a white silk blouse with lace trim and then a high-waisted pleated charcoal-gray skirt. Before she'd left Boston, her mother had advised, "You can wear either to mass on Sunday."

Her shoes came next. A pair of leather Mary Janes for special occasions. Finally the heaviest item, a pair of riding boots. Sturdy leather with pointed toes. Not jodhpurs, as she wore growing up, but Western-style. Women wore cowboy boots during the day in Las Vegas. Her mother hadn't seen her slip them into her suitcase.

Alongside her luggage was the hat box. She opened the top and lifted the tissue paper, revealing a black leather cowboy hat. She ran her fingers along the band and then secured the feather underneath. The hat brought her a sense of peace. It represented her way out when she felt trapped, mostly by the expectations of others.

A top shelf in the wardrobe provided enough space for the hat, now back in its box. She hung her clothing and lined up her shoes next to each other on the floor beneath.

Unpacking her nightgown and underthings, she slid them into an empty drawer in the small oak dresser, then folded a pair of riding pants and a ruffled shirt, tucking them behind the rest.

Josie placed her handbag on the small round table that sat under the window. The curtain had been pulled aside, revealing the street below. Railroad Avenue was lined with familiar shops and businesses, including the general store and a barber shop. At the end of the street was a saddlemaker. Only a handful of people hurried to the train as the last whistle sounded.

Two cowboys stood talking in front of the general store, laughing as a Model A drove past. The driver honked. One cowboy waved his hat in greeting.

Her glance fell on a third man, who stood apart from the others. He looked familiar. Obviously Native American. Dressed in brown pants and a natural linen shirt, he'd turned his back, revealing a long braid of thick dark hair. She noted his leather hat, the crow's feather tucked into the band, and the way his hand patted his horse's nose.

She suspected he was listening to the conversation between the two cowboys. He'd managed to make himself less conspicuous by tending to his horse.

Josie turned from the window as a knock came at the door.

"Who's there?" she called.

Lily Davenport opened the unlocked door and stuck her head through. "I've brought warm corn bread straight from the kitchen. You must be hungry."

Josie's heart leapt. Maybe there was hope to rekindle their friendship after all.

CHAPTER FOUR

Josie licked the butter off her fingers. "It's good to know the corn bread is still the best I've ever eaten."

"It's the chili peppers," Lily commented. "They dice the green ones. I watched so I could tell my mother. Sent her the recipe in my weekly letter home."

"I thought sharing Harvey recipes was a no-no?" Josie had never been that interested in what went on inside the kitchen. "I bet all the popular ones are kept under lock and key. In a secret vault. Under Freddy's bed..." Freddy being the son of Ford, the heir apparent.

Lily giggled.

Josie took another bite. "How did you do it, by the way?"

"I stepped out with one of the dishwashers," Lily said. "He got me in the kitchen, so long as I kept out of the way. I wanted to know what went on behind the scenes." She covered the empty corn bread basket with a linen napkin. "I have a good memory, so I wrote the recipe on paper as soon as I could. But now I want to know more from you. Did you meet the sheriff?" Lily's cheeks reddened.

"He's quite good-looking," Josie admitted.

"I know," Lily murmured. "But not interested in me. He steps out with women above our status. No Harvey Girls."

Josie sighed. "Not surprising. But he does have charm. Anyway, I need to get into the room where Trask's body was found. Can you help with that?" Aware that she was asking a big favor, she was prepared to be turned down.

Lily gazed out the window. "Passengers are heading to the afternoon train. Time for me to get back to work. I have evening rounds." She glanced at her watch that she'd pinned to her starched blouse. Josie felt the rebuff keenly.

It wouldn't do to nag her friend. She understood her reluctance. Plus if Lily got caught, she could be fired and sent away.

But then Lily surprised her with a quick nod. "Okay, I'll take you to the room. But on one condition. Wait until the train leaves the station. After that, Matron will be busy making inspections across the street at the Women's Dormitory. We will have a better chance of going unnoticed."

"I really appreciate this," Josie blurted. "And so you know, I'll explain everything—what happened to me, why I left in such a hurry. But for now, let's get a move on. I want to have a look at the room. I'm certain that the sheriff won't give me access. Do you suppose the maids have already cleaned?"

"There's a chance Mr. Trask's room won't be on the rotation as of yet," Lily explained. "We are understaffed, not like when you were here. Since the stock market crash, a lot of us were laid off. A few got married. A couple went to college on scholarships." She looked away as the hoot of the warning whistle filled the air.

Josie stood, brushing her hands against her dress. "That's our signal."

. . .

Lily slipped inside the room first, grabbing Josie's hand. "Hurry," she insisted.

Josie's eyes were drawn right to the unmade bed. "No service yet," she commented. A shudder came over her. *The last place Trask slept before his death.*

"This room is bigger than mine, that's for sure." Josie continued to look it over. There was a basin with a used towel on one wall. A dressing screen stood in the corner, next to the wardrobe. The screen was tall enough for the person behind to change clothes without being seen.

"This room is one of the preferred locations, next to a parlor on the second floor," Lily commented dryly.

"Nice view," responded Josie. "I'm surprised a salesman would deserve such special treatment."

Lily held her finger over her lips. "We don't want to be overheard."

Josie's eyes widened. "Would other maids know about the body?"

"Everyone knows. I heard talk at my break," Lily quietly added. "I think even Dolores knows—you know what she's like."

Josie, like all the Harvey employees, knew that Delores Delgado had worked her way up the ranks. "She's been an employee for Fred for so many years. I don't think she has a real life."

The Harvey Girls would comment, with a hint of competition, that Delores Delgado had more years on her employment pin than anyone else. She displayed it on her apron with great pride. Delores had a bigger salary, more traveling perks, and plenty of vacations to go along with her service.

"The matron saint," Josie said.

"Still worthy of her name." The corner of Lily's mouth raised.

Josie nodded and then continued to take in the room, this time more slowly. Her eyes stopped on the bed. The covers lay strewn over the side, one sheet draped on the floor. The hem soaked in a pool of dark liquid, probably Bobby's blood, now congealed in a circular pattern on the floorboards below.

She shuddered and directed her gaze toward a dressing screen that stood in the corner. Built on a carved wooden frame, the panels were embossed leather, both decorative and practical. The screen provided privacy but it also took up a significant amount of space.

She wondered: Was Bobby Trask the kind of man who needed privacy when he dressed? Probably not. But maybe a lady would, if she were interested in seducing him and wanted to play cat and mouse, dropping her clothing as she went, like a striptease.

A bright glare from the window cast a glimmer of the last rays of sunshine into the room. Josie blinked. *No time for dillydallying*, she reminded herself.

"Is this where you found the body?" She pointed.

"Yes," Lily whispered. "Face down on the floor, blood oozing from his temple." Josie could tell by the tremor in her voice that Lily had been unnerved by the whole experience. *Who wouldn't be*, Josie admitted to herself.

She turned back to Lily and noticed something lodged underneath her shoe. She pointed to where a paper protruded.

Lily looked down and shook her head. "I have no idea where I picked that up. Looks like a note or something."

Josie bent down and gave the paper a tug. She smoothed the wrinkled scrap to read. "At the church. Ten o'clock."

The handwriting was distinctive. Legible and printed in block letters. *It could be a man or a woman's writing.*

Josie's face flushed with excitement. "Did someone slip it under the door? I wonder if he read it before he, you know, died."

"Bobby could have dropped the note," Lily suggested. "If the window were open, it could have drifted under the bed. Then when we came in, I may have gotten it on my shoe without realizing."

"This is a note about a clandestine meeting at the church," Josie mused.

"It was most likely a woman." Lily sounded certain.

"Have a look at the writing."

Lily took the note to inspect. "I can't tell. Block letters could be either. If not one of Bobby's women, maybe one of his pals. They come and go a lot." She looked toward the door, her mouth tightening.

A loud voice came from the hallway.

"We need to go," Lily insisted. She reached for Josie's hand. "The mere hint of impropriety..." Her sentence trailed off. "On top of me being the one to discover a dead man. Who knows what Delores is up to."

The door opened wide.

"This room is strictly off limits." Delgado used her imperious voice, the one where she rolled the *r*'s to emphasize her displeasure. She also wore her triumphant expression, the one she reserved for getting Harvey Girls into trouble.

Josie flinched.

The matron saint, hands on hips, refused to budge.

CHAPTER FIVE

Josie extended her hand in greeting. "Hello, Miss Delgado. I am here on Harvey House business." She'd been instructed years earlier on how to speak and behave. Her mother hired a woman to give her lessons. Of course, she'd played down her carefully articulated voice when she was a Harvey Girl waitress because she wanted to fit in. But now she used it to push back Delgado.

The matron scowled, glancing at Josie's hand as if she were offered a smelly fish. Her lip curled. Josie dropped her hand. Finally Miss Delgado dabbed at her nose with a lace handkerchief. "I heard about your employment." She sounded disbelieving, as if what she'd heard had to be gossip.

Josie watched the woman carefully. How she folded her handkerchief into a square with the embroidered letter C in the corner.

"So you don't remember me." Surprise rang in Josie's tone.

"I know who you are. I just can't believe they'd hire you for the detective job." She sniffed. "Of course I called

Chicago to confirm. I was instructed to help you in any way I can." She sounded anything but approving. She looked Josie up and down. "Eventually you'll be shown the door, just like the time before."

"I must be your personal nightmare," Josie laughed. "Like the proverbial bad penny." She wasn't going to let Matron know that her disapproval still mattered.

It was time to include Lily in this standoff. "Miss Davenport will be helping me with my initial inquiries. Naturally I wanted to interview her first. All of this will be put in my report. Your cooperation included."

Delores shrugged. "You look quite different in that getup." She nodded at Josie's carefully tailored green dress.

"No more aprons and bows for me," Josie added with a cheeky grin. "But speaking of uniforms, we need to get Lily returned to her morning duties."

"Back to work, young lady. I'll be watching. Spit spot." Delores opened the door wider to let Lily pass.

"Nice seeing you again." Josie waited for Lily to scurry ahead before following her out and slamming it shut.

"That was a close one," Lily whispered. "I thought for sure she'd dismiss me on the spot. But you saved me." Josie waited for a thank-you, but it didn't come. Lily wasn't going to give her that, at least not yet.

Lily left Josie in the lobby. Josie wanted to thank her for the information, but she'd headed upstairs before she could.

From train, to basement, to the sheriff's office, and finally the victim's room. Josie wandered through the lobby, feeling the weight of her tired legs. Not sure what to do next.

Men reading newspapers were seated in worn leather

chairs. Ladies sat demurely close by, waiting for the first call to the dining room. Others already stood in a line for the doors to open. Josie made her way past, ducking her head to avoid being noticed.

I need to freshen up. She headed to her room.

The first thing she thought of once the door was closed, was how she'd love to take a bath. She laid her towel and washing kit on the bed. Wrapping a robe securely around her waist, she had everything she needed. Towel and washing kit in hand, she made her way down the hall to the shared bath. Fortunately it stood open.

Josie filled the clawfoot tub, exhaling as she lowered her body into the warm water. She leaned her back against the porcelain side. After a few minutes her mind circled. The sheriff was at the forefront.

He'd instructed people to clear out the crime scene and move the body, Josie knew. There was no sign of a weapon. But he'd missed one thing. That note. Josie felt satisfied that she at least had a possibly important clue he did not.

The bloodstain on the floorboards was an obvious sign of foul play. The quick way the sheriff got rid of the body, slightly curious. Then he'd been in such a hurry he'd left his notebook. *Why didn't I read what was inside?* Josie chastised herself. *What was he going to do, arrest me for unlawful snooping?* Her inability to stand up to authority, her obvious deference, had gotten in her way of learning more.

The memory of Cortez's look, his liquid brown eyes staring at her from across the desk. *He's certainly handsome.* She paused to run her washcloth over her arm. *I have to give him that.*

She squeezed warm water onto her chest. Her pulse quickened. Safe from the mesmerizing stare of Cortez, she made another mental note. *Don't be distracted by the chiseled chin and dark lashes and those eyes...*

Delores Delgado came next. Her refusal to shake hands. Her obvious disapproval of the Harvey Company hiring a former employee with a dubious past. Josie shivered. No wonder people were afraid of the matron. She felt her disdain in her heart. It made her jittery, wondering what punishment would come next.

She sank further into the water. It would take a firm resolve not to let Matron get the best of her again.

Finally she considered Lily. How much she'd missed her gentle and hard-working friend. Like many of the Harvey Girls, Lily sent money home. Things were tough for farming families. She had a clear understanding of her purpose in life, and Josie respected that.

Since money had never been a concern for Josie, she felt different. She'd answered the Harvey Girl advertisement on a whim, looking for adventure. Unlike Lily, who would have stayed home if her family didn't need her income.

Stepping out of the tub, Josie reached for her towel. She circled back on her feelings about the matron. It occurred to her that Delgado might be a suspect. Always on the prowl, checking every room. *Who's to say she didn't have a fling with Bobby herself? Now that would be rich...* But then her thoughts returned to Lily.

I'm not sure I deserve such a loyal friend. I know we've been thrown back together, but that doesn't mean we can pick up from before. Good luck or divine intervention? she wondered. Josie hoped that she'd get a chance to redeem herself in Lily's eyes.

She slipped on her robe. The gurgle of the tub emptying followed her out the door.

. . .

Seated at her table in front of the window, Josie licked the tip of the lead on her pencil. At the top of a fresh page, she made succinct notes on what she'd observed herself, not from secondhand witnesses.

She pulled the note out of her pocket to read again. Tapping the pencil on her chin, she wondered which church... There were several in Las Vegas. Then it occurred to her that maybe the meeting hadn't already happened, maybe it was scheduled for tonight.

She made a quick decision. *I'll start at the one church I know. If that's not the place, I'll look elsewhere.*

Once she arrived in Las Vegas, she attended Our Lady of Sorrows, a Catholic congregation in Old Town, every week. Going to church was the one promise her mother exacted before letting her leave Boston.

Josie closed her notebook. She pulled the curtain across the window. *Dinner first,* she decided. *But this time I won't be the waitress.*

CHAPTER SIX

The warm glow from the wrought-iron chandeliers illuminated the elegant Castañeda dining room. Crisp white cloths covered each table. They'd been meticulously set, with perfectly polished silverware, gleaming crystal glasses, and porcelain plates, each with the Harvey House insignia.

Harvey Girls, dressed in long skirts with high-collared blouses, moved smoothly across the wooden floor. Their starched aprons rustled. Like nuns, they kept their eye contact to a minimum.

The familiar walk brought up memories of her first days of Harvey Girl training. How she'd been instructed to move her body in such a way that you appeared to glide. Then came the bow-tying lesson. It had to be just so at the back of the apron, and the one under her chin required frequent adjustment. Before class was over, each girl stood in front of Matron to receive her curt nod of approval.

Lively notes filled the dining room, coming from the grand piano. Josie's spirit lifted to accompany the Scott Joplin rag. The low hum of conversation came from diners who were already seated. The player ended the syncopated tune, shifting to a modern version of "Embraceable You." The voices didn't stop.

The smell of fresh coffee scented the air. Fred Harvey was known for the quality of his brew, poured from polished silver carafes that were emptied and refilled every hour. Josie remembered the time spent polishing until her knuckles ached.

And what about those surprise visits!

Ford Harvey, son of Fred the founder, would pop in. He'd taken over from his father after his death and he still made the occasional unexpected visit. The train had a special whistle to alert employees Ford was minutes away. His father's reputation of spotting a fingerprint on a crystal glass from across the room was legendary. "He'd smash that glass on the floor," an employee had warned. "Make sure you're not the one who leaves the print."

Josie's eye traveled over the room. Servers pushed through swinging doors, balancing large trays laden with food. Roasted meats, fresh vegetables, and an array of pies and baked desserts. Fred Harvey's reputation was as polished as his silver when it came to food.

Everyone said that he'd brought a gourmet elegance to the old West. It included his generous hospitality, which was served up by a parade of attractive young women—the Harvey Girls.

"Just a moment, miss," the hostess addressed Josie.

This gave her time to look over the other guests who were arrayed in formal wear, with women in long dresses and men in stylized Western suits. She knew the clientele from before. Some were visitors to Las Vegas. Others were wealthy landowners and part of the local gentry. Josie was familiar with a few of the faces. She'd served them in the past.

Local ranchers took their families out to dinner for special occasions. It was common to request the same Harvey Girl to wait on their table. Those girls felt special. They also appreciated the tip left under a plate.

One large table in the back alcove accommodated a familiar set of faces. The DiWitts. Their land was prime property, nestled on the edge of the Great Plains, where they raised cattle and horses beneath the beauty of the Sangre de Cristo Mountains. They were the envy of the town and the most prominent family.

Josie had bumped elbows with the DiWitts and their hired cowboys when she was a Harvey Girl. Mostly at the rodeo. Never as their special waitress. Adelle, the only daughter, was always a subject of gossip. HNow Josie's thoughts returned to the rodeo, where she'd met Daniel and ridden Rio. Such good times.

Tonight the DiWitts had dressed for a special dinner out. Frank and his son, Frankie, wore tailored black suits, the crisp white collars accented with a handcrafted bolo tie. Mrs. DiWitt and Adelle wore elegant evening dresses. The older woman in burgundy. Her daughter in a shimmery light green.

Other diners glanced over occasionally before returning their attention to someone at their own table. Josie wondered what it would be like to be looked at all the time. When you ate and when you walked into town. She knew she'd not be comfortable with so much attention.

The DiWitt family only had eyes for each other this evening. They took their notoriety as their due. The men exchanged stories, while women nodded politely. The voices were pitched low and sounded well-mannered.

"Your table is ready, come this way."

Josie followed the waitress across the room. She ducked her head to cover her discomfort. The Harvey Girl left her with a small nod. Josie picked up her napkin.

She glanced up toward the mantel over the enormous stone fireplace. The evenings were too warm for a fire, but pottery lined the rough-hewn shelf.

"Menu, miss?" The Harvey Girl smiled.

Josie glanced over the day's specials, eager to try something new. The Santa Fe Roast Chicken with Red Chili Sauce sounded delicious. Since the Castañeda was known for using local merchants and butchers, the chicken would be moist and the skin crispy and golden. The sauce would also be made with the freshest ingredients.

Josie already knew all about the green and red chilis. The green was less spicy. The red made excellent decorations, often hung in merchant windows to invite customers to step inside.

Her glance lingered on the hominy. Known for its nutty and buttery flavor, she felt tempted. But before she made a choice, her waitress arrived. "Any specials not on the menu tonight?"

"Yes, miss," the Harvey Girl answered. "Chef Lansky's Blue Corn Enchiladas with Smoked Turkey are the perfect choice. There's a layer of freshly made blue corn tortillas filled with smoked turkey breast, then a rich cream sauce spread over the top, along with sautéed onions." She smiled. "All of this is baked to perfection. A regional dish and only available this month."

"The accompaniments?" Josie wasn't ready to make her choice until all was revealed. But she had to admit that being served felt intoxicating, especially in the elegant dining room of a Harvey House hotel.

"Spanish rice. Black bean puree. And of course, pickled red onions, my personal favorites."

"How could I resist," Josie teased. "Please add a piece of your delicious pecan pie for dessert. And two dollops of whipped cream."

The waitress took her order, then glided away from the table.

Josie glanced upward to the fireplace mantel again. She recognized the pottery now: Tewa geometric designs, like the ones Daniel had showed her. Eucalyptus branches had been cut and dried and placed around the pots as decorations.

The waitress returned after her meal with two polished silver pots. "Tea or coffee, miss?"

"I'll have the coffee. With cream and sugar, please." As the young woman poured, Josie looked over toward the DiWitt table, intrigued by the man who had joined them. Not just any man. A familiar face.

Mateo Cortez held a glass to his lips, smiling at a young woman sitting across the table. Josie felt an instant pang of jealousy. *He's rubbing elbows with the rich this evening*, Lily had warned her.

I need an excuse to stay and observe what's going on, she thought. *For my research*. But she also knew he made her curious for personal reasons.

"Will there be anything else?" the waitress asked.

"The pie was so delicious." Josie searched for an excuse. "I'd like another dessert. Maybe the piñon nut torte. I saw that on the menu." She knew that she'd surprised her waitress by ordering seconds.

"Of course, miss. I'll leave the coffee on your table. You can fill your own cup. I'll return with the torte."

Fortunately food had never been any issue for Josie. She'd been able to eat what she wanted for as long as she could remember. This brought comments, especially from her brother, who took after Father, more on the beefy side.

"You're gonna get fat, Josie," Charlie would say. "Keep eating like that, no man will have you. On the shelf you'll go. A spinster for sure."

When he'd make those remarks, she'd reach for another slice of cake, only to have her hand slapped by her mother. "He's right," she'd admonish. "You can eat like this now, but once you're courting..."

A man's strident voice made Josie look up.

"What's that I hear " Frank DiWitt yelled.

Forks hovered over food, staying in midair. Heads swiveled. Conversations died. All eyes turned to the DiWitt table.

Frank stood with both hands gripping the edge of the tablecloth. His gaze riveted on his daughter with blistering accusation.

Josie set down her fork to watch.

With a quick flourish, Frank DiWitt snatched a square of white linen from beside the sheriff's plate. Josie didn't know if it was a napkin or a handkerchief. The patriarch waved it under Adelle's nose, as if demanding an explanation.

"Sit down, dear," came the calm voice of the DiWitt matriarch. She reached to touch her husband's elbow. At the same time she scanned the room with the eye of a seasoned hostess. That look was meant for the others. Her way of saying, *Nothing to see here.*

Josie watched Mrs. DiWitt's other hand, which moved

with practiced ease. A flick of her wrist and she took the linen that her husband waved in Adelle's face and tucked it up the sleeve of her dress.

By this time everyone knew what to do. Frank lowered himself back into the chair. Diners resumed their conversations. The show was over. But there would be a lot of talk tomorrow, Josie knew. But Mrs. DiWitt had given her direction and no one dared to object.

By moving slightly to the left, Josie was able to observe the DiWitt table from the corner of her eye without being noticed. The sheriff smiled at Adelle. She looked away. He reached to touch her hand. She removed it immediately and placed it under the table.

Something important had just happened, Josie knew for sure. She could tell by how Mrs. DiWitt patted her husband's arm to soothe his feelings. How Frankie DiWitt looked away in boredom. And how Adelle wasn't interested in the sheriff's attention.

Obviously the sheriff had dropped a bombshell on the family. But what exactly, she couldn't say.

CHAPTER SEVEN

The following morning, Josie awoke with renewed energy. Prepared to pick up her investigation, she got dressed and headed to the lobby. Once outside, she dodged people struggling with luggage, running at breakneck speed toward the train.

A horse clopped along the road, pulling a wagon. A Model A Ford rumbled past. The horse whinnied a greeting, which caused Josie to smile.

She knew her way around horses, due to being sent by her mother to her cousin's farm outside of Boston. She'd helped with the family farm with no complaint. Josie found the work satisfying, more than anything her life in the city offered.

She'd taken to riding old Barney in the afternoons. At first on a dare, because her cousins didn't think she'd be willing, a city girl and all. This led to bareback rides, even in the rain. Such fond memories...

A wagon loaded with milk cans rattled to a stop in front of the general store. The farmer chatted with the shopkeeper, who was busy arranging baskets of vegetables and fruits near the street.

Josie nodded at them and kept moving. The San Miguel County Courthouse came into view. A man in his twenties locked his bicycle to a nearby post and called out, "Buenos días, Miss MacFarland." Her heart leapt in surprise that he'd used her name. She stopped to wait for an explanation.

"I'm Sheriff Cortez's deputy. He told me all about you," he said. "He described you very well. Muy bonita."

"Then the sheriff won't be surprised," she responded tartly. "I need to see him as soon as possible."

The deputy looked away. "Sigame, señorita." He led her inside the courthouse and stood behind the reception counter. "Me nombre es Tomas Rivera." Josie felt frustrated with his obvious attention. She wasn't interested in knowing his name or in being called pretty.

She took note of the tan-colored police uniform that included a matching shirt and slacks. His badge was especially formal. "Like I said, I'm here to see Sheriff Cortez about an ongoing investigation," she replied promptly.

He shrugged. "No hay problema," he said in a pleasant voice.

"As soon as possible," she added, feeling her chin tighten.

The corner of the young man's mouth twitched. He shifted into English. "The sheriff welcomes your interest. But he's not available right now. May I take a message?" He lowered his gaze to play with papers on the counter.

Josie fumed. *How about this, I'm going to make my way down that hall without an escort. Just watch me.* She tucked her handbag under her arm.

"Señorita," he called after her.

She kept moving. The sheriff's door was well marked

and standing open. Pushing the door wider, she stepped inside. "Good to see you again, Sheriff Cortez," she announced. "I need to discuss our case."

Mateo Cortez rose either out of surprise or politely out of habit—she couldn't be sure which. "Did you inquire at the desk? I'm very busy this morning. My courthouse deputy would have mentioned that, if you'd stopped and asked." His smooth voice made her wonder, *Does he always sound like a movie actor in a cowboy western?*

Josie squared her shoulders. "I want to talk to you about the evidence that was collected at the murder scene." She sat down in a chair.

"I cannot talk now." The soft edges had faded from his tone.

She didn't budge.

Finally his face softened. "Perhaps later today. This afternoon."

She suspected his good manners had won over his anger at being interrupted.

"I'll have more information then," he reasoned and then sighed. "I didn't expect you to take your job so seriously." He sat down in a huff.

"My employer knows I don't give up. That's why I was hired," she smartly replied. "They will expect a report by the end of the day. What will I tell them if the sheriff refuses to meet with me to share valuable information from the crime scene?" She quirked an eyebrow.

"Of course, señorita." He added a quick nod toward the door.

Josie rose. She knew she was being dismissed, but he'd agreed to a later meeting. That was something. "I'm available this afternoon," she said in a hesitant voice, as if she could barely manage to fit him in with her busy schedule.

They said their goodbyes.

On her way out of the courthouse, she realized that she'd learned a valuable lesson. The sheriff might refuse her request at first, but if she was persistent and mentioned the Harvey Company, he'd relent in the end.

It wasn't surprising. The Harvey Company was responsible for providing the majority of employment in Las Vegas. The sheriff was paid by the town, but Josie suspected that the Harvey Company might be slipping some money under the table to influence his decisions that worked in their best interest. Bread-buttered, her mother would say. Josie didn't doubt that Mateo Cortez buttered both sides of his locally made sourdough when he had the chance.

She walked briskly down the street, giving herself a good talking to. *I'm going to find that killer and bring them to justice with or without Cortez.* And then, as if to challenge her determination, thunder clapped from a distance. Josie jumped, hair rising on her neck.

She'd been so intent on tracking down the sheriff, she'd forgotten her umbrella. She ducked her chin to avoid the fall of rain on her face.

The abrupt change in weather was common in Las Vegas. Most people on the street opened their umbrellas; others ran for cover. The oppressive heat had given way to a deluge of rain.

A sharp metallic scent filled her nostrils. She shivered. The sky cracked open again, accompanied by a thunderclap so deafening, her spine stiffened. Fat raindrops pelted against the pavement. The sound of the rain drowned out the rest of the street noise. Only a horse whinny of alarm could be heard in the distance.

She dashed under a nearby awning, right as her heel caught on the uneven pavement. Arms flailing, she landed in a heap. Now soaked to the skin, Josie pulled her hat over her head right as a wagon driver shouted curses as his horse hurried past. Hooves clattered against the slick pavement. Lightning split the sky again. This time she was ready. She planted her feet firmly underneath her body and stood.

Josie felt a hand on her shoulder. "Get away," she yelled, shaking off their grip.

She looked up to confront her attacker.

A man with an amused expression, inches taller, looked her in the eyes. He wore a slicker that covered his shirt and pants. His leather hat with a wide brim had been pulled over his ears. A familiar feather lay tucked in the brim.

"Daniel." She shouted to be heard over the pelting rain. This time she didn't resist. He pulled her closer to the building, then smiled and lifted her chin. He adjusted her hat back over her hair, nodded, and then without a word, sprinted across the street.

Before she could call out, he'd disappeared into the crowd.

Josie knew that following Daniel would be useless. He was a Native and used to disappearing in plain sight. His hand on her chin and the care he'd taken made her throat tighten. He remembered her too.

The rain bounced along the pavement, coming down with less intensity. She ran her hands over her drenched clothing and swatted her cloche against the skirt of her dress, then pulled it back on her head.

Why didn't I wear my coat? she chided herself. *I didn't bring enough clothes.*

Josie could hear the lecture coming from her mother. "A lady must be presentable or she'll be judged." One of her mother's frequent reminders: *Clothes make the woman.* Now she was caught out due to her own poor planning.

The investigation would be hindered if she had to wait for her dress to dry. Wearing her Sunday best wouldn't do. Josie loathed overdressing.

She held her handbag to her side and walked a few feet farther. She stopped in front of the mercantile store.

I'll pick up some things off the ready-to-wear rack. Mother would be so proud.

CHAPTER EIGHT

An hour later Josie left the shop carrying a wrapped parcel with several items of new clothing. With the help of a salesgirl, she'd made careful purchases. An off-the-rack new skirt for everyday wear. She'd also ordered two blouses—both could be worn with the skirt—that would be delivered later.

"For a small fee, I can expedite the seamstress, since you're in a rush," the salesgirl had told her at the register.

Josie readily agreed. "When should I come back to pick up the items?"

"We can have them delivered. Sign here. So long as you live within the town limits."

"Oh, I do," Josie assured her. "You can find me at the Castañeda Hotel. Just tell them the delivery is for Josie MacFarland."

She inhaled deeply. The sun's returning light and the scent of wet sagebrush made her feel alive. The smell reminded her of Rio. His pounding hooves as they rode at breakneck speed, circling the barrels. She'd sure surprised Daniel that first day.

That feeling of exhilaration persisted as she walked

through the lobby, up the stairs to her room. She saw immediately that the Harvey maid had come and gone. The window had been slid closed to keep out the rain. She reached to lift the shade and then raise the glass.

She opened her clothes bundle and spread out the new items. With a sigh of satisfaction she glanced at her shoes. She spat on her hankie and rubbed the leather. *Good as new.*

Josie pulled her trench coat from the closet. She didn't want to be caught off guard again. Running her hand down the serviceable fabric, she felt more confidence. The coat defined her mission.

Once she'd draped her wet clothing over the chair, she reached for the recently purchased skirt and simple linen blouse. Now she felt even more determined. She'd managed another setback, refusing to give up.

Josie made her way along Bridge Street and past brick storefronts. She approached the bridge that separated Old and New Town Las Vegas. The Gallinas River rippled below.

Once she made it to the opposite side, she not only could see but felt the difference. Called Old Town by the locals, the air was thick with the smell of piñon smoke.

The spire of Our Lady of Sorrows rose ahead. The red adobe walls blended in with the Southwestern landscape. Though distinct in color, they belonged.

On her first visit, Josie became aware of the diversity of the congregation. Those who frequented the church came from different cultures. Some American Indian, mostly Hispanic. Some called themselves Mexican, a mixed-race people who'd lived in the area for generations.

Josie had only worshiped at one church until she came to Las Vegas. She'd spent every Sunday up until then at the Cathedral of the Holy Cross, come rain or shine.

Her parents were prominent members. Her mother was on several committees and in a prayer group. Mrs. MacFarland was often the first person that a parishioner turned to for solace and practical advice.

Josie had no intention of following in her mother's footsteps. But that didn't get her out of weekly mass. From infancy on, she'd squirmed her way through the service every Sunday. By the time she was seven or eight, she rarely listened to the priest, fascinated by observing other families. They sat on benches, not in pews with their name. Only the most influential sat in front, where the altar and priest were in full view, unobstructed by other members of the congregation.

Josie paid special attention to the children on Sunday, envying how no one yelled at them for being restless. This was because every Sunday she got into some kind of trouble. She'd hold her hands over her ears to ward off the harsh words of correction. Finally her parents agreed to stop reprimanding her, if only she'd lower her hands and behave.

Most of the children from less well-to-do families were comforted when they cried. She wished she could be held in her mother's lap instead of being shushed. And occasionally slapped. She didn't like to remember those times. But the sting on her cheek lasted far into the Sabbath.

She was well aware complaining would get her nowhere, because she'd get another lecture about the sin of being ungrateful; how other children would gladly sit still just to be in her place. Blah, blah, blah. Josie would look at those other children, who laughed with their siblings. They stood up and sat down at will. She doubted they ever wanted to be her.

The round-arched windows of Our Lady of Sorrows made her smile. Josie admired the twin bell towers, rising bravely toward the blue cloudless sky. Pilasters and cornices reflected a strong Spanish influence and brought a sense of old-world charm.

The wide stone steps led to the entrance of the church. It wasn't until she approached that she recognized uneasy guilt in the pit of her stomach. She didn't have the purest of intentions for making a church visit. *I wonder if God will mind...*

Once inside, Josie took a seat at the back. A dark figure approached, wearing a cassock that draped to his sandaled feet. He came closer. Josie held her breath, feeling ambivalent. She thought he'd have answers for her investigation, but she didn't know how to begin the conversation.

Priests often made her feel uneasy, the way they assessed her soul's health with their intense gaze. When he passed, she exhaled in relief.

Her mother had told her, "Priests always know what you are thinking. Best to behave." Before she could take a deep breath, the priest circled back.

He sat down next to her, leaving a respectable space between them. Pulling his cassock over his legs, he spoke. "I am Father Emilio Santiago. I haven't seen you for a while. You used to worship here, if I'm not mistaken."

"I had no idea you'd remember me." She felt genuine surprise. "We never met face-to-face. Were you the one to take my confession?"

"No, I did not have the opportunity to offer you spiritual insight." His voice had the familiar cadence of a fluent Spanish speaker. "But I did notice you, dressed as a Harvey

Girl. You usually sat with the families over there." He pointed. "You stood out because most of the other young women employed by the company chose to sit together, away from locals." He paused, a slight smile coming to his lips, and added, "The fancier seats."

Josie didn't disagree. But she did find it interesting that he'd noticed.

"Are you returning to your employment?" he asked gently. "I've been told that the young women who sign another contract are given an extended leave along with free train transportation. Maybe you've been traveling. To California, perhaps. I know that's a popular destination."

"Not exactly," she admitted. Her fingers unclenched. He'd disarmed her immediately with his interest. "I'm a little nervous telling you why I've been gone. You'll disapprove, and I don't have many friends here in town. I would hate to get off on the wrong foot with my priest." She inhaled sharply, realizing her mistake. By calling him her priest, she'd established a relationship that may not be true. He'd take that as free license to advise. His cassock aside, he'd not proven himself yet.

"Is this a confession, then?" He lowered his voice. "Do we need to meet over there?" He nodded toward the wooden structures nestled at the back of the nave.

If one didn't worship as a Catholic, the somber offer might have less emotional implication. But for Josie, who was raised on a weekly visit with a list of her sins twice as long as her arm, the wooden penitent boxes felt like a terrible reminder. Even the smell of polished wood and candle wax brought strong emotional memories.

She felt the fear, her stomach lurching. Every time she stepped inside the box it was the same. The catch in her breath when the door closed. Trapped. She'd lower to her knees, her face red with shame as she faced the lattice grille.

The mysterious figure of the priest on the other side only made her fidget more. She'd often confess sins she hadn't committed just to get out of the box faster.

"Not a confession, more of a clarification," she told him. The urge not to bother the priest, to save him for parishioners who really believed, also made her cautious. But deep inside, she had a need to reassure him that she wasn't a sinner. *Unless you count being a female detective...*

Confessing a small sin might be easier. It had worked when she was a child. One Hail Mary and she could call it a day. At least she'd avoid the "unsuitable" lecture that was sure to follow once she told him her new profession.

Josie reached into her handbag. Lifting her notebook, she turned to him. *He could have good information about my case. I can't let my concern about his opinion of my suitability get in the way.* She removed the scrap of paper from the notebook and handed it to him. His face remained calm as he read.

"May I hold this for now?" he glanced at the paper again.

Yes. For now," she replied. Then she launched into a staccato explanation. "I came by it in my investigation. In my capacity as a detective. Hired by the Harvey Company. Nothing nefarious, I can assure you.

"The Harvey Company thought a woman, a former Harvey Girl, would get to the bottom of a terrible situation. You may have heard. A dead body was discovered yesterday morning at the Castañeda."

"I see," he commented in a concerned voice. "You're not here to talk about the condition of your soul, your relationship with God. That is perplexing."

She felt even more foolish. So she spoke quickly to hurry up and get her words out. "But I failed as a Harvey Girl. I was too stubborn and didn't follow the rules. I thought they'd give me the boot for good, but apparently they had other plans.

"You must know that females can go places and learn things that men cannot," she continued. "Mr. Harvey has always seen the value of women employees. When his first waiters didn't turn up for work, against all opposition, he put out an ad to hire women. Mr. Harvey was far ahead of his time. He recognized the value of young females as hard workers.

"I couldn't believe my luck when they called me to help with this investigation. So I came west again, this time for a second chance. So here I am."

Her cheeks felt warm from embarrassment. Despite her intentions, she'd spilled her entire story to the priest. She couldn't be sure how he'd respond. She braced herself for the rebuke.

The priest stared into her eyes. His dark gaze softened as he seemed to assess the condition of her soul.

Josie shuddered. She clenched her fingers into fists. Before he could speak, she asked, "Are you sure you still want to be my priest now, Padre?"

CHAPTER NINE

Padre Santiago adjusted his cassock. Lifting his eyes, his weathered face broke into a slight smile. "Why don't we step outside into the courtyard?" he said. "Not the confessional box but a place where we can still have some privacy."

Not only had he not shown any disdain, he'd not tried to argue with her. A point in his favor. "Lead the way." She stood, embarrassed that she sounded so relieved.

An array of local flora filled the courtyard. A sand lizard scurried underneath a barrel-shaped cactus. One hardy rose brushed against a wooden bench. The blossoms were bright red. *A pop of color after the rain*, she thought. Josie remembered people sitting on the wood benches, taking a moment to contemplate nature and the church. But today it was just her and Father Emilio. He gestured with a nod for her to sit nearby.

A potential eavesdropper could linger and listen, she thought. But the beauty of the garden far surpassed the locked wooden box of her childhood. At least she felt safe.

"Even though this isn't a personal confession, will you keep what I'm going to share between us, or does that not apply to women who are detectives?" She knew she sounded angry. But that was because she didn't want to be refused.

"As you might imagine, señorita," began the padre, "I've never met a female detective. But I can assure you whatever you say will be held in the strictest confidence. Not because of your gender or your job, but because of my vow to God and the holy Catholic Church. You can confess your own sins and the sins of others freely in my presence." He looked over her shoulder, giving her a moment to consider his words.

"Glad that's cleared up," she answered tartly. Never one to flinch at the invocation of God or the one true church, she dove into the details of her investigation.

"Robert 'Bobby' Trask was found dead yesterday morning. My friend Lily was the first on the scene."

When the padre looked confused, she explained further. "Lily is a Harvey maid. She was always the one to give Mr. Trask his early morning wake-up call, a knock at the door.

"When he didn't answer, she used her key. That's what she was taught to do."

He nodded for her to continue.

"I was staying nearby in Santa Fe, awaiting my first assignment. I don't know how, but someone in Chicago was alerted about the death. I got a telegram. When I arrived at the scene, I was shown the body. I was told that the sheriff had already collected any evidence. I've been trying to talk to him, but he refuses to take me seriously. He's withholding information about the crime. I know he is."

She inhaled to catch her breath. "Oh, and one more thing." Josie nodded to the wrinkled note he held in his hand. "I got access to Bobby's room, where I found that note. Which is why I'm here. May I have it back now?"

The priest took the paper and read without comment. When he handed it back, he sounded wary. "Do you know who wrote this message?"

"I do not," Josie said. "I assume the mention of a church might refer to Our Lady of Sorrows. The location is close to the Castañeda, right on the plaza, in the center of town. I think my assumption is logical. Or at least a good place to start."

He nodded. "Go on."

"I also have the feeling this note isn't the first. Perhaps a way Bobby communicated when he stayed at the Castañeda. I assume he had connections that required a... How do I say it? More private meeting location. I have been told by a reliable source..." Josie's voice dropped off. She felt protective of Lily and didn't want to use her name, but she continued on, "That Bobby asked for the same room every time whenever he stayed."

Padre Emilio looked thoughtful. Josie felt her nerves jingle. "Have you noticed Bobby Trask in church, meeting with people late at night?"

The iron gate from across the courtyard clanked. Josie glanced to see who'd entered. Her heart skipped. Delores Delgado held a woven basket in her hand. She'd dressed in a shirtwaist, obviously her day off. A woven hat with a wide brim covered her dark hair. She closed the gate.

With a nod she greeted the priest. "Hola, Padre." Her voice sounded warm with affection.

"Hola," he called. Then he turned to Josie. "Señorita Delgado takes care of the plants. But we can wait until she's finished."

Josie felt her cheeks warm. Had she said anything awful

about the matron? She couldn't remember, she'd been in such a hurry telling him her story.

Josie turned her face away. Once she composed herself, she spoke. "Padre, I need to know who might have been meeting with Bobby." She kept her voice low so as not to be overheard.

Padre Emilio called out. "Señorita Delgado. Would you mind tending to the plants by the baptismal font? The ones indoors."

The matron scowled. But Padre Emilio kept smiling, not acknowledging her obvious irritation.

Delores disappeared through the side door into the church. Father Emilio turned back to face Josie. "I know a couple of people who met with Mr. Trask. Perhaps one wrote the note." He glanced away and back again. The use of "a couple of people" troubled Josie.

He hadn't been specific. Were there two or more? She recognized that he wasn't being entirely forthcoming. Was he protecting his parishioners?

Josie spoke with firm deliberation. "A couple of people... Do you have names?"

"Yes." The padre nodded.

Josie waited breathlessly. This was very important, the identity of the note writer would be an invaluable clue.

The priest smiled. "I can give you one name. Victor Lansky."

"He's the one famous for the piñon nut torte that everyone raves about," Josie said.

The padre's eyes rolled heavenward. "Delicious," he agreed.

"Can you tell me more about Chef Lansky?"

"I cannot say more." The padre stood and looked toward the side door where Delores had disappeared "Now I have to soothe the ego of one of my parishioners." He fixed his dark stare on her once more. This time she felt no inclination to fidget.

"I have more questions," she told him.

"Perhaps another time." He turned to go.

She watched him walk away, his brown Franciscan cassock trailing behind. Josie twisted her hands with irritation. *We were finally getting somewhere...*

He'd cut off her questions. Why? To protect someone. But he'd taken vows of poverty, chastity, and obedience. His worn sandals were only one symbol of the humility of his vocation.

Josie stood. She knew for certain that he'd left something out. The identity of someone else other than Lansky. But for now, she'd have to be satisfied with the new lead.

CHAPTER TEN

Josie was right on time for her meeting at the courthouse. Sheriff Mateo Cortez sat behind his desk. One strand of hair hung over his left eye in an appealing boyish way, having escaped the rest of his slicked-back style.

He smoothed it back with his palm.

Josie suspected he'd been tearing at his hair all morning, frustrated that he'd given in to her interview request. When she entered his office, he didn't try to hide his impatience.

"What exactly do you require, Miss MacFarland?"

He was a formidable man. His tone made her feel like a child, scolded by an outraged father. *Don't react*, she told herself sternly. She wanted to be less emotional and more logical. Without a doubt, Cortez was important to her investigation.

I need his approval, not his ire. That's tricky. I have a knack for getting on the wrong side of authority Her mind searched for the right thing to say as she ran her hands down her skirt to wipe the perspiration.

He tapped his desk with his fingers. She felt his exasperation, making her even more nervous. "Thank you for taking the time to talk," she said.

"I phoned Ford Harvey right after you left," he said. "Most interesting."

Josie felt the heat in her face. He'd called her boss. Went right to the top. That couldn't be good.

"Ford confirmed that you'd been hired. He told me to cooperate with your investigation." Cortez looked at her with his dark gaze. "So what is it that you want to know?"

She did her best to hide her surprise. But news that Ford Harvey himself backed her up buoyed her spirit. "I wondered about Bobby's personal items. The ones you collected at the scene."

Tempted to show him the note, she stopped herself in time. *Not until he shows me something first. Show me yours, I'll show you mine.*

"It's my job to collect evidence, the victim's belongings," he explained calmly. "None of them will be of any interest to you."

Josie wasn't going to be refused. She tried another tack. "I heard he was a salesman. Didn't he have a case with samples that he'd show customers?" It was her turn to glare.

"We found his case," the sheriff admitted. "Nothing unusual. It was made of hard leather, scuffed but still respectable. I've seen him open it more than once. He'd set up in the Castañeda lobby. People waiting for their room assignment or for the dining room to open would shop. He sold mostly... What do call them? Trinkets."

Josie paused, then asked, "Trinkets?"

"Bracelets. Cuff links. Belt buckles," he replied. "The more expensive items were special order. Finely etched with desert scenes. Saguaro cacti, hawks in flight, the kind of thing tourists associate with the Southwest.

"He also had bolo cuffs with fancy inlaid turquoise stones set in polished silver. Men like those. I have one myself," he admitted. "Crafted by the Diné and the Pueblo.

"Bobby liked showing off his wares to women mostly. Some would shove each other aside to get the right piece. Hombres como él simper saber qué decir," he added.

Josie quirked an eyebrow.

"Men like him always know what to say," he translated. "Ladies' men."

Takes one to know one, she thought.

"As for his personal clothing..." The sheriff folded his hands. "Nothing unusual for these parts. A business suit and a couple of shirts. Less formal pants for after hours. Rodeo attire. You wouldn't find anything of interest."

Josie resented that he'd made the decision for her. That his description was supposed to be enough. He leaned over to open a drawer. "I do have this box, if you want to look."

He slid it toward her.

Held together by a shoelace, it looked like a keepsake from Trask's school days.

She opened the lid to look inside. On top was an embroidered handkerchief with lace around the edges. She lifted it to her nose. It smelled of lavender.

Underneath she found an array of odds and ends. A silver concha button with the outline of a steer skull. There was a pocket watch with a long chain. Caught in the chain was a money clip, worn and slightly tarnished.

A lock of blonde hair tied with a blue ribbon came next. Maybe his mother's, Josie mused. Or maybe Bobby's hair when he was a child. A mother's keepsake. And then a small silver horseshoe charm. A gift from a Native? She had no idea. None of these items were more than a boy's sentimental keepsakes.

At the bottom of the box she found a faded photograph. A closer look revealed a smiling Bobby Trask, the man she'd seen on the table in the storage room.

He stood next to a man who wore a cowboy hat, brown leather cowboy boots, a white shirt, and an air of authority. Josie recognized him at once. Mr. Frank DiWitt, owner of the DiWitt ranch.

The photographer captured the men with hands outstretched, as if ready to shake and seal a deal. She handed it to the sheriff. "Is that the man I saw you dining with? I believe his name is Frank Diwitt."

Cortez's eyebrows shot up. "Yes, that's him. Bobby Trask liked to be seen with important people wherever he went. He'd sell an item and ask for a photo. A real wheeler-dealer," the sheriff added with a smile.

"Did Bobby show off his photographs?" Josie asked.

"To anyone." The sheriff scowled. "You didn't have to ask. His way of bragging."

"But this one photograph is kept with other sentimental items," Josie mused. "That has to have significance."

"That's true, señorita. I hadn't thought of that, but yes. Señor DiWitt's friendship is as good as gold in Las Vegas. Even Trask knew that. What's better than a picture standing next to one of the most influential people in town? One you could show around to make yourself look more important."

"What about this?" She held up the embroidered handkerchief. One corner had distinct initials: H. H. Josie had one just like it that she'd left at home. Every Harvey Girl carried a Harvey House handkerchief in her pocket. They were laundered and sent back just like the uniforms.

"That piece of evidence is our most likely lead to the killer. We found it at the scene." He leaned closer. "We suspect a woman. Hell hath no fury, señorita." Cortez eyed her. "We're following up on who might have seen Bobby last. He likely pulled the handkerchief from her fingers, staggered to the table, and slid it into his box of personal possessions before dying on the floor."

The sheriff sighed.

Josie thought his vision of the death scene overly dramatic. What kind of a man would think to put a handkerchief in a box before keeling over? Sounded like a movie, not real life.

The sheriff watched her face carefully, then he added with a note of triumph in his voice, "We have a suspect already. You may know her: Lily Davenport." His jaw tightened as he took the box and closed the lid.

Josie stared at him in stunned amazement. Her heart pounded in her chest.

"I have an eye witness," he said. "Along with the handkerchief, that's all I need."

Josie locked eyes with the sheriff. She wondered if he was telling the truth or bluffing about the witness. "Lily Davenport would never kill anyone. She can barely squish a fly, let alone bludgeon a man.

"No," she said firmly. "Lily wouldn't risk her reputation or her employment for even something so small as a quick cuddle from the likes of Bobby Trask."

"Not surprising you think that," Cortez said, his voice turning mild. "You're friends."

"Yes we are," she said flatly. "Best friends."

"Perhaps then, because you are best friends, you should excuse yourself from the investigation."

"Speaking of friends, what is your connection with Frank DiWitt?" He looked surprised, so she continued. "At one point your voices were loud enough to be heard over the entire dining room. Was there a squabble? Does Mr. DiWitt approve of you and his daughter?"

The sheriff looked away.

Gotcha, Mr. Lawman.

"I am a family friend," he admitted. "Since you're not local, you might not know that I often dine with people in the community at the Castañeda. My reelection is coming up in a few months. I do my best to stay connected to the most influential families. Frank DiWitt included."

"And his daughter," she added, her tone steely. *Breadbuttered*, Josie heard her mother's voice say again. The sheriff certainly knew which side his bread was buttered on. If Cortez and Adelle DiWitt were stepping out, the sheriff's reputation would only be enhanced.

Her mind whirled. But why would he want to make Lily his scapegoat?

Maybe a quick arrest gets him votes. Maybe it's to get me dismissed as an investigator. Would he have a personal vendetta?

Poor Lily, an easy target. A young woman without a local family. A Harvey Girl. No one would question the great Sheriff Cortez. The arrest would only confirm what many in the community thought anyway: that Harvey Girls were just waitresses with loose morals. As hard as the Harvey Girls tried, no matter how successful, there were the critics who still suspected they were neither moral nor upstanding.

Sheriff Cortez stood. "I hope this conversation has helped. You now know why I've withheld certain information. I have another appointment. May I escort you out of the courthouse?" He walked around the desk to offer her an elbow.

The display of false gallantry felt like a slap in the face.

"That's not necessary. I can find my own way. But before I go, what about the weapon? You didn't mention that you'd found it."

"Gun handle," he replied. "A Smith and Wesson. A distinctive pattern on the victim's skin. The gun was small. Would fit into the palm of a woman's hand." His eyes gleamed.

"Let me hazard a guess... A Model 10, approximately 1.9 pounds," she replied.

His eyebrows shot up. "You know the model?"

She'd made a quick deduction from his description. "Oh, I do. Very common where I come from. Women often carry one in their handbag for self-defense. Not too heavy. What was the pattern you found on the gun? Grips often have distinctive designs."

A look of appreciation came over his face. "A cross-hatch pattern," he admitted.

"Good," Josie said. "Now I have a clue that I can use. But hear me loud and clear. Lily Davenport is not the killer. Don't think otherwise. I will continue to investigate. Thank you for your time."

CHAPTER ELEVEN

Josie wondered if she'd missed a nuance or any important information. She reviewed her conversation with Cortez as she walked.

Her feelings had changed for the lawman. The initial attraction she'd felt had given way to irritation. Despite Ford Harvey's insistence that she'd been hired, Cortez had arranged for her to see only what he wanted her to see, to make Lily the target of the investigation.

That made the sheriff an obstacle, not an ally. Which made him less attractive in her eyes. She dismissed him from her thoughts.

Josie had two things to consider. Talking to Chef Lansky, of course. Since her recent conversation with Cortez, Lily became her most immediate concern. Josie would prove Lily's innocence by hook or by crook. Now was her chance to redeem herself. If she were lucky, afterward Lily would forgive her.

A solid plan took shape. Josie would find Lily and warn her about Cortez's intentions. Then she'd confront Chef Lansky. Getting him alone might be difficult, but once she did, she would lead him into a conversation about Bobby Trask. Play dumb. Flutter her lashes. Sprinkle on a few compliments about the piñon nut torte.

Getting to the truth would require a certain...what did her mother call it? Subtlety. But could she pull it off.

Striding through the entry of the Castañeda, she marched to the front desk. "Has Miss Davenport arrived for work?"

The clerk looked up with a sniff. "Who's asking?"

"I'm Josephine MacFarland. Fred sent me."

She observed his face carefully. If he showed any sign of cooperating, she'd feel she was on the right path. The young man's brow wrinkled.

Josie knew that the phrase "Fred sent me" had power. Not many people knew how it worked, the name-dropping for the Harvey founder. Because you had to be an employee and in the know. She'd tried to explain to her father.

"We just say, Fred, like he would be coming right around the corner."

"Ridiculous," he'd said. "Fred Harvey's been dead for years."

"But you don't realize," Josie insisted, "he's more a myth than a real person."

"Not logical, Josephine," her father insisted.

"Well let me explain," she'd responded. "Since 1898 Fred Harvey has earned respect from his employees. Those in the know used 'Fred' to show they are part of the team. From train conductors to the lowest of Harvey Girls. The first name for the Harvey House founder carried weight from the beginning. People still drop 'Fred' in a reverent tone, almost as if they are invoking the Lord's name. Everyone knows he's dead. He passed in 1901."

She hadn't paused because she knew she'd not get

another word in edgewise. So she rushed ahead, speaking as fast as she could. "But Daddy, his reputation continued to spread. Quality, discipline, and customer service became as familiar as his name. Americans loved him. He was known in Europe too.

"But when he got sick, Fred Harvey had a plan. He groomed his son, Ford, to keep the legend alive. The legend being all the stories about him, shared over the years. Plus the use of his first name, dropped casually in conversation. Like a secret code."

Josie stopped explaining to catch a breath. Her father rolled his eyes and went back to reading his newspaper.

But now she hoped the receptionist would play along. She jumped right in with a classic Fred story.

"Remember when Fred dropped that coffee cup right on the floor at the busiest time of day?" She waited for his response.

When he said nothing, she continued, "How he tested the quality of the china for cracks." Josie smiled. "How he insisted that the portion size of everything from meat to dessert was double that of any other eating establishment.

"People would scramble, dust pans would fly. Those were the days." She could tell that he was listening. On more solid ground, she kept spinning the story.

"I knew a guy once who told me lots of stories. I never knew Fred. But this man was fired on the spot. Instead of making fresh coffee every hour, he poured the dregs at the bottom into a customer's cup. Fred was furious. 'We only use the freshest coffee in my establishments!'" Josie used a deep voice to imitate the Harvey House founder.

Finally the lines on the clerk's brow smoothed. "Good ol' Fred," he said. "Miss Davenport can be found upstairs. This is her late shift. Look for a cleaning cart," he advised, turning back to his work.

"Thank you so much." Josie gave a quick wave as the next person stepped up to the counter.

Josie found the cleaning cart at the end of the hallway. She poked her head into the room. There was Lily, dusting and humming to herself.

She greeted her friend from the doorway.

Lily gave her a look and turned back to her work.

"I need your help." Josie stepped inside the room. "You can keep dusting while I talk."

Just seeing Lily at work made Josie feel better. She'd not been arrested. Maybe the sheriff was trying to show who was boss, threatening to arrest her friend.

Now that she watched her working away at her job, Josie felt reluctant to burden Lily with the news. *Hasn't she already found a dead body? She doesn't need the weight of thinking she's under suspicion too.*

"I need to find a piñon tree somewhere close by. In the town plaza perhaps," Josie began.

Lily kept swishing her duster. "Why not Hermit's Peak? Everyone knows that's the best place to harvest the nuts, especially this time of year."

Josie knew that the fall was a sacred time for Pueblo to hold ceremonies at Hermit's Peak. That the people would gather the piñon nuts and use the meat and shells as a part of their rituals.

"I don't want to interfere," she told her. "Is there another place I can buy them?"

"Try the farmers market," Lily suggested. "They sell to everyone." She folded her dust rag.

"The farmers market," Josie repeated. "Do you suppose Chef Lansky will be there, buying fresh food for the Castañeda kitchen? I'd like to meet him."

Josie held back her excitement. Maybe she didn't need a plan to get the chef alone in the restaurant. She could bump into him as if by chance at the outdoor market. Start up a conversation. Then ask about Bobby Trask.

Lily stopped. "All the Harvey Girls got an introduction when they brought him on, after you left. Plus I've seen him at the farmers market on several occasions." She bent to straighten the bed comforter. "We were warned not to bother him, that the kitchen is strictly off limits."

"He sounds quite snooty," Josie said.

"I suppose. The tall hat." Lily smiled. "What do I know... I'm not the best judge of character." She sent a side-eye in Josie's direction.

"You know plenty," Josie defended her friend.

Lily stopped to think. "The one thing I do know is the way he says 'willage' instead of village. Made the girls laugh behind his back."

She glanced nervously toward the cart outside the door. "I'd better finish. I hope I've helped." Her smile was rueful.

Josie wondered if now was the time to tell her she might be arrested. Her stomach turned. She just couldn't bring herself to be the one to upset Lily again.

"See you later." Josie bent to kiss Lily's cheek. "I'm heading to the farmers market. It will be open for a couple more hours." She hurried down the hall. *If I get to Lansky, maybe I can solve the case. Even if it's not just a threat and she is Cortez's number one suspect, she never needs to know. As her mother might say, ignorance is bliss.*

CHAPTER TWELVE

The Las Vegas Farmers Market was the place to see and be seen.

Josie walked into the stream of people, feeling the energy of commerce. Vendors called out prices from wooden stalls and makeshift tables. Friends greeted one another. She appreciated the array of fresh produce, the colors and smells. There weren't quite as many people as she remembered from before. Most likely due to the recent economic turn.

Sides of beef hung from wood poles. The sight of raw meat made her slightly queasy; she moved quickly past. Her favorite booths were the ones at the end of the row with delicious-looking, freshly made baked goods. The smell of yeast and sugar made her mouth water.

I'm not here to eat, she reminded herself. *I'm here to find Lansky and a bag of piñons.*

She'd start by looking for the Castañeda table, which might have a piñon nut torte for sale. He'd most likely be standing at the table. No chef dismissed an admirer of his signature dish. At least in her experience.

But then two men blocked the path in animated conversation. Josie immediately recognized Frankie DiWitt, wearing a chambray shirt with shiny pearl buttons. His bold laugh, confident and assured, drifted over the rest of the voices. Josie drew closer to listen in.

"I need the entire side of beef delivered to the Castañeda," the man told Frankie.

Alerted to the possibility that she'd stumbled onto an important transaction, Josie stepped aside.

"Certainly, Chef," Frankie replied. "Anything for the Harvey House." He leaned forward. "Would you also like a side of lamb? It's been freshly slaughtered. Will be very tender."

"Good idea. I'll work my menus around the meat." Josie felt her heart beat quickly in her throat. That had to be Lansky talking to Frankie. Who else would be called "Chef"?

"Bring the delivery to the kitchen, the alley entrance. I want it in cold storage and out of the heat." His European accent sounded much how Lily described. Now Josie felt quite certain she'd found her man.

Josie wasted no time. "Chef Lansky!" she called. "May I have a word?"

Both men turned away, as if she'd not spoken.

Josie's temper flared. Pretending to be alluring to get men to pay attention felt demeaning, especially for a detective. *Plus why bother*, she thought. *I'd most likely just be ignored.*

"I've been hired by the Harvey Company to investigate the death of Bobby Trask!" she announced in her strongest voice.

Now they looked up. The chef glanced down his imperious nose in her direction.

"I have no idea to whom you are speaking. I am a chef, not someone who converses with itinerate salesmen."

Josie hid her smile. "Well that's odd," she commented. "How did you know Mr. Trask was a salesman?"

He flicked his fingers in her face. "I'm busy." He turned away.

Josie wasn't done. She felt convinced he was hiding something. More than the secret ingredients to his famous piñon nut torte recipe, that was for sure.

Before she could speak again, a mariachi band began to play. This gave Lansky an opportunity to turn toward the music and walk back into the crowd. She reached out to grab his sleeve but then pulled back.

No use making a fool of myself when I can't be heard, she realized. *Okay, so Lansky isn't going to chat. I guess I need my other plan. Time to find those piñons.*

She spotted an herb and spice table. As luck would have it, there were bags filled with piñons.

Josie negotiated with the vendor. With the nuts tucked inside her handbag, she walked away, confident that her plan for the evening would go forward despite the chef's refusal to take her seriously.

The Harvey Girl hostess seated Josie in front of the fireplace. After spreading her linen napkin on her lap, she said, "I know what I want," before she could be handed a menu.

The waitress took her order. As soon as she slid past, Josie glanced out of the corner of her eye at the other diners. Not again. It was Mateo Cortez. He dined at a table for two, right across the room. His companion was none other than Adelle DiWitt.

Striking in her beauty, Adelle wore a high-waisted skirt that fell in folds over her legs. The elegant cream-colored blouse had to be made of silk. Diamond earrings and a diamond bracelet sparkled in the candlelight. This time she shared an effervescent laugh with Mateo. He looked quite pleased.

To Josie it seemed obvious that the sheriff was more than a family friend. He'd brought Adelle to more giggling using his charm and repartee. The tone of flirtation could be heard, even if the exact words could not.

They're stepping out, Josie concluded. *Not likely a secret since they're in the middle of the Harvey House dining room. Adelle's father must have given his approval. A notch in the sheriff's belt for sure,* Josie concluded. *He'll be a shoo-in come the next election.*

Her food arrived, piping hot. After arranging the cup and saucer, the Harvey beverage server lifted a highly polished silver coffee carafe to pour. Then she left the pot on the table and slid away.

When Josie finished her meal and put down her fork, her waitress appeared, this time holding a plate with a generous portion of piñon nut torte. The lavender drizzle had been artistically arranged over the whipped cream to the edge of the plate.

The beverage waitress came next and refilled Josie's coffee cup. "Will there be anything else, miss?"

"This should do it, thank you." Josie watched as the Harvey Girls retreated across the dining room toward the kitchen. It was time to put her plan into action. The one she'd contrived after being rebuffed at the farmers market. *I tried introducing myself,* she reasoned. *Now for my next idea.*

Josie assumed if she drew enough attention to herself,

refusing any offers by the Harvey Company to make things right, then she'd be able to storm away to have a word with the chef in person.

Once she was in the kitchen she could pull him aside and get answers to her questions about his relationship with Bobby Trask. She felt most certain that he would be caught off guard and be more willing to talk if for no other reason than to get rid of her.

After a generous forkful of piñon nut torte, Josie reviewed her plan. *Mouth closed, Josie. Be polite*, she reminded herself. Then she casually slipped a hand into her skirt pocket. *Operation piñon nut, full steam ahead.*

She deposited the previously saved piñon shells into the remaining portion of the dessert. A quick jab of her fork and they disappeared beneath the gooey surface.

She took another bite, then stopped mid-chew. Pushing back the plate, she clutched her jaw and then spat into her napkin. "Ouch! My tooth!" she called loud enough for everyone in the dining room to hear.

All eyes turned toward her.

Josie shot to her feet. "There are nut shells in my torte!" she claimed, her voice rising theatrically. "My tooth may be broken." She glanced around to make certain her audience was still looking.

She knew she was overacting. But isn't that what her high school drama coach recommended when the audience got restless?

She gave a groan, loud and dramatic, for good measure.

The Harvey hostess rushed to her side and took control with clipped efficiency. "Take this away," she snapped, thrusting the plate toward the waitress with a frosty glare.

Once she left, the hostess addressed the room. "The Fred Harvey Company prides itself on impeccable standards. The customer is always right. We will, of course, correct this situation immediately. Clearly a staff oversight. You'll receive another dessert on the house." She turned back to Josie. "If a dentist visit is necessary, we will cover the cost. I sincerely apologize for your discomfort."

Josie tossed her napkin onto the table. "I'm afraid that's not enough," she declared, holding her jaw with exaggerated care. "I intend to speak with the chef. This isn't the waitress's fault. It's his. He's responsible."

She turned and flounced toward the kitchen. Taken by surprise, the hostess didn't follow. Josie picked up her pace to burst past the swinging doors into the kitchen.

At first the kitchen help didn't notice her. They bustled past, intent on their work. Her eyes found the chef right away, with his ridiculously tall white hat.

"Chef Lansky, I'm here to file a formal complaint." Josie spoke over the din. He'd brushed her off one time today. He wasn't going to get another chance. "There were piñon nut shells in my torte!" She clutched her jaw for dramatic effect. "I demand an apology."

CHAPTER THIRTEEN

"You're lodging a formal complaint." Lansky's chin jutted. "No one is allowed in my kitchen without permission. You need to speak to someone at the front desk. I don't have time for petty accusations. Now go away." He flicked his fingers in her face for the second time that day.

Before Josie could launch into the questions she'd prepared, a familiar voice called from the dining room. Sheriff Cortez entered with a scowl. "I'll take care of this, Chef."

His formidable presence, even in his dining attire, made Josie gulp and drop her hand.

"Come this way, Señorita MacFarland." He nodded toward the back exit.

Outside in the alley, Josie's stomach jittered. Often her bright ideas ended like this. With her apologizing. She steeled herself for the dressing down.

"What were you doing in the kitchen?" he demanded. "And during their busiest time. I'm very certain your Harvey superiors will be quite concerned when they hear you've interrupted Chef Lansky at his work. He's a valued employee. Recruited from one of the finest kitchens in Europe. Did you think you'd be an exception, with your exaggerated complaint about a shell in your dessert?"

"I had no idea that I wasn't supposed to speak to the chef. I may have to go to the dentist." She held her jaw again. "But I admit I've caused a ruckus. Please let me apologize to the chef myself."

Cortez raised his index finger to scratch at the back of his neck. "I don't have to report this incident today, if you'll agree to never harass the chef again. Under no circumstances should you return to his kitchen."

Josie knew he'd blocked her again. Using a bunch of Harvey rules to keep her in her place.

"May I assume your silence is your promise? You will stay away from Chef Lansky?"

"You may assume what you wish. It won't matter what I say. Apparently you have enough authority to override me at every turn." Josie looked away.

"That's a harsh judgment," he said, sounding hurt. "You misunderstand my intent. I want my town to be safe. You must know that the rules are in place for a reason. Danger lurks around every corner. This is the Southwest, not Boston."

"Chef Lansky may be an important witness in my case," Josie insisted.

The sheriff cleared his throat. "As it happens, I do have information for you. I was going to tell you tomorrow, but since we're here right now..."

Her heart thumped against her chest.

"I've arrested Miss Davenport. She's in my custody. We found the weapon in her room and will proceed tomorrow with the paperwork required by the local jurisdiction. I have everything I need to close this case."

"I thought you already had the weapon in your custody. How could you have possibly found it in Lily's room?" Josie couldn't believe her ears.

"Here you are, Mateo." Adelle DiWitt came through the doorway. "Stranding me during supper is hardly the action of a gentleman." She cast a quick glance in Josie's direction.

"Especially when I find you with another woman in the alley. What is this about? I thought you were an honorable man." She stomped one elegant leather boot on the ground. *Just like a prize circus horse*, Josie thought.

"My dear." The sheriff's tone swelled with to charm right as he turned away from Josie. "Please accept my apology. My behavior is rude. If not for this woman's insistence that she see the chef"—he pointed at Josie—"I would never have left your side. Not for a moment, my dear." He took her hand, resting his lips on her palm.

Josie never liked palm kisses. She squirmed as she watched.

"Let me make this up to you," the sheriff said. He ran his finger over his full mustache. "Could I take you out tomorrow evening and try again? I hear the special will be Blue Corn Enchiladas with Smoked Turkey. You know we both love that dish."

Josie watched with fascination.

"What do you say, my dear? Am I forgiven?" the sheriff coaxed.

I'm not the only thespian in this group, Josie thought. *Look at him. What a performer. Oscar Wilde would be proud.*

Adelle sniffed. "As it happens, I am available tomorrow evening. But now I've completely lost my appetite. Please escort me home." The well-bred rancher's daughter lifted her head with a glare in Josie's direction.

CHAPTER FOURTEEN

Once the sheriff escorted Adelle back into the kitchen, Josie stood in stunned silence, her breath coming in quick gasps. She struggled to make sense of the sheriff's announcement that he'd already arrested Lily. And that he'd found the murder weapon in her room.

Without the weapon, she had a chance of convincing him of Lily's innocence. Initials on a handkerchief, distributed to every Harvey Girl, would hardly be solid proof. But now...

She should have warned Lily when she had the chance. Lily, who barely had a minute for herself. Who cleaned rooms and wiped scum from clawfoot tubs. Lily, who would never risk her job with the likes of a salesman with the reputation of a ladies' man, let alone murder a human being in cold blood.

The sound of pots and pans clattering in the kitchen brought her thoughts back to the present. The temperature had dropped with the setting of the sun. But that wasn't the cause of her shivers. It felt creepy to be standing alone in an alley. Anything could happen.

Josie walked toward the main street. Her stomach churned at the smell of garbage and urine. A cat meowed from behind a trash can. Headlights shone from a car ahead, driving straight at her.

For a moment she froze. Then she jumped aside. A black Packard with whitewall tires rumbled past, a Harvey Company Indian Detour sign on the side. *That's odd*, she thought. *It's too late to be picking up tourists.*

The car stopped behind the kitchen, and a man stepped out of the driver's seat and hurried inside. She walked out of the alley and back around to the front of the building wondering who it was and why he'd arrived so late.

A doorman nodded as Josie stepped inside. A few men lingered over newspapers and coffee. The scent of pipe smoke made her smile. Unlike many ladies, Josie didn't mind the smell. It reminded her of her father. She glanced toward a table where two men sat conversing. A familiar face caught her eye. He lingered behind the newsstand.

Her heart skipped a beat. *Daniel. What is he doing here?*

He nodded in her direction.

She walked calmly toward him. The closer she got, the better he looked. The familiar tautness of his body, mingled with the distinct smell of the desert and late-night rides. That mixture of mesquite and pine. Her breath caught. None of this had been apparent earlier, in the rainstorm.

Daniel had tied his black hair back in a braid. He wasn't obvious, but he wasn't invisible either. His eyes bored into hers, his face showing no emotion.

"I've been thinking about this moment, how we'd run into each other again," she said.

A flicker of warmth passed through his eyes, replaced by cool assessment. Then a slow nod. "Good to see you, Joe Mack."

His hand reached to pull her farther behind a tall palm, away from prying eyes. A quick memory flitted through her mind of how he'd lifted her into the saddle, grasping her waist with both hands. Once settled, he'd moved around Rio to adjust her leg and stirrup on both sides. Then he'd handed her the reins. The warmth of his hands, the confidence he gave her. That was what Josie remembered the most.

But now she didn't have time to reminisce. She took his hand in hers gave it a quick squeeze, then let it drop. "Lily's in trouble," she told him. "The sheriff arrested her." Her voice sounded unsteady. "She's not the murderer. Will you help me prove her innocence?"

His eyes flickered. "I heard," he said. "Came right over to find you." He glanced over her head.

She turned slightly to see for herself. She overheard a businessman discussing his schedule at the reception desk. Daniel's body grew still, and she wondered if he knew the man. Daniel gave a slight shake to his head. Once the man left, he spoke again.

"You want my help?" Daniel asked.

"If you know something..."

"I know a lot of things, Joe." The tone in his voice, quiet and teasing, made her stomach flip.

"Don't call me that."

His mouth twitched, not quite a smirk. "Why not? I'd say it still fits. From cowboy to Harvey House detective. Quite a leap. Even for you."

"Can I count on you or not?" Josie had no time to be looking back.

Daniel studied her for a long moment. "You left without saying goodbye," he said softly. "I was hurt." He looked away. "But then my grandmother pulled me aside.

When I told her, she explained, 'Some things aren't lost forever. Just waiting to be found again.'" Josie swallowed. The apology stuck in her throat. She was afraid if she said she was sorry, a floodgate of emotions would erupt, making her seem weak and vulnerable once again. *I'm always apologizing for something*, she reasoned. *Not this time.*

Daniel took a step backward. With a curt nod, he turned, making his way through the lobby toward the exit.

Her eyes filled with tears. She regretted what she'd done, leaving Daniel and Lily without a word. But now she accepted the consequence.

Back in her room, Josie rubbed her eyes. A difficult day in a dry landscape. Her initial plan to talk to Lansky had been thwarted by the sheriff and Adelle DiWitt. And then Daniel, waiting for her in the lobby. She'd not been prepared for her emotions. When he walked away, she'd nearly cried. Plus the bad news of Lily's arrest was foremost on her mind.

She got ready for bed, calling herself every name in the book. Selfish. Unreliable. Disrespectful. Disloyal. And finally the word she hated but often used in her own mind: sinner.

Her religious upbringing, always ready with a judgment, felt like an albatross around her heart. *Feel something, Josie. Anything but this.*

As tears ran down her cheeks, she thought of Rio. How they were a team. How the crowd, on their feet, roared with approval as they cleared the last barrel. The rush of emotion flooded her body. She wiped her tears, and finally the self-condemnation passed.

With one tug on the covers, she crawled between the sheets, her emotions spent.

Her eyes closed, she imagined the wind against her face. The pounding of hooves against the dirt. Even the smell of the dust and leather. Popcorn and sweat wafting in the air. Rodeo people calling to each other.

She felt her thoughts drift. Aware of her breath, even and strong, she knew the storm had passed. Her feelings had shifted, bringing a fresh perspective.

CHAPTER FIFTEEN

She woke the next morning with sun streaming through the window. Josie stretched and then groaned. The real world awaited her and she hoped she was ready.

After a quick splash of water from the basin, she rubbed a towel over her skin. This time there was little doubt: Lily was her first priority. *I have to find out where she's being detained.* Josie shuddered. *Surely Cortez didn't lock her up in a cell with vagrants and drunks.*

It would be so easy now just to give up. Run away like last time. But correcting a wrong required confession and the offer of penance. Maybe in the end, once Lily was free, she could also ask for forgiveness.

There was no guarantee. She had a slight hope with Lily. But Daniel was another story. What did he really feel beneath his calm exterior?

Josie slipped her green dress over her head. Since the rainstorm, it felt stiff and rough against her skin. She bent to lace her boots right when a note appeared under her door.

She began to read. Her heart quickened.

L at women's dormitory. It was signed with a simple D.

She felt her spirits lift.

Josie nodded to the doorman on her way to the street. She looked toward the Harvey House women's dormitory right across the road. Two Harvey Girls stood under the portico, chatting. Josie felt a pang. She missed the sharing of secrets and the camaraderie in the morning.

But now, without a Harvey Girl uniform, she doubted she'd be allowed inside. She didn't want to take the time necessary to be given legitimate access, explain again how she was a detective, only to be turned away. But she had another plan.

It was her memory the night before of riding Rio that gave her the idea. It had taken time for her to figure out how to get out of the dormitory and to the barn the last time. Once she committed to helping Daniel care for the stray pinto, she'd found an escape. The Harvey Girl curfew and the prying eyes of Matron held her back, but not for long.

It was a couple of other Harvey waitresses who explained. These particular girls were known to be fast. They certainly weren't sticklers for the rules. So once she pulled them aside, they were only too happy to help.

"Use the kitchen back door," one girl said. "My boyfriend meets me at the end of the alley. No one ever looks there." She took a puff on her cigarette and then laughed.

After that, Josie spent every spare minute with Rio at the barn. She never mentioned she'd made a friend who was a Native. Nor that she decided to dress as a cowboy and enter Rio in the popular barrel race.

If she weren't a Harvey Girl she might have ridden as Josie. It wasn't unheard of. But because of the Harvey

Company's strict policies, she had to disguise herself as a man.

Now she could use the kitchen back door again to sneak inside the dormitory and locate Lily.

Walking around the corner, she found the door ajar. Propped open, most likely by the cook. Josie ducked inside.

Like the night before, no one in the kitchen seemed to notice. So she didn't stop to look around, for fear of drawing undue attention. She made her way through the kitchen, taking light steps, eyes focused ahead. In the hallway, she executed the next part of her plan: hide in the linen room.

She closed the door behind her and took a deep breath. *That was easy*, she admitted. *You got inside, but now...* She stared down at her wrinkled dress. *You'll stick out like a sore thumb.*

A rack stacked with pressed white sheets drew her attention. Before she could inspect more closely, the door to the linen room flung open. Josie ducked behind the shelves, bending her knees to stay out of sight.

Delores Delgado hustled inside. She closed the door and checked her watch.

Josie held her breath.

"Miss Davenport is ready for her breakfast," came a young woman's voice from outside the closed door. "Do I deliver it to her, or is she coming downstairs to eat with the rest of us?"

Matron frowned and opened the door. "Miss Davenport is being held in my quarters. Deliver her breakfast on a tray, no frills." Matron sounded impatient. "I'll send over fresh linens. Don't forget. No one is to know she's staying here."

"Yes, miss," the young maid replied.

Matron closed the door. She turned to pull pillowcases from the top shelf. Josie crouched lower, letting out her breath slowly so as not to be heard.

Ahead of her was a stack of freshly laundered Harvey Girl uniforms. She sniffed the familiar odor of Rinso with a faint trace of bluing. This was just what she hoped to find.

Finally the matron finished taking inventory. After one more scratch on the paper, she turned to go. Josie waited to hear the linen room door shut before she stood. Her legs and back ached. She bent again to inspect the stack of uniforms.

The Harvey Company didn't expect the girls to launder their own dresses and aprons. They sent soiled garments out to a professional company. She selected one in her size. A bit short in length, but she wouldn't be visible for very long.

CHAPTER SIXTEEN

Inching her way along the corridor, Josie focused her gaze on the floor. Custody of the eyes, she'd been told by a nun at church. *Don't look at anyone else—this will keep you above the rest. Indifferent to their opinions. Safe.*

She held a stack of white towels as her prop. Two Harvey Girls giggled as they sauntered past, arm in arm. Josie knew her disguise was working. Not even a side-eye cast in her direction.

The matron's quarters were just ahead. A man stood in front of the door. Not just an ordinary man, but a giant of his species. He folded his arms in front of his chest, muscles bulging from his jacket. His dark hair was slicked back and neatly combed. There was a thin, slightly crooked scar running up the side of his face. *Could he look any more the mobster?*

She wanted to turn and run but realized it was too late when he called cut.

"Hey," he growled. "Whatcha doin' there?"

She kept her smile in place. With a determined step she walked toward him.

"I said whatcha doin'!"

She shivered at the menacing tone in his voice.

I can't run. I can't hide. I need to improvise. Josie looked over. "I have towels to deliver," she exclaimed in her brightest, most chipper voice.

"I ain't seen you before. I thought I knew all the Harvey Girls." He looked her up and down with an appraising glance. "When did you get into town?"

"Just last night." The lie came to her in a flash. "My first job. So I'm confused." She looked away. "I was instructed to deliver these to the head matron's room and I thought it was this one." She pointed, hearing a current tune in her head. I'm *Just a poor little lamb who's lost her way.*

"Right here." He gestured with a thumb toward the door. "I can take those for ya."

"Oh, I can't do that," she pulled the towels back. "Matron expects me to lay out the fresh linens and pick up the soiled ones. My first day on the job, you know. I don't want to get on her wrong side. Please, I won't be long."

He eyed her suspiciously but then nodded. "I get it. You gals are under that old bat's thumb."

This time her smile felt genuine. "So if you could let me in, I'll only be a minute. We don't want the old bat coming by to chew us out, now do we?"

She brushed past him and reached for the knob. When he didn't stop her, she walked inside. "Don't come in," she warned over her shoulder. "She's getting dressed."

She closed the door and latched the security chain.

By now, Lily had jumped to her feet.

Josie held her finger to her lips. She put the towels on the edge of the bed and turned to embrace her friend.

"I came as fast as I could," she whispered in Lily's ear.

Lily clung to her, body shaking.

"Shush, honey. Everything's going to be all right." Josie held her close. Once the tears passed, she took a step back while Lily dabbed at her face with her sleeve.

"Let's sit down at the table. I don't think he'll be able to hear us if we keep our voices low," Lily warned.

"You sit and I'll make myself busy. If he breaks in, at least I'll look like a real Harvey maid." Josie looked toward the bed and a small writing desk. On the other side of the bed was a nightstand that held a table and a lamp.

The washstand on on another wall included a mirror over the basin. She bundled the soiled towels and hung up the fresh ones. "If I have to make a quick exit, I'll have the dirty linens as an excuse," she whispered to Lily.

Her face puffy and lined with worry, Lily looked out the window, which faced the Castañeda Hotel. Josie suspected she'd not slept but sat in the chair all night. That she'd been up for hours, worrying and crying.

Finished with the linens, she perched on the edge of the bed. "Tell me everything. How you got here."

"Sheriff Cortez came to the hotel. He pulled me aside and arrested me on the spot. I haven't slept a wink since." Her chin ducked to cover more tears. Josie suspected Lily felt shocked and ashamed. "I didn't do anything, Josie. I swear."

"What evidence did Cortez have?" She knew what the sheriff told her, but she wanted to hear it from Lily.

"The gun, for one." Lily's eyes grew wide. "The matron found it in my room. She brought it to the sheriff. I guess it was the same one that killed Bobby Trask. Something about the pattern on the leather handle. And then they had a handkerchief."

Stifling another sob, she dabbed at her eyes with the corner of her apron and continued. "I don't carry a weapon,"

Lily insisted. "You remember how some of the girls had guns. But not me. I don't even know how to shoot one, let alone load the bullets."

"So someone planted the gun in your room. That's obvious," Josie concluded.

"I just assumed it was Matron. She's the one who brought it to the sheriff. She has keys to every room." A big sigh escaped her lips. "I denied it of course. I never would. You know me!"

"Even if it were yours," Josie reasoned, "did the sheriff explain what your motive would be? No decent woman, especially a Harvey Girl, would dare to ruin her reputation by stepping out with a salesman. Let alone killing him."

Lily sniffed and rolled her eyes. "Have you ever tried to tell someone you are virtuous? It just sounds like an excuse. The more I insisted, the worse it got. He could barely control his contempt.

"But then he came up with another bit of evidence. Something about leaving my handkerchief behind. I demanded to see it. When I pushed, he refused, said it was back at his office. Then he spun some story about a witness seeing me visit Bobby on a regular basis. How I'd come and gone late at night. I demanded to face my accuser, but the sheriff said no."

Lily's jaw set. Josie felt her fear but also her pluck. Lily wasn't going to take this lying down.

"So let me get this straight. You never were interested in Bobby Trask. You didn't step out with him or meet him in his room. Don't look at me that way, I'm not besmirching your reputation. I just want to hear your statement."

"Of course not! I wouldn't go out with him if he were the last man on earth. Bobby had plenty of women. He'd bribe them, even resort to blackmail, or so I hear. But I didn't like him. I refused to accept any of his trinkets. He soon gave up.

"I'd never ruin my chances of a good marriage by cavorting with the likes of Bobby Trask. You know that." Lily's cheeks flushed with indignation.

Josie patted her hand. "I just had to make sure."

"I'm engaged to a boy back home actually. I didn't get a chance to tell you before you left." Lily's tone sounded critical.

Josie felt the accusation, her chest tightening. "I'm happy for you."

"Well it's more like we're engaged to be engaged. As soon as he saves enough money, we'll make the announcement. Times are difficult with the farm. My parents are barely making ends meet. That's the only reason they agreed for me to work in New Mexico in the first place. I send nearly all of my earnings back home."

Josie wanted to believe that tossing away the life of a young woman like Lily must prick the sheriff's conscience on some level. She didn't think he was that much of a scoundrel. But now she wasn't so sure. Especially after seeing the hulk standing outside Lily's door.

"Have you ever seen that guy before? The one outside? He looks like a gun for hire."

"His name is Elias McCall. He used to work for Fred," Lily explained. "When we first arrived, he had a job on the railroad. An older guy who gets around. Rumor has it he's a gambler. Got into trouble and left the company. Now he's the sheriff's man."

A knock came to the door. Josie jumped to her feet.

"You been in there too long. Open up!" Elias McCall's fist beat on the wood.

Josie grabbed her load of soiled linens and rushed to

release the chain. Once she opened the door, Elias barged in, a gun raised in one hand. "I told you no funny business. Now get outta here." He shoved Josie into the hallway.

She gripped the towels to her chest and broke into a fast walk. Thankfully McCall didn't follow. Turning the corner, she slowed her pace and patted her hair back in place.

It wasn't until she safely returned to the linen room that she was able to draw a deep breath. *This detective work isn't for sissies*, she concluded, stripping off her Harvey Girl uniform. She folded the dress and apron and returned them to the shelf.

By the time she'd put her dress back on, she had her next plan. Confront the sheriff. He'd most likely sequestered Lily at the women's dormitory on the pretense that he intended to make things more official very soon. She felt a surge of hope. *I may have time to get her out of this mess. Get going, Josie.*

CHAPTER SEVENTEEN

Josie slipped out the back door of the dormitory. Her plan to confront the sheriff might not be as simple as she'd imagined. Finding him was one thing, engaging his attention another. Impulsiveness had gotten her into trouble in the past. But she rationalized to herself: *I get things done. No one can say I don't. Plus freeing Lily may be my only way to redemption.*

Her father made a habit of calling her on the carpet for the quick way she came to conclusions, acting without thought of consequences.

"Charley's the same," she'd say. "You'd have praised him for his leadership if he'd done what I did."

"Charles is a boy. My expectations are different." Her father, having done his duty, would turn his eyes back to his newspaper without further comment.

Josie stopped to glance at the bakery window. Bizcochitos filled one tray. Her mouth watered. The delicious memory of the local buttery light cookie with spiced anise and the dusting of cinnamon sugar made her smile.

The bell over the door jingled as she stepped inside.

Minutes later she carried a small sack of six bizcochitos in her hand. She made her way toward Plaza Park.

Located in the heart of Old Town, the park was a favorite spot for people to linger and for her to people watch. Shaded by trees, she could observe the comings and goings of the townspeople while enjoying her cookies. She found an empty bench near the bandstand and sat down.

Josie brushed crumbs from her lips and then reached into her bag for the next cookie. After licking cinnamon sugar off her bottom lip, she had time to think about Lily. How frightened her friend looked, and no wonder. That sheriff's man keeping her hostage. Josie shuddered.

She removed her notebook and pencil from her bag and made a few notes. *The only way to prove the gun doesn't belong to Lily is to find out who does own it. That's a must.* Josie knew this task would require knowledge from the community, knowledge she didn't have. People seemed to know their guns in New Mexico. They most likely knew what their neighbors carried as well.

I can keep explaining how Lily's family needs money, how she'd never risk her employment. But unless Cortez knew her, he wouldn't believe me. If only I could get him and Lily in the same room. He would be forced to pay attention.

After her last cookie, she made a decision. I'll head back to the courthouse, sit outside, and wait for the sheriff. I will beg him to go with me to talk to Lily.

She closed her notebook and crumpled her bakery bag. While she waited for Cortez, surveillance at the courthouse would be easy if she found a lookout spot across the street.

Outside the courthouse, she spotted a cluster of cottonwood trees across the street. The perfect place to sit and wait, she decided. Josie took the first available bench, placing her bag next to her. *Hopefully no one will join me.* She had no time for idle conversation about the weather.

Josie kept her eye on the courthouse entrance. Pulling out her notebook, she pretended to write. When she observed that nobody looked toward her bench, she set her writing implements aside and waited, no longer concerned that she'd be seen.

Twenty minutes passed and Josie felt restless. Her fingers tapped on the page. She hated sitting still.

Two familiar men exited the courthouse. *I know them.* She felt her pulse quicken. Frank DiWitt and his son Frankie appeared to be in a heated discussion.

Josie held up her notebook to block the bottom half of her face while she looked over the top. Father and son made their way toward a Ford parked on the street. Frankie's face had flushed red with emotion. The father's fists were clenched.

Interesting, Josie thought. *But no cigar. Where's the sheriff...*

She ducked her head to make note of the DiWitts' exit. When she looked up, she felt a jolt of surprise. Finally—Cortez himself.

The sheriff walked briskly from the courthouse, the midday sun glinting off of the silver star pinned to his shirt. His black Stetson sat low over his forehead. The gun on his belt jiggled against his thigh as he made his way down the street.

Josie quickly stood and hurried to catch up. She stepped in behind him, only a few paces back. After one block she called out, "Going somewhere, Sheriff?"

Cortez looked over his shoulder. When he saw it was her, he shook his head. "Not now, señorita."

"I want you to sit down with Lily and me to discuss the case. That way I'll be able to see the evidence." Josie picked up her pace.

Passersby glanced at her, but no one stopped. She broke into a slow run. "Excuse me," she huffed at a man she passed. She called out again. "It would be easier if you stopped so we can discuss the case like two adults. Plus, look at all of these people. They'll certainly conclude I'm a spurned lover if you refuse to speak to me. The gossip. Jeepers. I can't image what people will think."

He slowed his pace, pausing to adjust his belt. She came alongside. His voice sounded grim. "People in Las Vegas will reelect me on my reputation. Silly women chase me all the time. Now run along and pack your bag. Muy rápido."

CHAPTER EIGHTEEN

"Never mind about you, what about Lily? I've seen her, you know, in that women's dormitory. She's scared to death."

He raised his eyes and then lowered them, staring directly into hers. "I don't know how you got in the room, nor do I care. From my perspective, the case is closed. We have our suspect in custody. Like I told you last night, your services are no longer required."

"So you say," she admitted brightly. "But I have evidence to the contrary, which I will report to my employers. They won't be in any hurry to implicate one of their own, a loyal young Harvey Girl like Lily. Unlike me, she's never given them an ounce of trouble."

Josie had no evidence, but now was not time to parse the truth. She soon would have, if given half a chance.

"I have to go now." He looked over her head, his voice sounding less confident. She followed his gaze.

Above her was a wooden plaque for The Velvet Rose Tea Shop hanging over the door. She'd heard about the shop. Run by a Chinese woman named Madame Liu.

Other Harvey Girls whispered how they'd seen several

Las Vegas muckety-mucks frequent the shop. The girls had been warned by Matron herself that the tea shop was off limits.

At the time, Josie figured the warnings were overblown. Probably just another way to nudge the Chinese woman out of town. The local newspaper hadn't helped. They'd slandered Madame Liu, with nothing to back them up other than pure bias.

Like one woman selling tea was some kind of national threat. Sure, Chinese immigrants had built the railroads. Half the country owed them for that. But now that they stayed, made a living, opened up a shop or two, suddenly folks acted like something was being stolen right out from under them.

In Boston, a tea shop like this would've been a novelty. College girls, matrons in silk gloves, all sipping jasmine and acting cultured. But out here? In a place still trying to shake the dust off its boots? A Chinese-run tea shop wasn't considered proper. Especially not for decent girls like the Harvey Girls. Josie had never been good at following the rules, but even she knew the difference between harmless tea and small-town scandal.

The shop's door was painted red, the Open sign prominently displayed in the front window. Josie had heard that patrons were offered a variety of fragrant Chinese teas along with local treats.

She watched as the sheriff disappeared inside, the door closing behind him.

Her never-ending hunger and curiosity made her next decision obvious. She reached for the door handle. But then a cowboy stopped her with a tap on the shoulder. He tipped his white Stetson. "Excuse me, miss," he said, looking askance at the shop's red door. "That shop might not be safe."

"Okay, Tom Mix," she said sarcastically. She'd seen the actor in movies, and this man was the spitting image. Plus he seemed to think her business was his concern.

Aware that lingering outside might draw even more attention, she explained. "I'm meeting a friend," she assured the cowboy, and opened the door to the sound of a bell tinkling overhead. She entered without a backward glance.

The scent of herbs, lavender, sage, and rosemary wrapped around her the moment she stepped inside. Dried flowers dangled from a pole behind the counter, their faded petals whispering of summer fields. Warm spice lingered in the air—cinnamon and cardamom, two of Josie's favorites. Dark wooden shelves lined the far wall, each neatly stacked with glass jars, tea leaves promising more flavors with exotic names she'd never heard of before.

The counter beneath the shelves held an assortment of porcelain teapots, small cups, and a carved wooden abacus. Dangling strings of beads blocked the doorway next to the counter. *That must be the way to the kitchen*, she thought. *A private area, only for the infamous Madame Liu.*

She spotted Sheriff Cortez immediately. He sat at a table for two. *He must be meeting someone*, she concluded. Josie didn't acknowledge him. She looked away and waited.

"May I help you?" a Chinese woman Josie judged to be in her fifties greeted her. Her tone sounded cultured and precise. She spoke in clear English. Her gray hair had been tightly knotted in a bun at her neck. Two chopsticks were poked vertically into the center, tilted in opposite directions.

She wore a midnight-blue silk dress with rose embroidery that wound along the hem and collar. The dress hugged her figure, flaring slightly at the bottom.

"I'm here by myself," Josie explained, wondering if she'd be turned away.

"Over there. Table for one." The Chinese woman's voice shifted, her words now clipped. She gestured with an open palm. Josie took her seat. The woman lingered. "First time?" she asked.

"Yes," Josie replied.

"Jasmine for you," the woman said, tilting her head slightly. "I know."

Something in the way she said "I know" made Josie blink. She wasn't used to being studied so closely. The Chinese woman's eyes—deep-set, dark, and focused—made her uncomfortable.

Does she do this with everyone? Josie wondered. *Diagnose them and prescribe tea?*

"Jasmine would be perfect," she said at last. Then her gaze drifted downward. The woman wore a pair of scuffed cowboy boots, the tips peeking from beneath the hem of her skirt. Josie smiled faintly. "You must be the proprietor?"

The woman's expression shifted. Her eyes softened.

"I am Madame Liu. My shop." Then she drew herself up. "I do everything. I wait tables. Blend tea. Serve tea. Clean floor." She dipped her chin. "Pick up all the mess."

Each sentence was stripped bare, with no wasted words. A kind of defiance lived in their simplicity.

Madame Liu spoke again. "You that Harvey Girl detective."

Josie's jaw dropped. "How did you know?"

"I know." She nodded.

Josie leaned closer. "Did you hear about me from him over there?" She tilted her head toward the sheriff.

"Regular customer." Madame Liu glared and then nodded toward the sheriff.

The sound of the bell tinkling over the door made Josie look up. Madame Liu turned around. Josie followed her glance. It was Delores Delgado.

"Wait there," Madame Liu ordered.

Delores nodded.

After a whispered conversation, Delores made her way to the table where the sheriff sat. He immediately stood and pulled out a chair for her.

Madame Liu came back to Josie. "Sweet treats. On house. You pay for tea. Not free." She disappeared behind the beaded curtain into the back room.

Now Josie had the chance to get a closer look at the sheriff and the matron.

Delores had removed her stylish hat. Hair dressed in curls that surrounded her face managed to soften her features and accentuate her blue eyes.

"Buenos días," the sheriff greeted Delores. To Josie's ears it sounded like an invitation. Apparently Miss Delgado agreed. Her cheeks had flushed bright red with appreciation.

CHAPTER NINETEEN

Josie kept her eyes on the couple. She felt especially intrigued by the transformation of Delores Delgado, who wore a high-necked ruffled shirt of the finest silk. Her long burgundy skirt hung gracefully, the hem resting mid-calf.

They leaned across the table, eyes locked.

"Delores." Cortez spoke her name in an intimate way. "I'm happy you could get away."

"My day off." She seductively batted her lashes.

One glove came off, then the other. She set them aside. Then she arranged the folds of her skirt, casting him a side-eye. Sheriff Cortez's fingers pulled at the tablecloth as he watched.

The couple seemed oblivious to Josie's stare. She felt her cheeks flush as she continued to observe. The sheriff nestled his lips against Delores's bare palm, his mustache brushing her wrist. Josie's nose twitched. She could almost feel the tickle.

The matron not only looked entirely different in regular daywear, she wore very expensive jewelry. A gold watch and gold earrings. Even the comb in her hair was gold.

Gifts from a suitor? Josie wondered. Was the sheriff the giver, or were there others? She reached for her notebook.

Her pencil scrawled across the page. *Sheriff romantically involved with DiWitt and Delgado. Do the women know about each other?*

The beads clicked against each other as Madame Liu returned from the kitchen. She held a teapot and a plate of treats. Josie closed her notebook.

Steam escaped from the spout of the pot as she placed the tea and plate on Josie's table. The Chinese woman then turned abruptly and disappeared past the beads.

In just a minute, Madame Liu returned with another pot. Josie watched as she served the sheriff and the matron. When finished, Madam Liu bowed. She made her way to an empty small table in the opposite corner.

From there she could observe the door and the entire room. With her back straight, she eyed her customers, a wise look on her face.

Josie reached for a piece of toast. Cinnamon had been sprinkled over a thick layer of butter. She took a bite, self-conscious about the crunch. She wiped her mouth and averted Madame Liu's glare.

She ate every toasty bite and then lifted an almond cookie. After eating every treat on the plate, she opened her notebook again. The sheriff cleared his throat loudly enough for her to look up. He scowled directly at her and then turned his head back to his companion.

"I don't know what she's doing here," he said in a voice meant for Josie to overhear.

She wrote in her notebook. *Is Madame Liu's discretion sought for a price?*

. . .

An hour later, Madame Liu closed the door behind Delores Delgado. She cleared the table and then collected the money from the sheriff. "See you later," she said. He glared at Josie on his way out.

Now she was the only customer left in the tea room. Madame Liu turned the sign on the door to Closed. She walked to Josie's table.

"I'll get the bill," she said.

"Maybe you could help me, Madame Liu." Josie nodded. "You seem to know a lot about this town. A man is dead. I need to find out who killed him."

"I know," Madame Liu commented. "You're wasting time in my shop. Pay your bill. Then get to work."

Josie persisted. "I think you know more than you're telling. Especially about Sheriff Cortez and Delores Delgado. Do they come here often?"

"I am my own woman. I have a shop. I have lots of tea." She sniffed with dismissal.

Madame Liu watched her face. Josie felt her cheeks burn with frustration. But then her anger turned to something akin to curiosity. Madame Liu was different, more independent.

"Here's my advice." Madame Liu's dark eyes looked back and forth. "Worry less about enemy's opinion, more about your own."

Josie couldn't imagine what that meant.

"Think for self," Madame Liu insisted. Then she lifted the empty plate from the table, ending the discussion.

CHAPTER TWENTY

Madame Liu returned with a slip of paper. "Pay now. Shop closed."

Josie had spent nearly all her spare cash on more clothing, and now she was stuck. She dug into her purse, coming up with a few coins.

"Not enough." The Chinese woman pushed her hand away. "Pay later. I keep tab."

She wanted to know more about this curious shop owner. So she asked, "Do you find... Is life hard for you in Las Vegas?" She stumbled over her question, not wanting to offend.

"Not hard," Madame Liu replied. "I'm Apple-pie American wrapped in fortune cookie." She grinned and pointed to her door. "Time for you to go now, I have work."

On the walk back to the hotel, Josie got to wondering about Madame Liu's advice. *Think for self.* She felt it was important, but she wasn't certain how to apply the wisdom to her own life. She also wondered if Madame Liu's guidance wasn't just a decoy to avoid answering her question about the sheriff and the matron.

What about those two? she asked herself. They might be intimately involved, but there had to be more. Delgado could have planted the gun and the handkerchief in Lily's room. She had access with that set of keys. The handkerchief was one thing. They were a dime a dozen. But how had she gotten hold of the murder weapon? That was the question. Unless, of course, it belonged to her, and she was covering up her own involvement.

Unlike Lily, Josie had no trouble believing Delores Delgado would use the butt end of a gun to hit a man on the head. Given the right circumstances...

Josie kept walking. Past the Emporium, then the next shop. *Wait a minute. No more ladies' hats.* The display window and door had been boarded up.

She remembered her father's warning, right before she left. "I think there's something fishy about this detective job offer. Food is scarce. Workers are scrambling for jobs. Even Harvey has cut down his expenses. Everyone is firing employees because people cannot afford to travel like they used to. Why would they want to hire you? Makes no sense," he'd added with a huff. "I won't be close by to protect another one of your impulsive decisions." He'd sounded angry, but underneath, Josie knew it made him sad.

At the time she'd stubbornly refused to admit that he was right. But now she could see with her own eyes the economic downturn. With the exception of the farmers market, Telegraph Avenue wasn't nearly as prosperous as it once was. She blinked, wiping perspiration from her forehead. *Surely the government will step in to avoid an actual crisis. But I wonder when...*

CHAPTER TWENTY-ONE

Josie walked past the doorman into the hotel lobby. Businessmen chatted and smoked cigars. People waited in line to be seated in the dining room. *Some still have the wherewithal to travel*, she thought.

Josie made her way to the newsstand counter. A man with a cigar leaned against the glass. A puff of smoke circled his head as he turned the pages of his paper.

The counter was stacked with neatly folded glossy magazines and a selection of cigars. The *Las Vegas Daily Optic* caught her eye, the headline above the fold drawing her immediate attention.

"Rodeo Comes to Las Vegas. Thrills and Spills Expected at Annual Event!" She felt a stirring of excitement. Because the men in the photo looked familiar. Chef Lansky stood next to Elias McCall.

Lansky smiled while McCall glowered toward the camera. Josie shuddered, remembering when he brandished the gun. She picked up the paper for a closer look.

The men in the photograph obviously knew each other.

The way they stood together, posing for the camera. The smiles, so self-satisfied. Maybe invested in a horse or made a major winning bet. They had to be important enough for the newspaper to think their readers would be interested.

Her eyes scanned the background of the photo. This reminded her of a beginning algebra problem. If A knows B and B knows C, does A know C?

Could McCall be C, the third man, the one Padre Emilio refused to name?

Her pool of suspects now included Lansky and McCall. They were most likely the ones meeting with the victim in the church. But the question remained, why?

Her heart pumped wildly as she scrutinized the photo more closely. Lansky and McCall stood in front of a horse, who was tied to the corral fence a few feet away. His coat had a bold patchwork of chestnut brown and ivory. Her heart thumped. *That's Rio. And look, next to him is Daniel.* Though he held his face away from the camera, she'd know his body and distinct hat with the crow's feather anywhere.

She'd almost not realized the pinto in the background was Rio. He was no longer the bedraggled abused horse she'd rescued. This Rio's nostrils flared, as if he was looking for something in the crowd. His mane hung over his neck, full and even. His flanks had filled out.

"May I put this on my bill?" she asked the man behind the counter.

Josie awoke from her afternoon siesta feeling refreshed. She folded her hands behind her head and stared at the ceiling. Her thoughts turned to the newspaper. What were those three up to? More important, what were they hiding... *I need to talk to Padre Emilio again.*

Josie rolled onto her side and swung her legs over the bed. *Won't he be surprised when he hears I've discovered the name of the third man all on my own. There's no need for him to break the vow of the confessional. Maybe he'll have more to say.*

At the basin, a splash of cold water refreshed her face. One look in the small oval mirror assured her she was presentable. "I'm a Harvey House detective," she announced to her reflection. The words still felt empty, but she'd wasn't going to give up.

This time there was no line in the Castañeda lobby. The front desk clerk sorted through a stack of mail. A maid swiped a table with a feather duster. The doorman lounged against a wall, his eyes closed.

Sloppy behavior, Josie thought. *What would Fred say? Have the Harvey House standards for excellence slipped? Why isn't someone poking the doorman to stand up straight?*

The desk clerk looked up. "May I help you, miss?"

"My name is Josephine MacFarland," she began. "Do you have any mail for me?"

He blinked. "Let me check." He disappeared and returned holding an envelope. "Delivered this morning," he explained.

Her name had been printed in bold letters on the back. *Maybe a paycheck. That would certainly be welcome.* "Do you know who dropped this off?"

"I don't know, miss." He turned back to sorting the mail.

"Thank you very much." She sat in a nearby leather chair.

Upon opening the envelope, cash fell into her lap, along with a note. "Consider this your final payment."

Josie's heart dropped. Her services were no longer required. Just like that. Sheriff Cortez had warned her.

She counted the cash to find enough for a return trip to Boston.

She felt a sob in the back of her throat. The sheriff had gotten his way. Lily would go down for the murder. Josie would be sent home. And Las Vegas would still be the cowboy town that Cortez controlled.

CHAPTER TWENTY-TWO

She counted the cash in her lap again. A new plan formed in her mind. *What if...* she thought. *What if I don't go away just yet? What if I stay until they make me leave? I could still free Lily. Maybe find the real killer.*

The risk outweighed the long return home. Her mother taking over her life again the minute she stepped off the train. There would be a series of new suitors, followed by a slimmer selection of the most suitable, and finally an engagement. Father would huff and still be reading his paper.

I can't leave yet, Josie thought. *I haven't helped Lily. I owe her that.* Her jaw clenched. *I might need to make some extra cash. But until they toss me to the street, I can keep investigating.*

Josie skipped her lunch to lie back on her bed, listening to the voices in the street.

I have some cash from the envelope. But I don't know

how long it will last. I wonder if I'll be evicted from the dining room, once they hear I've been fired.

It would be embarrassing to be escorted from the dining room and tossed to the gutter. *But what choice do I have?*

She remembered the newspaper photo. But this time she focused on Rio. *That's it!* She had a plan. *I could resurrect Joe Mack. He can ride and win a big cash prize. I did it before, I can do it again. Then I'll have my own money. I don't need the Harvey Company.* She sat up with a big smile.

Staring into her closet, she found her pointed-toe cowboy boots where she'd left them, in the corner of the wardrobe. Smooth brown leather, with the silver button near a decorative strap around the ankle. She reached above her head for Joe's hat with the black ribbon band and the single crow's feather. The sight of the feather brought a smile to her lips.

Daniel had given her that feather for luck the first time she rode Rio and showed him how she could easily compete in a barrel race. The only obstacle was her Harvey Girl reputation.

"If I'm caught, they'll fire me," she told him. He'd come up with a solution.

"A couple of women have ridden the rodeo," he said. "Prairie Rose Henderson. She rode back in the day. Things are tough now, with people losing their money. But there's Della 'Dare' McAllister. I saw her just recently. She rode in a parade. Maybe not the barrels."

Josie wasn't convinced. "If I were a man, it would be different."

"My people have different names," he told her. "Tribal and English. Why not you? Two names. Josie MacFarland and how about Joe Mack? No one will recognize you as a

Harvey Girl if you put your hair under the hat. Buy men's pants and a new shirt, you'll look like a cowboy."

He'd persuaded her in the end.

Joe Mack rode for three glorious months, winning nearly every barrel race he entered. It wasn't until the last time, when he stepped up to take the first-prize money, that someone recognized Josie MacFarland under the hat. "That there's a female," they yelled and then disappeared into the crowd.

A day later, the matron confronted her. Followed by her dismissal.

Josie closed the wardrobe door. She had time to eat a meal in the dining room before getting dressed and heading out of town to the rodeo. She even had a backup plan, should the hostess want to boot her out before she ate.

I'll invite Padre Emilio to join me. No one would dare fuss with a priest as my companion. He's the perfect escort in a man's world.

Imagining two burly Harvey bouncers taking her by the elbows and throwing her onto the street still made her wince. Maybe during dinner, if that didn't happen, she could question the padre. Find out if Elias McCall was the third man.

CHAPTER TWENTY-THREE

Padre Emilio sat across from Josie. He smiled and spoke in his soothing voice. "I was delighted to get your note. It's a pleasure to see you looking so elegant." After delivering the comment he looked embarrassed at his own words.

He's not comfortable complimenting women, Josie thought. *But he feels it's expected.*

After a pause, he smiled gently. "This is my favorite table. I've dined here on many occasions." He lifted a cup from the saucer to take a sip of coffee.

"I like it here too," she said dryly. "Though this may be my last supper." She used the term deliberately, hoping to see him smile.

His eyebrows raised. "Surely you've not found your killer already. It's been less than a week."

She leaned across the table to confide. "I know who the third man was, that one who met with Trask and the chef."

"I didn't think it would take you very long," the padre said. "How about you ask me a few simple questions. That way I don't have to say the name, but we'll both know who we mean."

"I don't want to get you in trouble with the guy upstairs." She used her finger to cross herself.

"If your questions are asked to reveal the truth"—he leveled his gaze directly into her eyes—"I will not hesitate to confirm. The Old Testament states we are to do justice, love kindness, and walk humbly."

Josie reached into her handbag. She pulled out the newspaper and showed him the headline and the photo underneath. "I picked this up in the lobby. That man, the one shaking Victor Lansky's hand, his name is Elias McCall."

Padre Emilio coughed and glanced toward the fireplace. "The Tewa pottery. So elegant," he said. Then brought his gaze back to hers. "Mr. McCall and Chef Lansky do look like friends. They remind me of the men who would visit the sanctuary late at night. Most likely to pray."

Josie pressed him further. "Maybe you could tell me, being a long-time citizen of Las Vegas, what Bobby Trask, Victor Lansky, and Elias McCall could possibly have in common besides prayer. Surely not just their piety." She smiled.

The priest chuckled. "Yes, their interest in prayer is commendable. But don't forget, we are advised by Jesus not to pray in public, but alone in a closet. To preserve our humility."

"So if three men pretended to meet at night for prayer, that's okay with you." Josie was confused at the turn of their conversation.

"No, señorita. What I'm trying to say is that Mr. McCall told me they met for prayer. But I knew that wasn't the truth. I didn't get into their real business, but I am aware their intentions were hardly honorable."

She sat back in her chair, feeling a brief moment of

satisfaction. She'd received her confirmation. A firsthand witness.

After dessert Josie folded her napkin. "Thank you for this evening, Padre," she said in a quiet voice. "Perhaps we can have supper again another time."

"May I escort you to the lobby? It seems you're in a hurry to go."

"Escort me? Such a gentleman." She winked.

"I wasn't always a Franciscan," he explained. "The founder of my order, along with many of us, came from quite well-to-do families. I had another life, you know, before taking my vows."

"Look at you, Padre. Sharing your personal story with the likes of unsuitable me. I am in a hurry. If you must know, I'm trying to get out and stick you with the bill." She looked over her shoulder. "I'm no longer certain that I'm employed, you see. They've arrested a Harvey Girl for the murder, and I got my notice that the case was closed in writing."

"I see. That is too bad. I was so enjoying our friendship." He stood, offering her an elbow. "Let's walk out together."

It was nearly nine o'clock by the time Josie and Father Emilio parted ways. She hurried up the staircase and then down the hall toward her room. Her heart fluttered. She didn't know what excited her more, taking on the identity of Joe Mack or reuniting with Rio.

She pulled on one boot, then the other. Her britches came next. They felt stiff. It had been a while since she'd worn them. The ruffled shirt tucked easily into her pants. In front of the mirror, she braided her hair and then wound it into a knot on top of her head. The black cowboy hat easily covered her red hair.

Running her hand over her chin, she wondered if anyone would notice. *No stubble.* But then she dismissed her concern. *No one will look my way. I'll slip into the crowd. I won't be a threat. Just another young man at the rodeo, looking for fun.*

Opening the door, she peeked outside. It wouldn't do Josie any good if someone saw Joe coming out of her room. No matron nor a Harvey maid in sight. *Good*, Joe thought.

He closed the door quietly, dropping his shoulders into an unassuming slump. One more tug on the cowboy hat and he tucked his chin to his chest, making his way to the stairs. Joe didn't exhale until he walked out the back entrance toward the main street.

So far so good, he thought.

The rumble of an approaching truck caught his ear. He waved and the driver slowed down, brakes squealing. The driver called out, "Where you going, son?"

He deepened his voice to reply. "Rodeo grounds, sir. Are you going that way? I'd be much obliged."

The man chuckled. "Ain't every day you meet a fella so polite. Hop in the back."

Joe slung one leg, then the other over the side of the truck bed. Settling himself into the corner, he pulled his knees to his chin. The smell of alfalfa and dust filled his nostrils. As the truck rattled forward, he steadied himself with both hands.

The driver called out the open window, his voice cutting through the dry air. "You lookin' to ride or watch tonight?"

Joe kept his voice in the low register. "Maybe both. Got my eye on a young bronc. Soon as I get some money and the dust out of my teeth from last time, I'll come up with the entry fee and be ready to ride again."

The man chuckled. "Ain't that the truth. New Mexico gets into your skin. Mine's as dry as sandpaper. What's your name, cowboy?"

He flinched, realizing he wasn't ready to get that personal. But he didn't want to make the driver suspicious either, so he went ahead. "Joe Mack. Heard of me?" He made that last part sound like a joke, the words of an inflated young man ready to make a name for himself.

"Can't say that I have," the driver admitted. "Well, Joe Mack, you got some grit for sure. You live around these parts? Raised in Las Vegas?"

Joe knew when he was being tested. This time the evasion came easier. "Not anymore. Just me and the road." He sounded curt. That was the way of the Southwest. A cowboy code. You didn't need to talk or tell all the truth about the past.

When the driver didn't ask any more questions, Joe assumed he was satisfied.

The truck bounced along the dirt path. Finally the rodeo grounds appeared at a distance in the haze of dust. Brakes squealed, bringing the truck to a stop. "Good luck out there, Joe Mack. Show 'em what you're made of."

He hopped over the side again, boots landing in the dirt. Pulling down on the brim of his hat, he called out, "Much obliged, mister."

The truck rumbled away, leaving Joe standing alone. His pulse quickened. The sound of the rodeo announcer pierced the air. "Steer roping competitors can now enter the ring."

It's good to be back...

CHAPTER TWENTY-FOUR

Sounds of cowboys calling to each other and their horses filled the air as Joe approached the rodeo entrance. He made his way toward the livestock pens. A steer moaned, followed by the crack of a bullwhip. *Feels like home,* he thought, nostalgia hitting him in the gut.

The show ring was full with spectators in the bleachers. A collective gasp caught Joe's attention as the first rider was tossed off the bronco, left in the dust. His horse skirted away with a high-pitched whinny.

Joe's fingers twitched instinctively. Visceral memories of barrel racing, not just in his mind but his body as well. The sting of the rope against his palm. The power of Rio beneath his legs.

The announcer interrupted his thoughts with a call for the next competitor, followed by the sound of a gate busting open with another cheer from the crowd.

He walked past the corral toward the betting booth. A hulking figure with a flat cap counted his cash. Elias McCall, in the flesh. Joe's eyes narrowed. He wondered,

Who keeps guard over Lily while the sheriff's man enjoys himself at the rodeo?

Elias selected a few bills and stuffed the rest into his pocket. At the same moment, Chef Lansky walked around the shed. "McCall," he called out.

He wore a white shirt and fresh britches. Without his chef's hat, Joe wouldn't have picked him out of a crowd. But he didn't mistake him for a cowboy. The shirt was too pressed.

Lansky scanned the faces of passerby.

Joe edged closer, sticking to the shade of the building so as not to be seen. He felt his heart quicken. *One of them killed Bobby Trask. Must have been for the dough.*

Joe scuffed his boots in the dirt. He pulled a fresh toothpick out of his pocket and dangled it in the corner of his mouth. Resting against the side of the building, he could hear everyone who placed a bet.

Lansky stepped up to the window and handed over a wad of cash. McCall was next. They put their money down on the same horse, then walked away together. Joe turned his head to cover a laugh. *One thing I know. Those two aren't prayer partners. That's a couple of gambling pals.* He waited before stepping into the crowd to follow. Behind but still close enough to overhear.

"The crates arrived. Stored in the usual place. Everything's waiting for the transfer. What's stopping you?" Lansky asked.

McCall's neck flushed red. "The padre's been watching real close. I can only pretend to pray for so long. I even did a confession to keep him off the scent. I'll move the goods. Just give me more time."

"I saw him with that woman who calls herself a detective," Lansky said. "I thought we'd taken care of her."

"That's what I was told," McCall said. "I'll talk to the boss. Are we done here?" He turned his head to look at Lansky.

Fearful he'd be noticed, Joe stepped behind another man. He was close enough to hear the chef's answer. "Yeah, we're done."

McCall glanced over his shoulder. "Let's get out of here. People are too close. I feel like somebody's following us." He looked toward the grandstand. "Let's sit up there."

Joe made an abrupt turn in the opposite direction. He waited for the men to find a seat. Then he leaned against a corral fence to keep his eye out.

The conversation between McCall and Lansky confirmed his suspicion. He knew they both had something to hide, and it wasn't their prayer life. Maybe a black-market operation, where goods had to be moved from one place to another to stay ahead of the law. Crates. That would mean only one thing. Most likely liquor.

Four men left their seats on the top row. Joe made a quick decision. He took the steps two at a time to take one of the seats. From behind, he had a chance to look more closely at the other spectators. A familiar black Stetson caught his eye. *Sheriff Cortez*, he mused. *Oh yeah, and I know her too. Adelle DiWitt.*

And there's her daddy, big as life. Sitting next to...

He noted a resemblance between the older ranch owner and the younger man. Especially when they turned their heads. The same chins and a similar slope to the shoulders. *That has to be Frankie,* Joe concluded.

Adelle sat, the picture of poise. She didn't look toward the sheriff, who spoke in her direction. She turned her glance to her brother, who poked her arm. Adelle forced a smile. The brother scowled, his chin set in anger.

She's being reined in, Joe concluded. And then the rancher's daughter turned toward Cortez and smiled, while the brother leaned back to talk to someone behind him. *Just like I figured,* Joe thought. *Brother told her to pay more attention to her man.*

A Native made his way up the grandstand steps. His worn leather hat and the distinctive crow's feather made Joe smile. He stopped at the top row.

"Move over, Joe," Daniel insisted. He slid next to him. "What are you doing here?"

"I'm investigating for Josie," he retorted.

"I heard Josie was let go. Thought she'd be slipping out of town by now."

"Josie is no quitter." His gut clenched in defense of his alter ego.

"Like last time, you mean." Daniel shrugged.

"Are you ever going to forgive me? I mean, Josie?"

"We'll see," Daniel said. "Answer my question."

"I'm here to get back in the game." He nodded toward the ring. "I need some dough. But when I saw those two, I followed them here."

Daniel scanned the crowd. "You're watching the sheriff and the DiWitts?"

"Maybe." Joe moved his toothpick to the other side of his mouth. "I think that's more of a date right there. Miss DiWitt's being chaperoned by her brother, with Daddy looking on. I'm really interested in Lansky and McCall. They're sitting over there." He gestured with a nod.

"So you'll tell Josie?" Daniel smiled in his direction. He liked playing the game, that Josie and Joe were two distinct people.

"Yeah," Joe agreed. "Now I suspect that the sheriff is in cahoots. All friends with Bobby Trask."

"Cortez is getting up to go," Daniel said.

"Yup." Joe stood, stretching his arms over his head.

"Before you follow him, I have something I want to show you," Daniel said

A roar went up from the crowd. People jumped to their feet.

Joe made his way down the stairs, with Daniel right behind.

CHAPTER TWENTY-FIVE

As people moved past, Daniel pulled his hat from his head. He dusted it against his pants and then ran his finger over the crow's feather—a talisman of protection. He secured the feather more tightly in the band and set the hat back on his head. The crowd parted, allowing him to edge his way into the stream of people. Joe knew he was expected to follow.

After some elbowing and dodging, the barn stood ahead. A testament to endurance. A weathered structure that had survived rain, dust storms, and many a stampede. A group of cowboys leaned over a nearby fence. Joe scanned their faces. No one he knew.

A prize bull burst out of the shoot. He gave his rider a good run for the money before dumping him to the ground. The men laughed while the cowboy stood and staggered to the closest rail. He leapt over right as the bull rushed toward him, horns nearly grazing the seat of his pants.

Daniel opened the double barn doors and then beckoned for Joe to come inside. "Before you go any farther, come into my office. A few things have changed since the last time."

This news surprised Joe. Daniel had not had an office before. Maybe he'd gotten a new job. The DiWitts owned the barn and leased it to the rodeo.

Inside the office, there was a desk and chair. Sturdy pegs lined one wall. Ropes and harnesses hung over them. A small cot, tucked into a corner, held a distinctive black and gray blanket. One Joe knew was handmade by the Tewa.

Joe reached out a hand to lift a familiar harness off the peg, holding it between his fingers. "You kept it," he said.

"I was waiting for you," Daniel replied.

"Even after Josie..." He was going to say ran away, but he was stopped by Daniel's next words.

"I hoped Josie would come back." Then Daniel smiled, his face transforming to an expression of gentle understanding. "And Joe too." He held up his forefinger next to his middle finger, no space between.

Was the gesture about Josie and Joe. One and the same person. Or was he saying he felt close to them as well.

Joe didn't want to ask.

Next to the bridle was a braided rawhide rope. Joe reached for it, running his fingers over the leather. He'd thought of it often, how Daniel had given it to him as a gift that first time he rode as Joe Mack.

A sharp cry from a horse called out. The sound more like a cross between a coyote's yip and a rebel yell.

An unmistakable welcome, Joe smiled. He'd dreamed of this moment.

"Rio's done waiting." Daniel nodded. "I wanted to be here, to make sure you knew. He's still yours."

Joe coughed, his throat thick with emotion. He felt his memories strongly. That last barrel, the roar of the crowd. The judges staring with disbelief at their stopwatches.

Daniel grinned. Maybe he knew what Joe was thinking. "Just an unknown skinny cowboy, riding a beat-up pinto, setting a record-breaking time. No wonder you caught everyone's attention that day."

Joe hung the bridle back on the peg. Rio called again, this time sounding more insistent. Joe bolted out of the office door, down the middle of the barn, toward the last stall on the right. Rio, with his head hanging over the half door, nickered in a low voice.

Joe unlatched the hasp and slipped into the stall. He stopped for a moment to have a good look at the horse. Rio appeared the picture of health. The pinto's once-gaunt frame had filled out, his chest broad and strong, his muscles taut beneath a glossy coat.

The sturdy build of his quarter horse lineage was easily recognizable. The powerful hindquarters were known for speed and endurance. The deep chest promised stamina, and a refined head with intelligent dark eyes made him the ideal companion for ranchers and rodeo riders.

Rio huffed and pawed at the straw with one hoof.

Joe offered an open palm. Rio nuzzled and snorted his warm breath, making Joe smile. "I forgot your carrot." He owed the horse that much of an explanation for his long absence.

He patted his neck and ran his open hand down Rio's smooth flank. The pinto markings were striking. Rich chestnut splotches in a field of white.

A thick well-worn Navajo blanket lay across the horse's broad back. The deep pigmentation of indigo and rust-red patterns were familiar. Daniel had honored Rio by using a blanket he'd made himself. Also a Tewa design.

Joe lowered his face into Rio's neck, inhaling the warm

earthy scent. Rio flicked his ears forward and whinnied softly. Was Rio trying to tell him something?

Joe looked into his wide-set eyes.

Rio shook his head back and forth.

Joe's nerves tingled.

Then he heard a woman's voice call, "Stable hand!"

CHAPTER TWENTY-SIX

Do I hide? That was his first instinct. The Joe Mack disguise held up, but only when he kept a distance.

"Miss DiWitt," Daniel greeted the intruder.

What's she doing here?

Joe felt his heart sink. Well aware that Adelle DiWitt had seen Josie up close just recently, Joe thought he'd be recognized if she took a really good look at him. *She's no fool*, he concluded.

He ran his hand down Rio's nose to soothe the horse. "I'll take care of this," he whispered.

Joe peeked through a gap in the boards to watch.

Daniel stood very close to Miss DiWitt. When she spoke, he leaned even closer. He held his hands behind his back. This was a pose Joe hadn't seen before.

Adelle DiWitt played with a loose tendril of hair while Daniel's eyes followed her expression, a smile playing at his lips. Finally he spoke in a low voice. Joe couldn't make out the words. This was followed by light laughter from Adelle.

Rio nudged Joe's leg. As he ran his hand down the

horse's nose, he realized that Daniel and Adelle were friends. At least that's how it looked to him.

"I'm here to see my father's mare," Adelle said in a loud voice. "I'm to ride in the closing parade."

"She's ready," Daniel said.

Joe ducked down right as they passed by. A horse whinnied, and they disappeared into the stall together.

Rio nudged him again. Joe straightened up. In his relief, a fantasy went through his mind. If this were a motion picture, he'd do a quick getaway from the barn. Jump on Rio's back. Burst out of the stall. Wave his arm in the air and ride away into the open desert, where the sun would be setting over the mountains.

A shiver went down his spine. Just the thought of such freedom made him feel alive.

Joe had lots of fantasies about riding Rio. Most of them motion picture-worthy. But now he had to do something practical. Slip out of the barn before Adelle DiWitt came back.

He adjusted his britches. Opening the half-door slowly, he closed it behind with a wink at Rio. Then he stopped short.

"Who's this, then?" Adelle DiWitt came closer. Her hair looked disheveled. She brushed a curl back behind her ear. There was straw on her split riding skirt.

Her eyes swept over Joe's body, stopping at his face.

Perspiration broke out on his hands. He wiped them against his pants. The desire to run nearly overcame him, but he stayed, looking down at his boots.

"Hey, Joe." Daniel led a beautiful mare out of the stalls. She'd been groomed for the rodeo parade, her mane in braids with ribbons holding the ends. Daniel brought the horse up to Adelle, blocking her view of Joe.

"He's an old friend," he told Adelle. "We were catching up before you arrived." He pointed to the horse. "I saddled her and she's ready for a ride. Let me help you up."

Daniel offered his hands, fingers entwined, for support. She placed her boot right as he hoisted her on the back of the horse. Next he adjusted her stirrups, running his hand down the saddle close to her shapely leg. Then Daniel moved to the other side.

Joe observed Adelle's face. Her cheeks flushed pink, right as Daniel handed her the reins.

As they walked away, Joe had to admit Adelle looked like a queen, sitting on the beautiful thoroughbred.

As soon as she was out of sight, Daniel turned to Joe. "You'll have to ride Rio another time. I've got to saddle up the rest of the horses for the parade."

Joe frowned. He wanted to ask more questions about Adelle DiWitt. "See ya." He walked away right as Rio called out from the barn.

Joe had no trouble hitching a ride back into town. He had the driver drop him on Railroad Avenue. Joe nodded to the doorman and stepped into the lobby. He took two steps at a time to the second floor. With a glance over his shoulder, he made sure no one was coming before slipping into Josie's room.

The bed had been turned down. The curtains were drawn for the evening. He tossed away his hat and took off his boots.

Just like changing costumes backstage.

Now Josie stood in her undergarments. Her hand inched to a tight muscle in her back, easing an ache that came from holding her body so tall.

Reaching for her nightgown she realized that her day dress had been moved. *I know I hung it next to my church skirt... Did the maid look through my belongings?*

She calmed herself. It could have been worse if the maid had found her cowboy clothing. A deep breath brought calm. *It was a good thing I wore everything Joe owned and left nothing behind.*

Her nightgown slipped easily over her head. With a quick tug she brought the chair closer to the wardrobe. She stood and slid all of Joe's belongings, including the hat and the boots, to the back of the top shelf. Everything would be hidden from view.

Josie secured her bathrobe with a quick pull on the tie. Then she grabbed a washcloth and a bar of soap. The bathroom was located down the hall.

To her relief, there was no wait. An available claw-foot tub with both hot and cold running water. Nothing but the best for a Harvey House guest. She closed and locked the bathroom door.

Fred really was the king of hospitality. She watched the water level rise in the tub. It was only when she leaned back into the warm water that she remembered, *This may be my last soak before I go home in disgrace.*

She closed her eyes.

She paused to remember Rio. How he'd recognized Joe and called to him.

She ran a cloth over her arms and neck, leaving her face and shoulders for last. As the water grew tepid, she knew it was time to get out and dry off.

Back in her room, Josie dressed in a fresh nightgown. She turned down her sheets and lay in bed, appreciating the cool breeze from the open window. A freight train tooted in the distance. The clip-clop of hooves sounded hollow from the street below.

A night bird warbled as she drifted off to sleep.

CHAPTER TWENTY-SEVEN

The following morning, a prolonged train whistle woke Josie with a start. With both feet on the floor, she looked toward the window. The bath and sleep had left her feeling rejuvenated. Except for the day dress. The hair on the back of her neck rose at the thought: Maybe my room was inspected.

She looked around. At home she could depend on the privacy of her own bed chamber, but now, she realized, not in a hotel.

She'd been raised to feel safe. With men like her father and brother as her protectors, Josie wasn't used to suspecting everything and everyone. She didn't like the feeling at all. Another ignorance is bliss situation. She paused to chastise herself. *Am I really that stupid or just blind to everything that isn't about me?*

She slid the chair over for a quick glance on top of the wardrobe. Nothing had been moved while she'd bathed last night. She exhaled and returned the chair.

In just a few minutes, Josie walked outside the hotel

toward the bakery. Her cash was dwindling, but she had enough for one more cup of coffee and a pastry.

A line had formed outside the bakery. Men and women and a few children huddled together. All wore layers of worn, patched clothing. She suspected they used everything they owned on their backs. Just to keep warm.

Buddy, can you spare me a dime? echoed in her head. She watched two children play with sticks, pretending to have a sword fight.

At the front of the line she a familiar face caught her attention. "Padre," she called.

"Señorita MacFarland," he returned her greeting. "Come meet my old friend." He patted the slumped shoulder of the man next to him.

Normally Josie wouldn't approach a hobo. She'd been taught to look out for men who wore overcoats and scraggly beards. If someone held out a hand, her mother would move her closer and whisk past.

With the padre's smile, this time she didn't dare turn away. "This is Mr. Ventura," Father Emilio explained. "His circumstances have recently changed. He's a member of the parish council. I stop by in the mornings to catch up with him on the news. Mr. Ventura..." He turned to the man.

"Nice to meet ya," he said to Josie, then ducked his chin as if embarrassed.

"You too," Josie said politely. "I was going inside," she explained. "Do you suppose we could talk later? I need your advice, Padre."

"Of course," the priest said. "I'll be here for another hour. Maybe after that."

"Inside the church or the courtyard?"

"Find your way to the parish hall, adjacent to the sanctuary. You can't miss it. People will be lined up outside."

"Already?" She knew it was too soon for dinner.

"They're hungry and have nowhere else to go," he explained. "We stay open until the food runs out." Then he stared at Josie's face. She knew he was making a point, but she wasn't sure just what.

Her stomach growled. The padre motioned for her to go ahead of him. She nodded and walked inside the bakery without further thought.

The man ahead of her handed over cash. He made his way to the far corner to sit. Josie came next. She gave her order, still feeling the priest's disapproving stare.

After a quick walk, she found the parish hall behind the Our Lady of Sorrows sanctuary. The front window gave a good view to the interior of the room. Her glance stopped at the people standing behind a long serving counter.

They used long-handled scoops to dole out food. On the other side of the table, people held out their bowls, watching carefully. The end of the table held glasses and pitchers of water, along with a big pot of coffee and a stack of cups.

She felt slightly queasy, shocked that so many people were out of work and without food at the same time. Her father was right. Now she wished she'd paid more attention to his warning.

A line of people waited their turn outside. Some talked to each other. She noted a couple of men in business suits who had seen better days, children clinging to the skirts of their mothers. One girl wore shoes with her big toe poking out. Maybe she'd grown or maybe the parents couldn't afford a new pair.

Father Emilio appeared from across the courtyard. He

caught sight of her and came closer. "You see? They have no choice but to line up. There's nowhere else to go."

Josie felt a sweep of pity. "Are they all parish members?"

"Most are not," he replied. "But no one is turned away. Jesus calls us to welcome the stranger."

Josie knew her church in Boston preached the same. But she'd not seen the extravagant welcome so aptly applied until now. Shaking off her discomfort, she changed the subject.

"Padre, I need your help," Josie said.

"I assumed that's why you asked to meet me," he replied in a calm voice. "I don't have a lot of time right now. I need to check on my volunteers, bless the food, and ask God to bring comfort for those without a place to sleep. While people wait, I listen to their stories."

"I know, Father. I know there are people more needy. But I overheard a conversation last night. I think it was about your church. How items, not exactly legal, were being stored here. I wondered if you were aware?"

Lines appeared on his forehead. He seemed to be thinking. Then he made up his mind. "Come with me."

She followed him down the path toward the sanctuary, and then into a side door. They stood in the nave. "In answer to your question, I am unaware of such activity. If I were, I'd put a stop to it. But I do want to caution you. Passing on rumors will not serve you in the long run."

She felt her cheeks burn. "But isn't that exactly what you do? Listen to people confess all their dirty secrets. You deal in rumor every day."

"But I don't pass them on," he cautioned. "That's the point of the private confessional. People bring me the truth to hold for them, to find direction to make things right with their God," he reminded. "There's a difference."

"How do you know? Surely some people hide the truth from you, work behind your back. Maybe illegally."

Josie realized she'd stepped into his personal territory. And by the look on his face, he wasn't used to being questioned.

"I'm not here to judge. That is God's business," he said quietly. "But perhaps I need to hear more."

She took a deep breath. "I overheard Elias McCall talking to Chef Lansky. He said right out that he wasn't in church to pray. That he was late moving goods because the padre kept watching. He was asking for more time. So I assumed..."

The priest nodded. "Like I said before, I've seen them together at night. I hoped they were praying, but I suspected... A pickup, you say? Did he mention anything specific?"

"He did not," Josie admitted. "But I think finding out is very important. Where would such items be coming from? How and where would they be stored? And Padre, they may be bootleggers. Have you thought of that?"

"There are hidden chambers in this old building," the priest shared. "The first place that comes to mind hasn't been looked at for years. At least to my knowledge. In fact, I've never been down to the underground chamber myself. I don't suppose anyone's been there for decades.

"I heard rumors when I first arrived that there was an ancient underground burial chamber. Most of the priests are buried in the outdoor graveyard, along with a few notable parishioners. So I dismissed the rumor. I was too busy keeping up with the day-to-day problems.

"I assumed in earlier times there was concern about grave robbery. Which would explain the buried tombs."

Josie glanced toward the front of the church. "Where's the entrance to this sealed chamber?" she asked.

He rubbed his chin. "Finding the room may take time. Time I cannot afford to lose. I'm busy with hungry people who are in need. The dead can wait." He glared at Josie.

"This isn't about the dead," she explained matter-of-factly. "It's about finding a killer. Someone who may be dealing in illegally obtained goods. A Mafia connection maybe. Surely you've thought of that. Las Vegas isn't immune. But go back to your work, Padre." Her tone was tart. "I'll take it from here."

Padre Emilio sounded unhappy. "I did my best to discourage you. You are a difficult person, señorita."

She held her arms folded over her chest.

"I will show you the way, but I only have twenty minutes," he warned.

CHAPTER TWENTY-EIGHT

Josie and the padre stood shoulder to shoulder on the altar, facing the empty pews. She could imagine a sea of faces, expectant with hope, staring at the one man they thought had answers. A humbling perspective. *But does he really know all the answers?*

She'd seen many different priests growing up. Heard the gossip. She felt quite certain that they were human and subject to human frailty, just like the people they served.

Take Father Emilio, for example. Perhaps he didn't know about the clandestine operations happening under his nose. But there was an equal chance that he turned a blind eye. That every morning when he pulled on his brown cassock, prayed, and then examined his soul, he might conclude that turning a blind eye was good for his congregation.

"The sacristy is this way." He walked behind the communion table. She followed him to a narrow door where she knew the elements were stored. *The body of Christ shed for you. Blood of Christ...* echoed her in mind. She'd heard the words every week for as long as she could remember.

Shed for me... She shuddered. The Eucharist held many memories for Josie, including a sense of foreboding. She knew better than to share her doubts with her parents. Never with a nun or a priest. *Just keep 'em to yourself*, she'd concluded. *Otherwise there would be more Hail Marys.*

She knew from communicants class that priests, shielded from the laity, blessed the wine and bread in the sacristy. Shrouded in their robes, they would emerge at the beginning of each Mass. The embodied representative of the Holy Mystery.

The cloying smell of incense caught her nose. The weekly celebration of the Eucharist came flooding back. The ritual had taken hold of her in ways she couldn't explain and didn't entirely trust.

"We keep our vestments and mass supplies in there," the Father explained, breaking into her thoughts. He pointed to a line of wooden cabinets and a series of drawers.

Josie knew along with vestments, that chalices, and candles were also inside. She averted her eyes, feeling a flush come to her cheeks.

Priests dressing and undressing qualified as an impure thought. An urge to cross herself made her shrug. Then her eyes drifted upward. A crucifix hung on the wall above. The sight of Jesus's body spread on the cross made her inwardly cringe. She never believed that a truly loving father would send a son to such a death. But again, she knew better than to express her doubt to anyone.

"Where does that door go?" Josie pointed.

"There's a hallway that leads to parish offices," he explained. "It allows me to enter and exit the sacristy without being seen by the congregation. If you keep walking, you'll find another door."

Recognition sparked in his eyes, as if he'd just thought

of something. "If you walk out that door and go half a mile, you'll find a Harvey Company garage where they park the Indian Detour vehicles."

"I remember hearing about them." But then Josie wondered, *Is he thinking what I'm thinking?*

"Don't you have to get back to the soup kitchen?" She couldn't wait to walk out that door.

The town's edges looked a little ragged. Step far enough past the depot, the hotel, and the tidy dining room, and Las Vegas started to lose its polish. Dirt roads replaced sidewalks. Faded signs leaned against buildings. Many looked half-abandoned.

Josie kept walking.

The high-noon sun made her blink as perspiration rolled down from her forehead. Then she caught sight of a low-slung building. *That has to be the Harvey property.* Memories of the sleek black and red cars parking in front of the Castañeda, ready to take tourists to the local pueblos and mesas, came to mind. The drivers in uniforms and the tour guides talking nonstop about locally approved history.

Only today there wasn't a uniform or a Harvey vehicle in sight.

The wide garage doors stood slightly ajar, as if someone forgot to lock up. Or maybe they didn't care who wandered in. Josie hesitated, the faint smell of gasoline and desert dust filling the air. Her boots crunched over gravel as she moved closer.

Inside, the place was half in shadow. Rows of touring cars, their paint dulled with dust, lined one side of the building. On the other, stacked crates leaned against the far wall. Ordinary at first glance, but there was something about the mismatched wood and the faint sharp smell of alcohol that tickled her nose.

She stepped closer to make out the stenciled lettering on the nearest crate. The label read *Imported Glassware*. Josie sniffed. *A bold lie, if I'm not mistaken.* She brushed her hand over the crate. The boards were rough, splintered at the edges, most likely not something the Harvey Company would approve to ship delicate glass deliveries.

The lid shifted under her touch.

She pulled it up, just enough to peek inside.

Dark glass bottles, neatly packed in straw. Whiskey, by the look of it. Maybe worse. Bootleg liquor, hiding in plain sight beneath the Harvey Company's polished image.

A door slammed somewhere behind her.

Josie's pulse jolted. She dropped the lid, heart thudding, and slipped behind one of the touring cars, just as footsteps echoed on the concrete.

CHAPTER TWENTY-NINE

Right as she prepared to whisper a prayer and cross herself, a voice echoed

"Señorita MacFarland." The *r* curled off the sheriff's tongue like a challenge. "I know you're in here. Have I caught you at an inconvenient moment?"

Josie might have laughed, if she hadn't been so busy trying to catch her breath.

At the wide garage doors, Sheriff Cortez stood, a hazy figure in the dim light. "Come this way," he urged, his voice calm, as if they were simply taking a stroll.

It didn't take a second invitation. Josie darted out from behind the touring car, heart pounding like a war drum.

"How did you know I'd come here?" she asked, breath catching as she reached him.

"Never mind that." His eyes sparkled with quiet amusement. "I'll escort you back and then we'll have ourselves a little chat." He nodded toward the lot beyond the garage. "Ladies first."

Wonderful. Nothing like getting caught red-handed,

crawling around company property to liven up her afternoon.

Outside, under the blistering sun, Josie found her voice. "Have you come to your senses and let Lily go?"

"Why would I do that?" He arched a brow. "I've been too busy keeping an eye on you." His tone was dry. "You're turning into quite the inconvenience, señorita. You've cost me a lot of time today."

He fell into step beside her, their boots crunching on gravel. "Stopped by the soup kitchen," he added. "Padre Emilio mentioned you'd been around. Said he left you at the church. The man seems quite fond of you." He shook his head as if mildly baffled. "But then I saw the garage lights and figured I'd better check."

His gaze drifted toward the building behind them. "Imagine my surprise. Stacked crates. Locked door left conveniently ajar. And the faint sound of someone trying not to breathe."

Josie's cheeks flushed. "Just part of my routine investigation," she replied, flashing her best smile.

His eyes flicked down to her dusty skirt, her scuffed boots. The corners of his mouth twitched. "Why don't we have a cup of tea and a proper conversation? In my office."

"Am I under arrest? The door was open, you know. I just stepped inside."

"I don't seem to have enough evidence to arrest you," the sheriff admitted.

"I know," Josie said. "Let's have tea at The Velvet Rose instead. That seems to be a favorite of yours."

The sheriff groaned softly. "You're impossible, señorita."
"So I've heard."

"Not the tea room." He gestured toward the street. "My office. The courthouse. The sooner, the better."

. . .

Josie and the sheriff stared at each other across his expansive desk. Cortez leaned back in his chair, the picture of authority. Not one hair on his head was out of place. He smiled, waiting for her to speak first.

Josie swallowed. Even if she could put aside his good looks, it was that naked appraisal in his eyes that left her feeling like putty in his hands.

Despite her best intentions, she found herself captivated by his charm. She fidgeted in her chair. *No small talk*, she told herself. *Get right to the point.*

"Did you have me fired?" She glared. "What did you do, call your buddies in Kansas City? That's where the Harvey Company has its offices. Did you tell them the Trask case was solved? That you'd arrested the killer?" Her face flushed.

His eyebrow rose. "I did hear that you received a dismissal. That they no longer require your services. But it wasn't me. Since I haven't officially booked Lily Davenport, I was waiting to let them know."

His statement sounded genuine enough. But she wasn't going to give him an inch. "Another lie," she said flatly, watching his expression.

His eyes narrowed. She'd hit her mark. He didn't appreciate being questioned.

"I'm not surprised you don't believe me," he retorted. "But tell me, how did they dismiss you? What makes you think you were let go?"

"I was sent a letter with just enough cash to take the train home. I assumed my room and dining privileges were no longer paid for and that I had to leave immediately."

"Did you bring the note with you?"

"I didn't," she admitted.

"Maybe if you weren't so busy inspecting garages, you'd remember what's more important. You could have brought it to me. I'd have told you that I didn't call the company. Describe the note to me," the sheriff insisted. "Every detail."

"The envelope was addressed to me. The note was handwritten with block printing."

She felt herself hesitate. Why did he want to know?

"I've seen the printing before," she admitted slowly.

He leaned forward. "Where was that?"

"Lily and I discovered a note in Bobby's room. You missed it somehow. The block printing on that note was similar to the printing on my dismissal letter."

The sheriff sounded eager. "Why didn't you tell me? That may have been important evidence."

"We weren't exactly collaborating then. You sent me away, remember?" Now it was her turn for a *why didn't you*. "Speaking of which, why didn't you tell me that you're so chummy with Delores Delgado? I might have mistaken you for lovers, watching you at the tea room."

She caught a flash of anger in his eyes right before he turned away. When his gaze returned, he'd composed himself. "About that..."

"You seem to be quite close to Delores." Josie was tired of lies and excuses. "Hand-holding across the table. All cozy over a pot of tea. How long have you been seeing her?"

"We have a long-term acquaintance," he admitted. "I'd appreciate it if you didn't tell Miss DiWitt, since she and I are ready to announce our engagement. Her father wouldn't be pleased. Neither Miss DiWitt nor Miss Delgado know about each other. I'd prefer to keep it that way."

It seemed the sheriff had plenty of women to cast his warm brown eyes upon. Josie's jaw clenched.

"The note you describe," he said, changing the subject, "maybe it didn't come from your employer."

She wanted him to be right, for it to mean she'd jumped to conclusions. She'd been in such a turmoil, worried about failing, that she'd not realized the significance. The similarity in the writing.

"Maybe you're right, and that's why I haven't been thrown to the street."

"That would be most unfortunate." To give him credit, he looked genuinely distressed. Then he spoke earnestly. "I admit the idea of a lady detective bothered me at first. But now I can see you have a certain persistence. You've made some connections that might make you a valuable asset. Padre Emilio must be in your confidence. I trust his opinion."

"Now that we're collaborating, she sent him a glare before continuing. I might as well tell you, there were some interesting crates in that garage. Ones without glassware inside," Josie nodded. "They were filled with liquor. Whiskey. Some fancy labels."

The sheriff didn't look surprised.

"If you already knew, why haven't you arrested the bootleggers? Is that why you won't admit that Lansky and McCall are the ones?"

The sheriff huffed. "My work in law enforcement is only as good as my sources. I can't arrest everyone who breaks the law. Only the most desperate criminal gets put behind bars."

Josie glowered. His ridiculous explanation only made her more frustrated.

"So you're saying that Lily Davenport is the worst criminal on your streets? Not the two bootleggers right under your nose?" She continued defending her friend. "Why, Lily doesn't even know how to shoot a gun, let alone conceal one in her room. Someone must have planted it there, knowing you'd arrest her."

The sheriff looked away. He cleared his throat and then turned back. "You know this for a fact? That Lily isn't familiar with guns?"

"Yes." Josie felt a surge of confidence. She'd finally gotten his attention. "When we trained together, we were told that it might be a good idea to keep a weapon around. Some of the locals weren't at all accepting of Harvey Girls.

"Matron gave us a lecture on protecting ourselves. She suggested the small Smith and Wesson. But Lily flatly refused to purchase a weapon. She's a churchgoing Christian and the most innocent of girls."

The sheriff looked thoughtful.

"Who found the gun in her room? You never mentioned." Josie wasn't giving up.

"I'm not at liberty to say." His voice dropped off.

Corez's evasiveness no longer mattered. She'd had enough. At least he wasn't as confident about arresting Lily as he was the other day.

Maybe he's wondering if it could be the matron herself who killed Trask. Someone who walks the halls of the Castañeda, who has keys to every room. And one who never misses a chance to point the finger and blame a Harvey Girl.

CHAPTER THIRTY

With their interview over, Josie made her way out of the sheriff's office and walked briskly down the street toward the Castañeda. The sun baked her head as she approached the courtyard. Today, two men sat at a wrought-iron table. They leaned toward each other, deep in conversation.

Josie recognized the Harvey kitchen supervisor. She'd seen him on many occasions, going in and out of the dining room. She ducked behind the fountain to listen.

He spoke in intense tones, nodding his head. The other man, listening attentively, looked more like a stylishly dressed hotel patron. Each word from the Harvey employee brought a bigger smile to his face.

"I'd expect nothing less," the patron said.

"If that will be all, Mr. Johnson, I'll see you this evening. The Governor's Suite. Around eight o'clock."

"That would be perfect. Tell Freddy and Kitty that I say hello."

With the conversation concluded, the Harvey employee rose.

Josie ducked farther into the shadow. One lone caw

from a crow overhead made her look up. The bird dipped downward, skirting the outside of the fountain. After a brief dip in the water, he lifted his wings to soar away.

She watched the hotel patron fold a newspaper in half and place it under his arm, then make his way toward the Castañeda lobby. Josie followed close behind. Once she was inside, she made a beeline to the reception desk. "Any mail for me?" she asked the employee.

"Miss MacFarland. I'll check." The young man disappeared into a back room. When he returned, he shook his head. "None today," he stated.

"By the way, did you happen to see who dropped off the note for me yesterday?" Josie fluttered her eyes, doing her best Delores Delgado flirt-with-the-sheriff imitation.

"It was delivered by a courier," he said. "No one I know."

Josie smiled. "How long have you lived in Las Vegas?"

"Just short of a year. Not that long." He hesitated and then added, "Sorry I couldn't help."

"I'm just wondering who my secret admirer could be," she said, hoping he'd believe her.

"I'll keep a lookout if he shows up again." The young man blushed. "Your safety is the utmost priority at the Castañeda Hotel."

And you sound fake as a lead nickel, Josie thought.

"One more thing." She placed her hand on the counter. "A man greeted me outside in the courtyard just now. Well-heeled. Important." She blinked her eyes seductively. "He seemed a bit forceful. I avoided his advances, of course. But I'd like to know which room he's in to make sure I don't, you know, run into him by mistake."

"Did you catch his name?" the clerk asked.

"I believe he's called Mr. Johnson."

He nodded. "That would be Johnny Johnson. He's a

wealthy businessman who frequents the Castañeda. I'm sorry to hear about his unwelcome advances. I'm most certain that Mr. Johnson wouldn't want his wife to know."

Josie caught the young man's meaning instantly. He'd shared personal information that she could use if necessary. "And the room?" she asked, using her most persuasive tone.

"The Governor's Suite," he said. "But you didn't hear it from me."

Josie knew about the special accommodation, which was reserved for very important people. Politicians and executives frequently passed through on the Atchison, Topeka, and Santa Fe Railroad. They often stayed in the Governor's Suite.

"Thank you so much." She smiled as a goodbye.

Everyone has a secret, she concluded. *If I find out what it is, then I can barter effectively. Knowing who, besides the sheriff, holds the purse strings in Las Vegas might be really helpful.*

She only had to think of Delores Delgado and the sheriff hiding away at The Velvet Rose Tea Room. She'd heard her father say many times, "I'll scratch your back, if you'll scratch mine." Not to her, of course, but to the men he dealt with every day. Now she had something on them both. Something she could use when the time came.

Back in her room, Josie reached up to grasp her handbag from the the wardrobe, taking a moment to look inside. Everything seemed hunky-dory, just as she'd left it. A quick scan of the rest of the room revealed her notebook and the pencil between the same pages.

Her bed had been made, the coverlet pulled up. She tugged the curtain closed to block out the strong midday sun, then wrote in her notebook, listing everything she'd heard that day, beginning with her chance meeting with Father Emilio earlier in the morning.

By the time she was done, she felt hungry. Though she had no desire to eat in the dining room again, her choices were limited.

Some concern still lingered that she might be thrown out of the Castañeda without ceremony. But now that the sheriff had denied any involvement, she felt less convinced that the note came from the Harvey Company. *Someone was trying to frighten me. I need to find out who. Because they may be the killer.* Her mind wandered.

I must be getting closer to Trask's murderer if someone wants me out of the way that badly. Plus, handing over that amount of money... Whoever it was, they weren't poor.

So the dining room it is. And then afterward, I'll mosey on over to the Governor's Suite. I want to know what's happening this evening that requires such careful planning. Sounds like a party. A good place to serve booze. Maybe of the bootlegged variety.

Splashing water over her face, she reached for the fresh towel. Her skin felt dry from the harsh climate. *Vanishing cream will fix that.* She spread a thin layer over her face and her forearms, then changed into a clean blouse and skirt.

A loud whistle filled the air. Josie felt happy. She'd thought she'd be heading back to Boston on the evening train. But it now looked as if she still had a job.

CHAPTER THIRTY-ONE

Josie savored each bite of the piñon nut torte. The honey-lavender cream topping had been swirled over the top, tasting like heaven in her mouth. The dining room hummed with activity, offering ample opportunity to observe without being noticed.

Kitchen doors swung open. Harvey Girls balanced trays loaded with plates. Josie watched, savoring the last bite of her torte, as they made trips from table to kitchen and back again.

I have to get this recipe, she concluded. *Maybe then Mother would give it to our Cook.* She rose and made her way across the room. Now that she'd done this a few times, she felt more at home. Just another guest. Except Fred picked up her bill.

Upon returning to her room, she opened the door with purpose. She hung up Josie's dinner skirt and blouse. Now it was time to alert Joe Mack.

She pulled on the riding pants and buttoned his shirt. One look in the mirror convinced her that with a little bit of luck, Joe could go without notice.

He stood in front of the oval mirror to fix his hair. Pulled back with pins and then arranged under the leather hat, no one would know about Josie's crop of rich red curls.

A quick tug to the brim and his green eyes were slightly hidden. He took the matchstick and stuck it in the side of his mouth. "Howdy," he mumbled, shifting his tone to a lower register.

Half an hour later Joe set up his surveillance spot in the hallway, leaning his back against the wall. With a newspaper in front of his face, he looked like a bored cowboy, spending time until the evening rodeo.

A woman's forced laugh came from down the hallway. Joe glanced over the top of the paper. Adelle DiWitt walked next to her brother, both dressed to the nines. But the closer they came the less comfortable she appeared.

The young rancher's exquisite leather boots had been tooled by a real craftsman. The pointed toe had silver on the tip. Inlaid turquoise designs were secured to the calfskin. He sported a bolo tie with an engraved silver clasp that matched the silver cuff links on each wrist, all featuring a steer skull with the letter *D*.

His fancy boots and the silver jewelry set off the white shirt and Western-style tuxedo perfectly. Joe was impressed and felt a stab of envy. It must be nice to have that kind of money.

Frankie offered his arm to Adelle, but she shook her head and brushed his elbow away. Then he removed his black Stetson and frowned. "Put on a happy face," he growled.

"Certainly, brother. Whatever you need." Her tone sounded clipped with undisguised resentment.

Adelle had also dressed for a fancy party. Her tall, slender silhouette was encased in a bias-cut evening gown that fit her to perfection. Her hem length had dropped since the earlier flapper days, but her lips were still enhanced with bright red lipstick forming a Cupid's bow.

Frankie reached for the door and rapped loudly with his knuckles. Adelle stepped aside. She turned her head, her glance falling on Joe Mack. "Fancy meeting you here," she called across the hallway.

He tugged on his hat to cover his eyes, pretending he'd not heard. Then he pulled his newspaper up to shield his face. But he could feel Adelle's stare.

"We've met before," she called out. "In the rodeo barn. You're a bit skinny for a cowboy."

She continued her assessment. "No beard." She rubbed her forefinger over her own pert chin. Joe knew she wasn't going to stop talking. He lowered his paper.

"Good to see you again, miss. You've dressed in a fancy getup and are looking real fine. That sapphire diamond bracelet—a gift from an admirer?" He hoped his admiration was enough to deflect her attention.

"From my father," Adelle replied. "When I came home from London, he presented me with this bracelet. Finishing school. Such a bore." She rolled her eyes.

Frankie done with his conversation with the doorman. He called over his shoulder. "No time for chitchat, Adelle. Let him be."

She must have heard his words not as a request, but as a command. She gave a quick nod to Joe. Then reaching into her clutch, she removed a card and stepped across the hall. "You can reach me here." she whispered. "We can talk another time."

Joe slipped it into his pocket. When he finally glanced toward the open door, he saw Elias McCall. *Of course he'd be the doorman.*

"I'll just be another minute, brother." Adelle's forced tone was not lost on Joe.

"Hope you have a nice night," she said, before turning to go. Adelle flung her shoulders back in defiance. This time she took her brother's offered arm.

"Do I need to tell you again?" he began to scold. "Don't go picking up stray cowboys. Remember what happened the last time. Behave like a lady and all of this will go as planned."

Elias McCall stepped away as the elegant couple passed.

McCall wore a dark suit, white shirt, and black tie. With the door still open, he announced, "Mr. Frank DiWitt, Jr. and Miss DiWitt."

The voices in the room stopped. Then the partygoers greeted the couple, giving Joe a moment to look inside.

Before he could assess the situation, Elias McCall stepped into the hallway looking up and down it like a passenger waiting for a train.

Joe glimpsed the partygoers again. They all held a cocktail glass or a flute of champagne. Uncorked bottles in cooling buckets stood on the bar. *There you go*, Joe thought. *Plenty of booze for that lot.*

"You have somewhere else to read?" McCall called over.

Joe's response was interrupted by the sound of rolling wheels over hard floors.

A line of Harvey Girls, dressed in uniform, pushed polished glass and mahogany carts. Dishes lined the shelves, some topped with silver domes. "You're late." McCall held the door open.

The smell of lobster made Joe's mouth water. *I hope they're fresh*, he thought. *Transported by train; a Harvey specialty.*

Another Harvey Girl pushed a cart with crystal carafes. Porcelain bowls rattled. Next to the bowls were hand-folded cloth napkins, along with polished flatware.

"Hurry up,' Elias McCall muttered.

Finally the doors closed. The last of the Harvey Girls pushed their carts back down the hall. Only then did Joe exhale a sigh of relief. Folding the newspaper under his arm, he knew he'd seen enough. Up until now the lavish parties had only been a rumor.

Special Harvey Girls with impeccable manners were chosen to serve and sworn to secrecy. Like most rumors, employees heard the gossip but weren't sure what was true. Now he'd seen for himself. The array of liquor bottles. People holding glasses. The specialty food items accompanied by the distinctive laughter brought on by inebriation.

He knew serving liquor in one's establishment was strictly against the law. That the amount of liquor and the number of guests indicated illegal activity. Bootlegging.

He left his post to stop at the stairway leading to the lobby just as Sheriff Cortez, dressed in a Western tuxedo, made his way up. Joe stepped aside to let the sheriff pass.

Along with his distinctive Western-style close-fitting tux jacket, the sheriff wore a bolo tie, snugged securely under the collar of his white shirt. The decorative clasp, designed from sterling silver, looked one of a kind. Distinctively Navajo, there was a coral stone, shaped like a diamond, at the center.

Joe hurried down the steps. "Buenos días, Sheriff," he greeted Cortez. He kept moving, his chin tucked to his chest. The sheriff was dressed for a big party, most likely headed to the Governor's Suite to enjoy the best hospitality the Harvey House had to offer.

CHAPTER THIRTY-TWO

Josie put away Joe's cowboy attire and slumped on the side of the bed. Fatigue swept her body, her shoulders drooping toward her chest. She bent over to hold her head in her hands. What had she gotten herself into?

The day had been filled with unexpected adventure. But the memory of Elias McCall standing at the door made her shudder. If he hadn't been so busy, he might have confronted Joe Mack.

She lifted her head, remembering how Joe had gotten her into trouble before. It could happen again. What about Adelle DiWitt and that card she'd shoved into Joe's hand?

Josie stood and rifled through Joe's pants pocket, coming up with the card. She took note of the details. Constance Adelle DiWitt was printed across the top. *Very fancy*, Josie thought. *I bet not many women carry these cards in Las Vegas.* Then, remembering that Adelle had spent time abroad, she knew why. *It's more of a custom to have a calling card across the sea.*

She looked closely at a familiar ranch insignia. The steer skull with the large letter *D*. Frankie had the same emblem on his cuff links. And on the decorative collar of his bolo tie.

A phone number had been handwritten on the back. *A wealthy family like the DiWitts must have a phone line,* she concluded. *Is this an invitation to give Adelle a call?*

She slipped the card into her notebook. *Where would I even find a phone?*

The desk clerk will know. I'll ask pretty please

Josie suspected that Adelle had seen beneath the Joe Mack disguise. The observant young debutante was no fool. Much more than a pretty face.

But there was something else about the card. She turned it back over. The rancher's daughter was not called Constance. Everyone used her middle name to address her, even her brother.

Delores Delgado came to mind. How she'd dabbed at her nose with that lace handkerchief Josie's first morning here. In tears over Bobby Trask's death. That lace hankie also had a large letter C embroidered in the corner.

Now she wondered, *Why would Delores Delgado carry a handkerchief with the initial C? That would only make sense if she had another name like Adelle.*

Josie yawned. *Time for bed,* she decided. She lifted the bedspread and slipped under the sheets. Sleep arrived quickly, a release from a very eventful day.

The next morning, Josie arrived bright and early in the dining room. The Harvey Girl hostess greeted her with a smile. "Are you Miss MacFarland?"

Josie felt her cheeks flame. *Is this where I'm escorted out because I haven't paid my bill?* Before she could turn and run, the hostess spoke again.

"Miss DiWitt said to look out for you." She gestured with her hand, inviting Josie to follow.

She'd not expected Adelle to take the initiative after slipping the card into Joe's hand. *This must be important,* Josie thought. Adelle sat at a table for two. The hostess pulled out the extra chair.

Miss DiWitt nodded and lifted the silver coffee pot. She raised an empty cup and saucer with the other hand. "Do sit down," she said quietly. "We have a lot to discuss."

Josie spread the cloth napkin on her lap.

"I've ordered for us already," Adelle said. "A Big Four. I hope you like duck eggs. My friend Chef Lansky always sets aside several, should I arrive for breakfast. I swear he'd chase a duck down the street just to get me fresh eggs." She chuckled at the expression on Josie's face.

"I've never had a duck egg before," Josie admitted.

"Oh they are the bee's knees." Her companion smiled. "Well, not literally. You know what I mean."

Josie was familiar with the expression, but she was surprised it came from the lips of the ever so sophisticated Miss DiWitt.

"I realized as soon as I left you in the hallway last night that you might not have access to a telephone. I told the Castañeda manager on the way in that you were to be given full privileges henceforth. All you need to do is ask and they will take you behind the counter where it's located. Complete privacy, by the way. Part of Fred's hospitality."

Josie's stomach churned. She'd been right to suspect that Adelle wasn't fooled by Joe Mack. Fortunately the debutante wasn't going to make a big deal about it. Their meal arrived before Josie could say thank you.

A large plate held the oversized duck-egg omelet. Since it took four eggs, the breakfast was known as the Big Four.

The omelet was surrounded by four slices of thick bacon and four small roasted potatoes.

"And here is your toast," the waitress said, placing a smaller plate close by. "I'll alert the coffee server to freshen your pot."

Miss DiWitt reached for her fork. She pointed to the bread plate. "I love sourdough. I hope that's okay with you."

Josie smiled her approval.

The two women ate in silence. Adelle chewed with dainty precision, followed by a quick dab of her napkin to her lips. Josie looked furtively around leaving the food untouched, keenly aware of the staring eyes of the other diners. Finally, brushing aside her self-consciousness in favor of her appetite, she picked up her fork.

After a few bites, Adelle reached for the coffeepot. "You'll get used to it, the staring." She filled Josie's empty cup first. "I get that kind of attention all the time because of my father."

"I see," Josie said. Though her family was firmly middle class, she'd never felt particularly important like the young debutante.

Adelle nodded over her coffee cup. "I think you might need my help and I also require yours. Am I correct in assuming Lily Davenport is a chum? The one they arrested for Bobby Trask's murder?"

Josie looked up in surprise. "You know about that?"

"Oh darling, I know nearly everything that goes on in Las Vegas. Why do you think brother Frankie watches me so closely?"

Josie detected the note of disdain. The brother and sister were obviously at odds more often than not.

"I don't ask permission," she explained, "about who I date, for one. Plus Frankie doesn't want to leave me unattended because I may spill the beans about his illegal enterprise."

When Josie only stared, Adelle continued.

"The bootlegging. Surely you know." She put down her cup. "That's just the icing on the cake. My life is a terrible inconvenience to my brother. Father has put him in charge of keeping me in line ever since I returned from Europe. A regular watchdog, that brother of mine.

"But enough about him. We need to do something about your friend Lily. I can help with that. I have a certain connection with the sheriff." She batted her eyes seductively.

"Not to put a bee in your bonnet or give you false hope, but I think darling Mateo is just about ready to release Lily on his own. I just need to give him a little shove in the right direction. Which I'm fully prepared to do. Today, if you'd like. Just say the word."

"Will there be anything else?" The Harvey Girl stood at their table.

"Fresh coffee," Adelle said. "We'll be here a while. Please bring it over and then skedaddle. We don't want to be disturbed." She looked to Josie for approval.

There were questions that Josie wanted to ask before she could accept any more help. "Why would you care about Lily? She's a Harvey Girl. Not from your side of the tracks. Plus I know you saw Joe Mack."

CHAPTER THIRTY-THREE

Adelle poured another cup of coffee for herself. She nodded toward Josie, then she took a sip and answered her question. "I did hear about Joe Mack. A year or so back. Saw his last ride when he won the barrel race and the big cash prize.

"After that no one heard from him. I figured he left town. It's not as if Las Vegas will hold anyone for too long. Then when I ran into him at the rodeo—oh, I knew. A woman in disguise. But I didn't put two and two together until last night at the Governor's Suite."

For some reason, maybe Adelle's ease, Josie no longer felt worried. "So you got curious and gave me your card."

"More than curiosity, darling. I'm bored here, as you can well imagine. Your dual personality intrigues me."

Josie didn't know what to say.

"I just need a friend. Someone who isn't conventional. Are you game?" Adelle asked.

This overt offer of friendship surprised her. And to be frank, it felt welcome. Maybe not so much for personal reasons, but for Lily. "Sure," she said. "I'm game. I suppose you miss your old life, away from your father's grasp."

"Boy do I ever." Adelle's eyes lit up. "I arrived here a few months ago fresh off the boat from England. I spent a couple of months in Chicago after that. I stay at the Palmer House whenever I'm in town.

I stepped out with Freddy, Fred's grandson, during my stay. He's quite the host. He cuts quite a rug too." Her eyes grew misty. "Under other circumstances we might have gotten together, but alas, he only had eyes for Betty."

The confession brought Josie some relief. In just a brief moment, Adelle managed to create bond between them. Plus she'd heard that Fred Harvey's grandson, Freddy, had stirred up quite the scandal when he married seventeen-year-old Betty Drage.

She was a well-known equestrian, her father a former famous British Royal Horse Guard officer and polo player. Her family had rejected any possibility of her relationship with Freddy at first.

Betty's mother was heir to a major Midwestern grain brokerage and was a social phenomenon in her own right. The first woman in Kansas City who ever smoked a cigarette in public. Everyone in town wanted her advice. She was the last word on personal style and home redecorating. Josie wondered, had Betty's mother ever dressed as a man before her marriage? She hadn't realized that other women felt as she did about the restriction of gender.

Miss DiWitt leaned closer. "Betty's mother nearly derailed the couple early on. She thought Freddy the most frightful bore. Too old, for one. Sent Betty to a Paris convent until the girl stood up for herself." Adelle's laugh tinkled above the other voices in the dining room.

Josie smiled. She felt a warmth that often accompanied a new friendship. A day ago she'd expected to be unceremoniously ousted from the Castañeda, and today she was having breakfast with Adelle DiWitt, the Las Vegas debutante.

"They have no children yet," Adelle added quietly. "Imagine a little Freddy or a Fredericka running about." Her genuine tone of sadness caught Josie off guard. *I wonder if Adelle and Freddy were more than friends...*

"But back to your question." Adelle shifted to a more chipper tone. "I know you used to be a Harvey Girl. That you were let go. Something about being caught past curfew. I also know how you dressed as a cowboy to ride in the rodeo. And that you are as close to your horse as you are to a good friend. I was shocked when I ran into you—I mean Joe—at the barn. I had no idea you'd returned to Las Vegas. But like I said, I put two and two together."

"You looked top-drawer riding that thoroughbred." Josie wanted to compliment Adelle, her way of saying thank you for the offer of friendship. Up until now, she hadn't realized how lonely she felt.

Adelle grinned mischievously. "The parade was grand. The horse is up for sale. Father makes a good living on his livestock."

By the third pot of coffee, and lots of talk about horses, Josie felt a certain glow. It had been so long since she'd shared a meal with another woman. Finally they both rose from their seats, and a hush came over the dining room.

They walked together toward the lobby as the gaze of the other diners followed. But then all eyes shifted toward the kitchen. The room grew quiet. Josie turned to see what had changed.

Chef Lansky, resplendent in his double-breasted jacket, clean starched apron, and tall pleated hat, had exited his domain. He peered over the diners, as if looking for someone. His eyes stopped on Adelle.

With long strides, he made his way across the dining room in their direction. Josie stared as Adelle blushed like a schoolgirl.

"I expected to see you last night," he said, his voice tinged with concern. "Have you had any more troubles?" His thick speech sounded uncommonly romantic to Josie's ears.

Adelle batted her eyelashes at the chef. "Victor, dear, I had another engagement. Frankie is such a beast. He insisted I go with him. He's such a watchdog."

"He's an infant," Lansky retorted. "We'd never treat our women like that in my country." Then he lowered his voice. "Tonight, then. The usual place: Our Lady by ten o'clock."

Josie's heart skipped a beat. It seemed it wasn't just the bootleggers who met at Our Lady of Sorrows in the night. Unless the chef and Adelle were praying... Josie smiled to herself.

The church also served as a place of clandestine assignations. She wondered if that included stolen kisses in the back pew. No wonder Adelle blushed.

But wasn't she taking quite a risk meeting with the chef? Surely she knew the consequences if the sheriff found out. Her father would disapprove. Her brother as well. Josie felt a certain admiration for Adelle's navigation of her social life despite society's expectations.

"Of course, darling," Adelle whispered. "And why don't you bring a friend? Josie will be accompanying me this evening. That way I can ditch the watchdog. We'll all go dancing."

Chef Lansky scowled. It was obvious that he'd not intended it to be a double date. "I'll find someone for her. It won't be easy. Make sure she dresses up." He gave a short bow to Adelle and then turned on his heel.

In the lobby, Adelle spoke to Josie. "That settles it," Adelle nodded. "I can't wait to go out on the town with you. We'll meet at the church. Wear your best. I'm certain this will be an evening to remember."

"What about Lily? You mentioned that you'd speak to the sheriff on her behalf."

"I nearly forgot." Adelle tapped her chin with her forefinger. "All right, then. Let's head to the police station now. I'll have a word. But I can't take forever. I have an appointment with my dressmaker." The doorman smiled.

"Good morning, miss," he said politely. Then he eyed Josie but didn't offer her a greeting.

They made their way down Telegraph Avenue. After walking in silence, Josie's curiosity got the best of her. "Do you use Our Lady of Sorrows often? With others or just Chef Lansky?"

"Women need to vary their meeting places, especially in small towns. So not that often. Otherwise I'd get spotted and word would get back to my father. What an exhausting way to live." She stepped around a man sitting on the corner, who held out his hand.

Josie wished she had a dime to give him.

Try as she may, she'd never had a minute of the freedom Adelle spoke of. Her father was much more strict. She'd taken the job as a Harvey Girl after many arguments and lots of door slamming. But she finally got her way.

It must be nice, she thought, *to be a rich rancher's daughter, sent to Europe for the season. Dressed in the latest fashion.*

"The sheriff's office is through that door." Josie pointed.

Adelle looked Josie up and down. "I am well aware."

She sounded offended. "He's my fiancé, you know. Once he gives me the ring, we'll be setting a date for our wedding."

Josie realized her mistake. Knowing the sheriff's location brought Adelle's ire. Some girls were like that about who they stepped out with. She'd not make the same mistake again.

CHAPTER THIRTY-FOUR

"Matteo," Adelle murmured. She lowered her eyes seductively. He pulled out a chair, with a quick glance toward her posterior.

"I'm honored that you're visiting me in my workplace." The sheriff sounded beyond honored. More like flabbergasted, if Josie were to guess.

Probably only because he was the consummate gentleman, he gave a curt nod in her direction as a greeting. Then he returned to his place of authority behind the desk. Josie seated herself next to Adelle.

"I'm very disappointed in you, Sheriff." Adelle had somehow managed to make "disappointed" sound naughty. This mystified Josie, how certain women made every comment feel like an invitation.

"Lily Davenport has been kept under lock and key for far too long," Adelle continued. "Even you must agree, Mateo, my dear, that it's time to release her."

It seemed Adelle could be both direct and disarming at the same time.

Cortez's eyebrows raised. "Has this one made a nuisance of herself, putting ideas into your pretty little head?" He scowled at Josie.

"We both know I have a mind of my own." Adelle smiled.

Josie was beginning to feel like an observer of an Oscar Wilde play. Both had memorized their lines, performing for her benefit.

"We had plans for dinner tonight, did we not?" Adelle openly assessed the sheriff. Her eyes lingered on his hands, then his belt buckle.

Josie suspected there was more on the menu than food.

"I'm looking forward to our meal." Cortez's admiration shone from his eyes.

"Darling, I am so happy to hear you haven't forgotten," Adelle said. "I could take that time to discuss Miss Davenport's situation then, if you're too busy this morning. But maybe we can settle it now to give us more time for our meal."

His lips tightened. It was obvious to Josie that Mateo Cortez had no intention of ruining his evening with discussing a case. He shifted his glance back to her. She could feel his wrath and knew he blamed her for the unfortunate downfall of his romantic evening.

"Surely you're ready to admit that mistakes were made. The arrest of Lily Davenport. The gun in her room. Josie tells me Lily didn't even own a gun," Adelle continued. "Perhaps another one of Bobby's friends shot him. Some disgruntled customer, more than likely. Imagine a Harvey Girl like Lily Davenport having the courage to kill a man like Bobby." The tinkle of Adelle's laughter made Josie wince.

"I really must put my foot down." Adelle pointed the toe of her expensive leather boot. "Release Lily now. Please."

He looked toward her boot with a loud sigh. "Such a beautiful foot," he commented. "I'm busy this morning. Perhaps I can release her tomorrow. After our dinner."

Josie suspected he didn't want to appear weak and that he needed to save face. Biding his time before agreeing with Adelle would seem more manly. She wondered what would come next.

"Oh, I know about how busy you are, the only sheriff in Las Vegas. Such a difficult job in this small provincial town." She tapped a dainty finger to her chin. "Unfortunately, I just remembered that I'm also busy. Maybe that dinner won't work out tonight. Another time, perhaps?" She glared at the sheriff.

Josie saw him wince.

Back and forth, the rancher's daughter and the town's sheriff played out their roles. Josie felt trapped. *Just cut to the chase. Be done with it. Jeepers.*

She hid her impatience by keeping her eyes focused on her lap.

But Adelle DiWitt, rancher's daughter, London debutante, woman who knew Fred Harvey's family personally, had no intention of losing this tussle.

Josie's interest picked up. She watched Adelle closely, wondering what would be her next move.

After all, Adelle had the upper hand. Her attention was highly sought after, especially by the opposite sex. She wielded the powers given to her—status, beauty, intelligence—with admirable finesse.

Finally it was the sheriff who gave in. "I suppose I could consider releasing her today." He looked away and then back at Adelle. "For you, my darling."

"I want to hear your promise that you'll release Miss Davenport," Adelle insisted.

His jaw tightened. "I'll have Lily Davenport transferred to her own room before lunch and drop all charges." Now he sounded unhappy. "Does that satisfy you, darling? Enough to put aside other plans and have dinner with me tonight?"

"Oh, I'm so pleased." Adelle's expression completely changed. Her face lit up, her eyes sparkled. Yet she obviously knew better than to overplay her hand.

Josie wanted to clap as the final curtain fell, but instead she crossed her fingers. Maybe Lily would be released after all.

Adelle turned to Josie. As if on cue, they stood together. "How about eight o'clock?" Adelle suggested, turning back to Cortez. "For our dinner."

The sheriff's face flushed with...was it relief or anticipation?

"We really have to go now, darling Mateo. I have an appointment with my dressmaker, and Josie will run straight to the women's dormitory. She'll want to help Lily back to her own room."

"Yes," he sighed. "I'll send over my deputy to release her right away. Miss MacFarland can meet with her friend."

Josie said goodbye to Adelle outside the courthouse. It wasn't until she stood in front of the women's dormitory that she realized Adelle had made a date with Lansky and with Cortez on the same night.

"The sheriff said I was to let you in." Matron opened the door for Josie to enter. "I'll bring tea," she added. "Miss Davenport is anxiously waiting for you."

Josie edged open the door to the parlor. Lily turned from the fireplace, her face glowing. "Josie. I'm free!" She stretched out her arms for an embrace.

The stress and strain of the last few days had taken a toll. Lily's frame felt fragile in Josie's arms. "I came as soon as I heard," Josie said "Please sit down. The matron is bringing us refreshments."

"Probably so she can listen in," Lily muttered. She sat in a floral armchair next to the fireplace. Then she arranged her wrinkled Harvey dress around her knees. The apron had lost its starch. Even the bow at her throat was askew.

"You must be gasping for a bath," Josie said.

"I am," Lily admitted. "But back to work tomorrow. No rest for the wicked."

"I'd think they'd give you a day or two off under the circumstances," Josie replied.

"It's not such a bad thing. I want to keep busy. This has been an ordeal. But I have so much to tell you." Lily leaned forward right as the parlor door opened. Matron carried a silver tray.

"I was able to bring fresh biscuits." She arranged a basket along with the teapot, saucers, and cups on the table.

"Thank you," Josie replied curtly.

"You're an angel, Miss Delgado." It was clear to Josie that Lily knew better than to bite the hand that fed her biscuits and tea.

"Would you like me to play a tune on the piano?" The matron nodded toward the upright instrument in the corner, where sheet music stood on the stand.

"We'd like to be alone," Josie answered quickly. *Enough of this polite nonsense.*

"Not that we're in a hurry to get rid of you," Lily jumped

in with an excuse. "Josie is tired. She's made every effort to secure my release. A true and loyal Harvey Girl."

The matron shrugged. "Not a Harvey Girl any longer," she commented with a sniff.

CHAPTER THIRTY-FIVE

Once the matron closed the parlor door, both women burst into giggles. "Nothing's changed. Spies everywhere. Now that you're a free woman, it seems you're back under their thumb," Josie said.

Lily agreed. "The Harvey rules are still the rules, though not quite as strict as when we first trained. After being kept hostage with the sheriff's man, I will appreciate the security of my own room and my job."

As Lily poured herself another cup of tea, the reference to Elias McCall got Josie thinking. With his threatening size and the gun he carried, he looked like a man who could easily kill another man who got in his way.

He'd be strong enough to transport those crates. He'd lift and stack and get them from the railroad to the Harvey garage. And then he'd deliver them to the Castañeda kitchen to be stored. She felt a shiver up her spine.

Did the sheriff know his right-hand man was involved in a bootlegging operation? She suspected he was fully aware, and that was at least one reason he wanted to close the Bobby Trask case quickly.

Cortez. A law unto himself. He managed to be in the middle of all the goings-on in Las Vegas. He associated with criminals and the businessmen of the small town, moving from source to source gathering the necessary information. He picked and chose who to arrest, at his own convenience.

She wondered if Cortez was getting kickbacks from the bootlegging operation. There was no Carrie Nation to breathe down his neck and get her name in the headlines.

Now she wondered how far the sheriff would go. Had *he* killed Trask? His moodiness made Josie think he might be hesitant, until his own needs got in the way. That would be three main suspects, all in bed with Trask and his bootlegging operation. Lansky. McCall. And now Cortez.

And even though he had a soft spot for her, Padre Emilio might be involved. He told her about the Harvey garage. That seemed transparent, but maybe he had an ulterior motive. Hadn't Cortez shown up right afterward? Nearly scaring her to death.

Maybe there was a case of expensive wine in one of those crates. Good wine would be used for the Eucharist and maybe for other things. Like when the bishop visited, or at the end of a long day of feeding the poor.

Didn't Our Lady of Sorrows need money to operate the soup kitchen? Maybe the padre kept the illegal activity secret, the right hand not knowing what the left hand was doing, so that he'd have money to serve the needy.

But would he kill a man? Josie knew that was out of the question. The padre might be an accessory but not the one to raise a gun to brutally attack another human being.

Finally Josie considered Delores Delgado. All cozy with the sheriff that day in The Velvet Rose Tea Shop. As the head matron of the Castañeda, she was in a prime position to report everything she heard and saw to Mateo Cortez.

Despite his obvious infatuation with Adelle DiWitt, he still was a man who basked in the gaze of another woman's adoration.

Josie felt herself blush. Despite her better instincts, she was not immune to the sheriff's allure. He had a certain charm and devilishness that appealed to her. She'd love to be the recipient of those adoring dark eyes. To know he was sending those admiring glances to her posterior.

"Wool gathering... May I pour you another cup of tea?" Lily asked.

She'd used the same expression Josie's grandma did whenever she caught her lost in her own thoughts. Josie smiled.

"One more cup," she said. "Then I'll let you go. I'm sure you want time for a warm bath and to resettle in your room. I have a few things I need to do."

Lily poured while Josie explained.

"I have a date tonight. Arranged by my new benefactor, Adelle DiWitt. You have her to thank for your release, by the way. The sheriff ignored me, but he's engaged to her, so she made him see reason. Anyway, I have nothing to wear for my outing."

"Is it a blind date, then?" Lily looked interested.

"Adelle never mentioned a name. I'm to meet her at Our Lady of Sorrows later this evening. Chef Lansky is her date. Mine is yet to be determined." She didn't mention that Lansky was a main suspect and that she planned on doing a little sleuthing along the way.

"Sounds like fun," Lily sighed.

"I didn't bring a fancy dress," Josie admitted.

Lily's face lit up. "How about I bring you an outfit? I have a hat and heels. I'll bring my sewing kit. It won't take a minute to lower the hem." She looked her friend up and down.

Josie heard the old lilt in Lily's voice. How could she refuse such a generous offer?

"I've collected several second-hand items that are perfect for going out. I'll pack up a few things. Then after my bath and a rest, I'll come right to your room. This will be fun!" Lily looked like a different girl, her cheeks rosy with excitement.

"You're a lifesaver." Josie smiled.

A quick knock came to the door. The matron stuck her head inside. "May I refresh your tea?"

"I'm just leaving." Josie whisked past the matron without a backward glance.

CHAPTER THIRTY-SIX

Josie was sitting on the edge of her bed when the knock came at her door. "Come in." Lily stood in the hallway holding the handle of an oversized suitcase. Josie opened the door wider to let her through.

"I've brought everything I have." Lily swung the suitcase onto the bed. She smelled of lilac and lemon. Her hair had been washed and brushed back, falling in curls to her shoulders.

"You got your bath." Josie smiled.

"And a rest. Matron brought dinner to my room. That was a surprise. I think she might be feeling a bit guilty."

Josie eyed the suitcase. "So what did you bring? I can't wait to see."

She wondered if Lily knew how nervous she felt. Everything in her wanted to cancel the date and say no to Adelle. But under the circumstances, this might be her only chance to talk to Victor Lansky. He'd blocked all other avenues.

The lock on the suitcase snapped open. Lily lifted the lid. "You have underclothing, I presume?"

Josie nodded. "My underthings are most suitable, even

Mother would approve. I have a girdle and stockings too. Just like a real Harvey Girl." She chuckled, remembering her training from Delores Delgado. The matron would slap each young woman on the rear to make certain they'd not forgotten that important foundational garment. A girl would be sent back to her room to change with a firm talking to if her fanny wiggled.

"Show me what you've got," Lily insisted.

Josie took off her dress to stand in her girdle, drawers, and chemise. Lily frowned and then rummaged through the suitcase.

"You are not going on your first blind date bound up like a Sunday roast," Lily said. "Take off the girdle and the chemise and see what I have."

Josie giggled. "According to the matron saint, I'm entering hussy territory."

Lily held out her hand. "Here, this is called a brassiere. It covers the top. And without a tight girdle, you'll be able to dance and breathe and eat pie. Which are all important on a first date."

The cream-colored garment had simple stitching and a tiny bow at the center. Two cups were gently curved and the cotton felt soft against her fingertips. "It doesn't look like much." Josie slipped her arms inside as Lily clasped the back.

"That's the point. It's liberating. Trust me, once you try it on, you'll never go back."

"I'm warning you, if this date goes sideways..." Josie kicked her girdle across the floor. "I'm blaming the undergarments."

"Blame all you want, honey, but do it with good posture and circulation."

Now she stared down at her legs, perplexed. Once again

Lily rummaged through her magic suitcase. "Here you go. The finest of silk. We can't have you going bare-legged." She handed over two stockings and a garter belt; at Josie's questioning look, Lily showed her how to hook the belt and then the stockings.

Josie rolled her eyes and smoothed the seams along the backs of her calves.

Another costume. Not Joe Mack the cowboy, but Josie the girl-out-on-the-town.

"I don't even know who my date is," Josie insisted. "Surely you don't think I'd be going home with him tonight. That he'll see all this?" She swept a hand over her new underthings.

"Of course not, darling," Lily retorted. "But you'll be able to run away at least, should he become handsy, and not hindered by that tight-fitting monstrosity."

Lily drew a midnight-blue dress from her suitcase and held it in front of her. "Look at this!" Her voice sounded far away as she ran a finger over the fabric. "Made from the finest silk. A tourist left it in her closet. She didn't leave a forwarding address, so I kept it for myself."

Josie took the dress and slid it over her head. It felt cool and luxurious. The shimmery blue fabric fell below her knees, to her ankles. Lily adjusted the back, then the front.

The dress enveloped her figure, clinging to her body. Josie touched the fabric with a sigh. "This is exquisite." She turned to face her friend. "Does it look all right?"

"Better than all right." Lily tugged gently at the alluring cowl neckline to expose Josie's collarbones. "You look come hither," she said. "Not full-on sexy but enticing enough to catch any man's eye." She stepped back for one more assessment. "That's it for the dress."

Now Lily dropped a wine-red embroidered shawl over

Josie's shoulders. "It can get a bit cool in the evenings," she said.

Josie felt completely transformed. No longer the outspoken detective from Boston nor the rodeo cowboy, but a mysterious femme fatale. A stranger. A woman of intrigue. "I like this," she sighed.

Lily placed a long string of pearls around her neck. Then she looped them in a knot, allowing the bottom half to fall to Josie's waist. "Something to twirl while you're doing the Lindy," she explained.

She'd guessed Josie's biggest hope. That the evening would include dancing. Something she didn't get to do with an actual partner back home. Wherever left alone in her house, she'd practice in the drawing room, using her brother's collection of records on her father's gramophone.

She'd let herself go, imagining how she'd amaze her partner, always a college boy just a bit older. Her skin prickled with anticipation. Maybe tonight she'd be able to dance and show off her steps.

"Sit down," Lily instructed. "Let's do your hair and makeup. I brought my favorite scent. It's called Shalimar. I discovered it at the back of a drawer when I was cleaning. A woman left it behind by mistake months ago."

Lily lifted the small cut-glass bottle. Removing the stopper, she took a sniff. Then she moistened her finger with the scent. She leaned closer to apply it strategically behind Josie's ears and on each wrist. She left one drop at the hollow of her throat. "Now you'll smell delicious when he whispers in your ear or holds you close for a slow dance."

Josie gasped with pleasure. The rich scent, jasmine and rose, filled her nostrils. "This is quite lovely," she admitted.

"You won't know yourself once I do your makeup," Lily said. "Just give me a sec and I'll find my bag."

. . .

"All done," Lily claimed. She stood back for Josie to look at her skin and lipstick. Then she dangled a pair of teardrop crystal earrings in the air. She clipped one to each of Josie's lobes with a smile.

"The earrings sparkle like the clutch."

Josie watched with fascination as her friend dropped a mini compact, a lace-trimmed hankie, and a slim silver cigarette case inside the small purse. "I don't smoke," Josie insisted.

"I know, honey. But you can pretend. If your date is a bore, you can sit at the bar and do your detective work. No one will realize you're listening in, especially if you have a cigarette holder." Lily dropped one inside the purse.

"You think of everything," Josie agreed.

Lily lifted Josie's chin in two fingers. "Now don't forget, you look better than any other woman in the room. I know you've been dying to get this over with and talk about the murder. Give me the scoop."

It was good to be known that well. Josie realized she did have questions for Lily. "I'm wondering about Bobby Trask."

"Honestly, I didn't know him personally, but he was a gadabout in Las Vegas. Lots of women coming and going from his room. I kept my mouth shut, you know. Fred's training, to not divulge the personal lives of any of our residents. But I couldn't help but notice."

"Have you ever wondered if a woman killed Bobby?" Lily continued. "If any one of his paramours found out about the other—why, it's not impossible."

"It has crossed my mind," Josie admitted. "Delores Delgado for one."

"I suppose." Lily nodded. "It's not like she's ever done

anything remarkably kind for either of us. She could be a killer. That's enough murder about her, back to you." Lily spun Josie toward the mirror. "You must have plenty of men on your list of suspects. All the more reason for you to ditch your date and sit at the bar and pretend to smoke." Lily made an effort to sound light, but Josie heard the concern and touch of fear in her tone.

Josie snapped the sequined clutch closed.

"Give us a twirl, girly. There you go. You're all ready for a night on the town." Lily stood back to admire her creation.

Josie felt the sheer fabric wrap around her legs. A quick glance at her face and hair in the small mirror made her feel giddy. She didn't recognize herself.

Her red mop of unruly hair had been turned into the current style. Finger curls hugged her head, lost tendrils tucked away neatly with a sparkly pin. For once she looked quite elegant and sophisticated. Maybe not her mother's cup of tea, but she knew even in Boston she'd get a few glances from the most eligible men.

Even her skin looked flawless. Lily had dusted her face with rice powder, making her complexion look smooth. Her pouty lips were a complete surprise. And then her eyes. Lily had artistically plucked and penciled her eyebrows, leaving them slightly arched. Josie's green eyes smoldered with excitement.

"Where did you learn all those tricks with the pencils and eye shadow?" she asked.

"I had a friend, nearly your height, who was a showgirl. She explained everything to me." Lily sounded wistful. "But she left a few months back. I never heard from her again. Those were her heels." Lily pointed to Josie's feet.

That would be two friends who left Lily, abandoned her in Las Vegas. "Was she, you know, in the family way?"

"Not that she said," Lily replied. "Just up and left."

She didn't want to make things worse, so she changed the subject. "I can't thank you enough. Even the heels…" She glanced down at the t-strap champagne-colored shoes. "They fit perfectly."

Josie executed a quick swing step and a twirl. "Good enough for dancing, that's for sure."

"Look at you." Lily smiled. "Off you go." Her voice sounded wistful.

"Maybe we can go dancing the two of us next time," Josie offered.

"I'd love that!" Lily's face brightened.

"But only if you have enough duds to dress us both."

CHAPTER THIRTY-SEVEN

The side entrance to Our Lady of Sorrows stood ajar. Josie stepped inside at exactly ten o'clock and waited for her eyes to adjust to the candle-lit interior. A shiver of anticipation tickled down her spine.

A woman sat at the front of the church toward the altar. She wore a bright magenta-colored shawl, her hair waved tightly against her head. *That must be Adelle*, Josie thought.

Adelle DiWitt looked up at the sound of Josie's heels clicking against the stone floor. "There you are. Right on time. Don't you look like the cat's meow."

"You're not so bad yourself."

Adelle looked stunning in her slinky black silk dress. The neckline dipped over her substantial cleavage. *Heaving bosom*, Josie thought. That's what the forbidden romance novels would write.

She sat next to her in the pew. "Not here yet."

"They'll be here shortly," Adelle assured her. "Thank you so much for agreeing to this evening. I had dinner with Mateo earlier. He was such a bore, wanting to know how I came to know you. So many questions." Her mouth was in a tight line of displeasure.

"I appreciate what you did for Lily," Josie commented. She thought another thank you was due, considering she'd gotten nowhere with the release of her friend on her own.

"Think nothing of it." Adelle sounded confident. "We girls have to stick together."

"Can you tell me more about my blind date?" Josie had been dying to ask. Plus she wondered what her mother would say. Accepting a date from a man she didn't know was strictly forbidden. The very idea made her feel jittery, reckless even. She'd stepped into the risqué world of ruining her reputation.

"Is my date a friend of the chef's?" Josie wanted to know in the worst way.

In the past she only dated men approved of by her mother. She'd gone out with a few suitors, mostly because she'd gotten to the age where marriage had become a looming necessity. Her mother didn't want her lingering about, growing stale. Like a loaf of old bread. Dry and crusty. That's what her brother always said when the topic came up in his presence.

"He's a friend of Victor's," Adelle explained. "You've seen him about. He works for my father, so I could never date him, but that doesn't mean he's not a catch."

The sound of voices came from the side entrance door. Victor Lansky appeared first. He looked dapper in his double-breasted blue suit, with his hair slicked back and a red carnation in his breast pocket. Without the chef's hat, he reminded Josie of a foreign fashionable businessman.

His companion loomed behind him, at least six inches taller. His broad frame filled the doorway. Massive shoulders pushed against the fabric of his pinstripe jacket. His wide face was impassive. Josie's heart stopped.

Elias McCall.

Oh no. He's the last man I want to go out with. Despite my fancy dress and makeup, he might recognize me from the rodeo and realize that I'm Joe. Her fists clenched. What was Adelle thinking!

A quick glance toward Adelle's beautiful face explained. She wasn't concerned at all. It wasn't as if he'd brandished a gun at her. Adelle turned on a wide smile that she directed at the men. "Hello, darlings. We're ready. Eli, I'd like you to meet my new friend, Josie MacFarland. You've seen her in passing."

The hint of mischief in her voice angered Josie even more. *There's nothing funny about going out with the sheriff's man.*

Victor Lansky pulled Adelle to her feet. He planted a quick kiss to her cheek and then stepped aside. It was Josie's turn to greet Elias. She shuddered and avoided his penetrating stare. She stood on her own, ignoring his hand.

Feeling betrayed and angry all at once, her heart beat wildly. *He's enormous. I can't overpower him physically. No jokes about the undergarments now. There's no way I could possibly outrun this giant.*

Her mind whirled. *It wouldn't take too much for him to thump me over the head and haul me away. Once Adelle and Victor leave, he'll be free to do the dirty work. The cleanup man.*

He could carry me across his shoulders and dispose of me without looking back. He's strong enough and mean enough. No one would even ask where I'd gone. I've already disappeared once. People would assume that I'd run away again.

As her thoughts wildly raced, Josie felt her cheeks burn.

She couldn't run away this time. What if Adelle told Mateo, and he arrested Lily again? Everything depended on her keeping calm.

Josie refused Elias's offered arm. She walked stiffly beside him, wondering how she was going to get out of this awful situation.

Victor and Adelle walked ahead arm in arm, chatting together like old friends. "Shall we?" McCall offered his arm again. Josie shook her head no.

"Have it your way," he mumbled. He followed the other couple, leaving Josie with little choice but to tag along.

Victor and Adelle took a side alley and stopped behind the Frontier Meats butcher shop. The rich scent of smoked sausage and aged ham clung to the night air. A single gas lamp flickered overhead, casting shadows against the adobe walls.

Victor rapped twice on the mission-style door. He paused and knocked one more time. *Must be a code*, Josie thought. A door panel slid open, revealing a shifty set of eyes. "Who sent you?" came the demanding voice.

"Uncle Fred," Victor answered with practiced assurance.

The panel slid shut. The door opened, swinging inward with just enough space to let the two couples inside.

A dimly lit corridor stretched ahead. The scent of smoked meats gave way to the strong odor of whiskey, cigarettes, and wafts of perfume. Their footsteps echoed against the stone floor as they descended a narrow staircase.

Victor was still in the lead with Adelle. Josie gripped the rail. McCall was so close, she could feel his warm breath on her neck. She had no chance of escape now.

At the bottom of the stairway, people and laughter filled the room. A golden light cast from a chandelier overhead created a motion-picture atmosphere, what with everyone dressed in their finest attire.

A jazz piano stood in the corner. Functioning more as a table, the cover for the keys was closed. Empty glasses and bottles had been strewn across the top. A gramophone's loud music filled the room.

Two waiters circled, both wearing crisp white shirts with black tuxedos. They held trays with drinks. One woman sat on a stool at the end of the bar. She dangled a cigarette holder as she talked to a man who stared down the front of her dress.

Adelle and Victor wasted no time. He took her hand and they disappeared onto the crowded dance floor. Josie anxiously looked around the room for an exit. She felt her arm grasped from behind. "Shall we?" Elias McCall leered.

His face loomed closer. He spoke quickly into her ear. "Play along, lady detective. Don't say a word." He gave her a gentle nudge toward the dance floor.

She blinked. The tone of his voice surprised her. No longer harsh. Even in the noisy room he sounded different. His eyes pleaded. She had feared his close proximity, but now she felt the opposite. He was trying to tell her something.

Or was he just trying to bring down her defenses before he made his move? She yanked her arm away.

He reached again, his grip viselike on her upper arm. "Let's dance." He spoke lightly but forcefully, pulling her onto the floor.

The record stopped and the dancers groaned. But then a familiar tune blared from the gramophone—"Ain't Misbehavin'." The energetic and playful jazz tune was Josie's favorite. The very one she practiced at home.

Despite her fears, she tapped her toe to the infectious rhythm. Elias dropped her forearm and offered his hand again, his eyes pleading. *So he really wants to cut a rug*, she thought. *Maybe this will be my last dance before he has his way with me, but oh well. I'll go out strong.*

She felt his warm fingers clasp around hers. Releasing her last resolve to run, she gave in to the moment.

Elias moved closer, his eyes on hers. A short nod and then he broke into an elegant swing step. His massive body transformed into something agile and fluid. All of his limbs moved with ease to the eight counts of the popular dance. After a few lively steps he released her hand, freeing Josie to spin away. She spun back immediately into his arms, mesmerized by his expert direction.

Perspiration rose on Josie's forehead. Her heart raced with exhilaration. Moving quickly into the Charleston, she'd forgotten all of her fears. She playfully kicked her legs to challenge him. He smiled and kicked his legs higher, his body bouncing to the beat.

Close to his chest once again, she felt his steady heartbeat. He gave her a slight push to nudge her away, only to bring her back, as if they were attached by an elastic band.

The tempo picked up right as Elias led her to a side-by-side dance step. Through unspoken agreement, both acknowledged to give it everything they had. Their knees bumped, arms swinging in unison side to side. Josie threw her head back to laugh aloud. She didn't give a pin what Elias McCall did for a living. He could dance.

As Elias kicked higher, he looked up at the ceiling. When he glanced down, he grinned at Josie. The smile utterly transformed his face. No longer the intimidating sheriff's man, he looked at ease and in his element.

She synchronized her moves with his and then ducked under his arm. On her return she felt her curls release from their pins. "Ain't Misbehavin'" reached the last refrain just as Elias pulled her into his arms. By the final notes he dipped her back, into a graceful arc. Breathless and smiling, she returned to stare him in the face. "For such a big guy, you can sure shake a hoof."

His smile felt like sunshine. He took her hand without a word, making his way across the dance floor.

Here it comes, Josie thought. *What mother warned me about. But I got my dance and at least I'll die happy.*

CHAPTER THIRTY-EIGHT

Elias led her up the stairway, past the door, and into the alley behind the butcher shop. She yanked her hand, but he refused to let go. "I have to tell Adelle I'm leaving," she said, her voice coming in rasps.

"She already knows," he called over his shoulder. "Just hurry. I don't want anyone else to notice and get in our way."

His insistent voice was surprisingly not threatening. *Adelle already knows. What could that mean?* Confusion twisted Josie's insides. It was the dance that made everything different. She thought the sheriff's man was one thing, then he became something else entirely.

The joy on his face, how he spun her around, his laugh when she got the steps just right. *Surely he's not a killer.*

She'd always put stock in her ability to judge people. She'd listen to their tone, not just the words. Sometimes she'd know a person's feelings before they did. Then she'd watch body language for confirmation. She could tell a lot about who people are by observing how they move. And their eyes. The expression. When they look away. When they stare over your head. When they take you in with a full glance.

But Elias McCall, he put her confidence in her own ability to the test. From the horrible sheriff's man to the exuberant dancer, the partner she'd always dreamed of, in no time at all.

With quick steps, he pulled her along toward the main street. Finally he released his grip. "Let me explain," he said. "Just gimme a chance. Then if ya want to leave, I'll escort you back to the Castañeda. No matter what you say, I don't wanna have you walkin' alone after dark. It ain't no place for a lady."

He sounded genuinely concerned. Josie felt her previous judgments fall away. Even the bulge in his jacket where he kept his gun no longer alarmed her. Because he admitted himself that he was protective.

"I bet your mama had to tell you to stand up straight when you were young," she quipped. His shoulders had slumped as he lowered his gaze to look into her eyes.

"All the time." He nodded. "I was the tallest of my brothers and the baby boy. They picked on me because she liked me best. But my ma was no pushover. I'd come home crying and she'd box my ears. Tell me I could take any one of them in a fight, if I put my mind to it." His voice sounded soft when he spoke of his childhood.

Josie's heart warmed.

"But you're not gonna take me on now, are ya? Not after our dance. We hit it off, right? Or did I just imagine?"

Josie's chin jutted out. "Stand up straight, big boy. You've got my attention, dragging me out of the speakeasy."

His reached to adjust his bow tie with a sheepish smile.

Admit it, Josie, you don't even know this man—not really.

You only know who he's paid to be. What he looks like on the outside.

"So why am I here?" she asked. "Why would Adelle go to the trouble of setting us up?"

"Adelle got a bee in her bonnet," he explained. "I had nothin' to do with your friend's arrest. All the sheriff's idea. I'm just the hired help."

This confirmed Josie's observation at least. Which gave her confidence. "Go on."

"I tried to keep Lily safe. Never made a move on her. Promise." His eyes searched her, as if asking her to agree.

"How does Adelle fit into all of this?" Josie prodded him.

"She knew that the sheriff wasn't taking you seriously. That made her mad. Once she ran into you as...Joe Mack? You're a cowboy on the side." He grinned. "Wish I could have seen that. Anyway, once she put Josie and Joe together, she butted in and got involved.

"Your friend, she ain't no killer. Anybody can see that. Adelle knew the only way to keep Lily safe would be for you to find the actual man. So she told me to help out with the evidence. Plus it doesn't take no genius to know that Cortez never tells all the truth."

He sighed deeply, a look of shame crossing his face. "It was Adelle's idea to arrange the blind date. Then I'd dance you off the floor when no one was lookin'. After that we'd head to the sheriff's office. It's dark. I have the keys." He reached into his pocket. "A perk of being the sheriff's man."

Josie's heart pounded against her chest. This would be a real break in the case, if she could only trust him. She'd be able to read what the sheriff found at the crime scene. But she wasn't ready to trust him quite yet.

"I already have a few suspects. You included." She watched his expression carefully.

Elias looked grim. "I'm not surprised. That's why Cortez told me to keep an eye out, up close and personal like. But you need to know. Bobby Trask was in cahoots with lots of wheeler-dealers. He had a special operation with Lansky. Bootlegged liquor and goods for the Harvey Company. I was the guy who lifted and transported the crates. Nothin' else. Honest." He held up his fingers in a Boy Scout salute.

"Like I said, Cortez is at the bottom of this, arresting your friend too. He musta been really angry when you came to town. Smart young filly." He grinned at Josie. "The boss man doesn't want you anywhere close to digging up more information and naming names. I don't think it's personal, but there's no use getting on the wrong side of him. I should know. He pays me to keep his nose clean."

Elias looked away, a flush coming up his neck. Then he admitted, "I'm pretty good at my job."

Josie had suspected as much. Despite his charm, Cortez was a formidable adversary. "I want to see those files and everything he has on Trask," she said.

His shoulders slumped, she assumed it was relief. Now that he'd convinced her, she'd come along willingly. "Walk with me," he said. "I'll get ya there safe."

Elias held a flashlight to illuminate the sheriff's office. He focused the beam on a row of file cabinets on the far wall. Then he nodded. "I know which drawer to start with."

He opened a drawer and flipped through folders as Josie watched over his shoulder. "Here it is: Bobby Trask." He lifted the file and slammed the drawer shut.

Josie sat at the sheriff's desk. Elias held his flashlight over her shoulder to help her read. The file was thick with papers. At the back there was a ledger. The kind that bookkeepers used to record money transactions.

But first Josie scanned the notes of the crime scene. Not one word recorded about Trask's clothing or more personal belongings. A disappointment. "Nothing new there," she told Elias.

A report from a Dr. Meta Christy caught her attention. Trask was in reasonable health. He'd been bludgeoned by the butt end of a Smith and Wesson and left to bleed out. The design on the leather had a distinct pattern, which was found on Bobby's skin. The local doc did not recommend an autopsy.

The last note included a number and a receipt. "There's a box of belongings," she told Elias. "But wait. Here's a photo of the contents. See the label?" Nothing in the photo was any different than the sheriff had showed her before. Replacing the information back into the folder, she closed it and set it aside.

Finally she came to the ledger. Thick and rectangular, the ledger had been bound in brown leather, now cracked. The gold embossing along the side was barely legible. Josie could smell the old ink and the waft of tobacco. She opened the cover.

Trask used a fountain pen. His scrawl was surprisingly florid, with curlicues on the capital letters. Each page was ruled in green and red. Clear columns were indicated: *Date, Item, Amount, Recipient*. Some of his notations trailed off as if he'd been in a hurry and hadn't finished.

A name or two had been scratched out, replaced with an initial or vague reference: *CL* and *Frankie D*.

Elias drew her attention to a particular set of initials. "Take a look right there, why don't ya."

Josie took the flashlight from his hand. She read aloud.

"We have Chef L and abbreviations. *HP Reserve.1890. Green Rose.* And then a list of prices. Looks to me like Trask was the buyer." She thought about what she'd seen in the Governor's Suite, realizing he was most likely in charge of organizing and procuring the food and liquor.

"Like I told ya." Elias nodded.

"But there's more. If you follow the prices, you can see that Trask increased the cost for every transaction, especially in the past few months." She flipped a page and then came back to the most recent.

"Not just for alcohol but pieces of specialized jewelry. What do they call that... Inflation."

"Like I said, I'm just the muscle. But I noticed that Trask had plenty of dough to spend in town. He dressed real spiffy. Always had a lady on his arm. Dripping with jewelry from his collection."

"And here's another note. About the meetup place." Josie pointed. "OLOS. That has to be Our Lady of Sorrows Church. So that makes sense. But do you think he was splitting his extra profit with the chef and Frankie?"

When Elias shrugged, she turned back to the ledger.

Josie's attention shifted back to Frankie. She didn't know much about Adelle's brother, other than how he protected her. Josie had another idea.

"Maybe Bobby was killed over some argument about the profit share. Was he keeping back more for himself? The chef got angry, or Frankie DiWitt did, and hit him over the head. Then they ran before someone discovered his body. Had someone intervened, Bobby might still be alive."

Josie stared at McCall. "You were around them all the time. Do you mean to tell me you never heard them argue about the money? Not once?"

He looked down at her and sighed. "You got me. Those

two were always at it. Like my brothers. But it didn't end up in a fist fight. More like a few businessmen disagreeing."

Elias nodded toward the ledger. "Hey, look at that. Ain't that Adelle's brother? He made a few of his own special orders." He pointed to the jewelry column.

Josie began to read. "Frankie has just been added to my list of suspects." She closed the book. "Put this away, I've seen enough."

He replaced the ledger and slammed the drawer shut.

Standing in the dark, Josie had one more question. "But I need to know the truth. How involved were you in this sideline?"

"Not me." Elias sounded firm. "I'm not stupid. I'd lose my job for skimming. The sheriff would can me. I think Trask, Lansky, and Frankie were the brains behind the whole operation. All three had more money than I ever had. Fast women. Bettin' on the horses. Rubbing elbows with the law-di-dah. Not my style.' He lowered his face and stared at her in the dark. "I dance. And now I have a new partner. That's all I need."

Josie could feel the emotion in his words. She knew if she hesitated, he'd lean in for a kiss. And now wasn't the time. "Let's get out of here," she said. "I've seen enough."

CHAPTER THIRTY-NINE

Once outside Elias offered her his arm. She took it willingly, still thinking about the new evidence they'd found. He kept her close to his side as they walked toward the hotel. Right as they rounded the corner a familiar laugh caught her attention.

"That's Adelle," Josie said. "See, over there."

"Date night's over," Elias mumbled. "Do you want me to go get her for a chat?"

Josie shook her head. "I don't think so. She's probably got other plans. Plus I need my beauty sleep. I want to think about everything that's happened this evening and pick up my investigation early tomorrow."

She turned to face him. "You've been quite helpful."

Before he could answer, a low uneven rumble came from down the street. A Ford truck pulled up along the curb. Josie took Elias's hand and pulled him closer to the building. *Who's picking Adelle up at this hour?*

Adelle DiWitt opened the door to the truck. Swinging her body inside, she disappeared in a cloud of silk and high heels, her laugh wafting on the air before the door slammed shut.

Josie turned to Elias. "Who's driving?"

Elias glanced toward the curb. "That's a DiWitt truck from the farm. A cowboy hired by Old Frank. Or maybe junior got tired of being Adelle's bodyguard. I bet he got someone else to do the dirty work tonight while he's playin' poker." He eyed Josie with a look of mischief.

"You know they keep tabs on her—that Adelle DiWitt's one marriageable female."

Josie nodded. "Since she's beautiful, smart, and quite funny."

"Not just that." Elias scowled. "She gets herself tied up with a lotta different men. I bet Mr. DiWitt can't wait to sell her to the highest bidder. From what I can see, Cortez may seal that deal."

"I suppose," Josie sighed. Adelle's love life appeared to be in constant flux.

But what interested her more was that Elias seemed to be holding back something else, maybe his own opinion.

"You sound doubtful, Mr. McCall."

"A rancher knows to keep his brand pure, you gotta have a mare and a stud from the same line. Breeding Adelle to the sheriff, a man with russet skin, no matter how deep his roots go, doesn't feel right to me. Out of, what would you call it, character."

He shrugged. "I suppose that after marriage, Adelle's bad behavior will be her husband's problem. Like a pony that refuses to get broke. Only the rider is to blame."

"They had dinner earlier," Josie said. "The sheriff and Adelle. Did you know?"

"Nope." He sounded less than happy. But his dismissal

made Josie wonder if he wasn't still holding something back. Josie pushed further to make sure.

"She had two dates that I know of and now, driving away in that Ford truck, that could be a third. She'd be called a siren where I come from." Josie could almost hear her mother's proclamation in her head.

He scratched his chin. "She's a busy one, that Adelle."

Puffs of exhaust spewed from the tailpipe as the truck disappeared around the corner. The back of the driver's head was visible through the window. She held her breath. Adelle sat close to him, which made Josie notice the width of his shoulders and the dark hair that had been braided Native-style. A shiver ran down her spine. *Oh, Daniel. You too.*

She turned to Elias. "I really must go. Thank you for the...interesting evening."

"How about a date tomorrow?" he asked. "We got some more dancin' to do..."

"We'll see. Right now it's beddy-bye for me."

She felt his eyes follow her as she walked away.

The rap of keys against her door brought Josie abruptly awake, and she rolled over. Another rap came, this one more insistent. With a groan she slid her legs out of bed. "Who's there?" she called and then shrugged one arm into her bathrobe.

"It's me," Lily said.

Josie opened the door and Lily slipped past. "I can't stay long," she explained. "But I wanted to know how your blind date went."

Josie smiled. "Not one bit like I expected. Let's just say, he sure can dance."

Lily's eyes widened. "Good to hear. I need to check in with Miss Delgado. Once I get myself organized, I'll come back. We can have a chat then."

Josie sent Lily on her way. She'd not told her about Elias McCall being her date. She didn't dare. Lily would be outraged that she'd danced with the sheriff's man. And then she'd lose any good will they'd recently established.

The clothes she'd worn the night before lay strewn over the back of her chair. Josie folded everything in a neat pile. Waiting for Lily gave her time to write down important details about the investigation. List her suspects, their motives, and opportunity to kill.

She drew a line through Elias McCall's name. Now she had Chef Lansky, Mateo Cortez, Delores Delgado, and Frankie DiWitt. Adelle might be mad about a couple of those, but Josie wanted to be thorough.

She turned her thoughts toward timing. The opportunity. Lily found the body on her early rounds at 5 a.m. He was already dead. Delgado came next. She'd alerted the sheriff, who showed up quickly. He arranged to have Trask's body transported to the storage room. Then came Josie's part.

I got the telegram before dawn. I immediately packed and got a cab to the Santa Fe Depot. The train left the station left right at seven. It arrived in Las Vegas in good time, nearly four hours later. Around eleven. Right at the beginning of the lunch hour rush.

Even thought it was just across the street, It took me at least half an hour to navigate the crowds and walk to the entrance of the Castañeda. By the time I reached the storage room... She stopped to count on her fingers. *He'd been dead eight hours maybe. Give or take.*

Satisfied that she'd made a good account of the timeline,

she started another journal page, scribbling *Means* at the top.

The doctor's report indicated that Bobby was bludgeoned with the butt end of a Smith and Wesson. The marking on his wound matched the pattern of the butt end of the gun. *But where is that gun?* So far Cortez had only spoken of it. He said it was found in Lily's room, but that was his word alone. He didn't have a photo in the file or the actual weapon.

Josie didn't doubt Trask was bludgeoned by a gun, but she still wrestled with why. Maybe the answer was in who Bobby was, his personality. Hadn't she just been shown how a person could look like one thing and turn out to have an entirely different side? Thoughts of Elias came to mind. Josie smiled, thinking of him kicking his leg high into the air to egg her on.

She wrote *Victim* on a fresh page. It hit her between the eyes. Why hadn't she put him first? To know the victim is to get a glimpse into why he might have been murdered. *Now that was a mistake*, she thought. *I should have started with inquiring more about Trask right from the beginning.*

Instead of being discouraged, she corrected herself. *No time like the present. Remember the ledger.* Bobby was meticulous when it came to his note-taking and his money. Not surprising. Everyone was since the stock market crash and the country's plunge into financial crisis.

But Bobby also knew to disguise his sales with stars and initials. She wouldn't call it a code exactly, but it was effective. Plus there was evidence that Chef Lansky and maybe Frankie DiWitt were his partners.

On the final page she wrote the heading *Opportunity*. If she could find evidence of any suspect in his room the night of the murder, then she'd be able to deduce the killer.

She looked away. Her eyes moistened. For the first time since she'd seen the body, she felt sorry for Bobby Trask. *No one deserves to die that way. He was like everyone else, trying to make a buck.*

All the people around Bobby made money from his dealings. Why wouldn't he be resourceful and want to make a little for himself? He must have had the jewelry designed to order, paying a Native American a little bit of a markup. Josie assumed that was the case, though she didn't have actual proof.

He was the middleman, offering tourists what they wanted. Just like Fred Harvey, now considered a pillar of the community.

She wondered if Bobby's business went wrong when he raised his prices. She knew from experience that corruption crept in bit by bit. It probably started with him holding back a few extra bottles from each shipment. Just to make ends meet. Maybe he'd offered to pay his bootlegging pals a bit on the side. But it wasn't enough. One of them got greedy or just plain angry.

She rubbed her eyes with the back of her hand. It was hard not to think of Bobby as a victim. Then she reminded herself, *I need to find his killer. Not exact revenge or even bring him to justice.*

One of your partners turned on you. She felt convinced. *Maybe you argued, then fought. A gun was pulled. He hit you and then ran away.*

Confidence returned to Josie. She'd have her murderer soon. She could feel it in her bones. Then she'd report back to the Harvey Company and hear, "Job well done."

With a last scribble in her notebook, a knock came to the door.

When Josie opened it, she found Lily holding a tray

with a pot of coffee and two cups. She placed the tray on the table and then sat on the edge of the bed while Josie poured.

"You won't believe this," Lily began. "Miss Delgado stopped me in the hall. Blah, blah, blah. She started right off lecturing me on the propriety of a Harvey Girl, how my arrest brought down the standard for all the other employees.

"I tried to explain that I'd been unfairly accused, but she wasn't having any of it." Lily's eyes brimmed. "I hate being that person, you know. The one everybody thinks let the team down."

"She's a tyrant of the first order." Josie comforted her friend. "And she may be covering up her own involvement. Have you thought of that?"

"What do you mean?" Lily wiped away her tears.

"I didn't say so yesterday, I was so excited by your release, but I saw Miss Delgado having tea with Sheriff Cortez. They were quite intimate." Josie described what had happened in The Velvet Rose Tea Room, leaving out no detail.

"Is Matron one of your suspects?" Lily asked.

"She's always around," Josie said. "Spying on the Harvey Girls. Most likely spying on the hotel guests. I bet she tells Cortez everything she sees. Who knows, she may have been blackmailing Bobby herself. Things got out of hand and—"

"An informant and a blackmailer." Lily looked shocked. "I never thought she'd stoop to such lows." She sounded skeptical.

"That's right. So even if she didn't kill Bobby, she may know who did. Think back, Lily. Do you remember if she was on duty that night into the next morning?"

"Mr. Trask requested his usual early morning wake-up,

so I tapped on his door. When he didn't open it, I used my key."

Her eyes held a faraway look. "I did wonder if he deliberately didn't answer, to get me to come in. You know, to make it look like I was interested in his affections.

"But then I told myself I was being too sensitive. That Mr. Trask needed to get ready for the train. That was all."

"So you didn't see anyone leave his room earlier?" Josie asked.

"No. I'd been on duty since four thirty. No one in the hallway for sure. I'd have noticed."

Josie opened her notebook to scribble. When she finished, she had another question. "Do you think Miss Delgado may have been watching? She was right there, Johnny-on-the-spot, after the porter. She sent for the sheriff so quickly."

"I see Matron so often I don't know her actual work schedule. I think she practically lives at the Castañeda." Lily sniffed.

"What do you mean?"

"Have you forgotten? When you were here, every time you'd turn around she'd pop up with her accusing face, as if she couldn't wait to catch you doing something wrong."

Josie sighed. "So many Harvey Girl rules." She jotted in her notebook. "My goodness, Lily. You may be on to something. Maybe Miss Delgado does live here. A room of her own, perhaps?"

"I don't think the Castañeda would give up the price of one room's lodging, even for the matron saint." Lily's brow crinkled. "But what about the closet where the linens are stored? She's the only one with a key. No one else ever gets inside. Strictly off limits."

Hadn't she just seen Daniel's make-do office in the

barn? Matron could be living out of the linen closet to what, save money? Not impossible.

"How would we ever know?" Lily asked.

"What about this? We spy on her for a change." Josie felt her skin prickle.

Lily's eyes grew round. "No one has the nerve to spy on the matron saint." She stood. "I'd better get back to my shift." Before she left, she turned around and said, "I never got to ask about your date. Who was the lucky young man?"

Caught between a rock and a hard place, Josie knew if she lied, and Lily found out, she might not get another chance. Her voice trembled. "Elias McCall."

"I don't believe it!" Lily looked livid, her face turning red. "After all that work with getting you ready, you go out with my jailer."

"He's not what you think!" Josie defended him. "He's a big softy underneath that exterior. He's just an employee of the sheriff, not a bad person."

Josie tried to say more, but her words got lost in the slam of the door.

CHAPTER FORTY

Josie paced in her room, deep in thought. Had she made a mistake defending Elias to Lily? If only she'd waited on that, given it a little time, maybe Lily would feel differently. But now the rift between them felt twice as wide.

A rattle came at the door handle. *Maybe Lily's come back.*

The door inched open. Delores Delgado stuck her head inside. "I saw Miss Davenport leave in a huff. But you're still here. Did you two have a spat?" She looked rather pleased. When Josie didn't answer she added, "I was just checking."

Instead of leaving, she came all the way in and closed the door behind her. Josie's skin prickled.

"It's my duty to check up on the maids. I admit, I've been paying special attention to your accommodations." Delores looked around with a distasteful sniff. "Smells like debauchery in here. Stale perfume, and look at that." She pointed to the pile of clothing left from the night before.

Josie held her tongue.

"You came in quite late, Miss MacFarland," Delgado

continued. "No respectable woman would be out until the wee hours."

Josie's chest tightened. She knew losing her temper would only give the matron more power. *She's one of my suspects*, Josie thought. *I have to handle her carefully.*

Miss Delgado launched into another one of her speeches. "The behavior of all the Castañeda guests is my concern. You must leave immediately. I can't have you influencing my staff."

Biting her bottom lip, Josie thought carefully about her next words.

"I'm looking into the night when Bobby Trask was killed." She ignored Delgado's demand and used her calmest voice. "Since you were on duty, you most likely saw people coming and going from his room."

Delgado jingled the keys in her hand and cleared her throat. "I did see people. But that wasn't uncommon. Mr. Trask had friends in Las Vegas. He was a frequent guest, stayed in the same corner room every time. He had the same expectations each time he visited. I made sure that he got early morning wake-up calls, and the special hospitality treatment that Fred was famous for. Along with the turndown service he had a private bath located close to his room. I kept an eye on him." Her voice trailed off.

"You must have been tipped well for that service," Josie said dryly.

"We're not supposed to take tips from guests," Delgado retorted. "Maybe the bellboys, but not the maids...or the matron," she added as an afterthought. "But yes, he did offer me money at first. When I refused, he gave me lovely gifts. Mr. Trask traded in Native jewelry and fine linens, you know. I have a collection of monogrammed hankies. He'd bring one on each visit. I didn't buy any of that Native jewelry. It's not my taste."

Josie remembered Matron's handkerchief. But then she'd dropped her surprise in pursuit of other inquiries. "What about his visitors the night in question?"

"He went out at nine," Delores replied. "He was in a hurry. Most likely heading to the last service in the dining room. I called after him, but he didn't hear."

"Had he already received his turn-down service?"

"I attended to it personally after he left," Delores said.

"Did you find anything unusual in his room?"

"I don't spy."

"Oh come on, Matron. I know you better than that. Look at the way you spied on me. I suspect you know my wardrobe better than I do."

"I did find a note on his desk," she admitted with a scowl. "He'd scheduled an assignation at the church. Most likely one of those soiled doves that he tended to keep company with." Josie flinched at the phrase "soiled dove." A Western way of describing a woman of ill repute.

"Did any of those 'soiled doves' visit Mr. Trask in his room that evening?" Josie asked.

"As I told the sheriff..."

Josie's ears perked up. Miss Delgado finally admitted that she reported to Cortez. "Do continue."

"Miss DiWitt was the only one. She visited Mr. Trask around midnight. All dressed up, smelling of perfume, laughing loud enough for me to hear from the hallway. I think she'd been drinking." She touched her nose with distaste.

"When did Miss DiWitt leave?" asked Josie.

"Only a few minutes later. I watched the two of them stand in the hallway, brazen as you please. She kissed his cheek and swept down the hall. He watched her go. The poor man was besotted, I can tell you that."

So Adelle had visited and then left. "What did you tell the sheriff about Adelle's visit? They are engaged."

Matron sniffed. "They weren't engaged then. But Sheriff Cortez needed to know who he was dealing with," she explained. "The little tramp. But no, I don't really care about who he's engaged to. At first he didn't believe me about Adelle, but I had evidence. It wasn't until later that I suspected someone else.

"After all the fuss, I gave the sheriff something I'd picked up in Mr. Trask's room that night. I found it on the floor and was going to have a quiet talk with one of the maids afterward.

"It was a lace handkerchief with H. H. embroidered in the corner. Since Lily Davenport was on call and always serviced his room, I knew it belonged to her." Delores's eyes brimmed with tears. "The sheriff took the evidence from me and he arrested Miss Davenport soon after."

Delores reached for the door right as Josie blurted one more question. "Did anyone else visit Bobby Trask after Miss DiWitt?"

"Chef Lansky and the sheriff's man, Elias McCall," she stated flatly. "Just those two."

"Around two o'clock," Josie clarified.

"Yes," Delgado confirmed. "Trask called out goodbye to them as the door closed. His voice could wake the dead."

"Before you go," Josie began, "what time did the men leave Bobby's room?"

"I suspect they played some poker. In fact I saw a bottle in the jacket pocket of the sheriff's man. That's what they were up to." Her lip curled. "The men left around three in the morning. I remember thinking Mr. Trask would get very little sleep before his wake-up call." The matron sounded impatient. She turned to the door. "I have to go. Good day."

Josie had enough information, so she didn't stop her from leaving.

Now I've got something, she realized. But then she felt a sudden thirst come over her. She ran her tongue over her cracked lips. Everyone knew to drink more liquids in the dry climate. She'd been so busy, she'd forgotten.

I could sure use a cup of jasmine tea right now. All of this thinking and writing has made me parched.

CHAPTER FORTY-ONE

Madame Liu poured a cup of jasmine tea for Josie. She left the pot on the table. "This time you pay." She nodded for emphasis.

"Of course," Josie agreed. "Thank you for the cookies."

"You pay double for those. Fresh out of oven." The Chinese woman's precise no-nonsense words made her meaning quite clear.

Josie knew the proprietor of the shop had the right to charge whatever the market would bear. An American ideal, drummed into her by her father. Just ask Fred Harvey, the man from England who turned American travel and cuisine on its ear, using Native customs and handmade crafts to his own advantage.

"Put them on my tab," she said briskly. *Like everyone else, I'm short of cash.*

To her delight, the older woman's mouth twitched. "A tab. That make you a regular customer now." She moved away from the table.

Josie munched her first cookie. The delicious taste of almond burst in her mouth. When Madame Liu returned, she gestured to the empty chair. "Would you like to join me?"

"You want company?" Madame Liu looked surprised.

"I need help," Josie admitted. "I remembered you told me to think for myself. Please, if you have a moment, sit down. I think you might be the best person to advise me with my investigation."

Madame Liu pulled out the chair and sat primly on the edge. "I good judge of character," she admitted. "I see you try. Too hard. You need to watch more. Wait before jump. My advice." She rose, but Josie kept talking.

"No, no. Not just that." Josie glanced at the bottom of her teacup. Residue of the jasmine leaves made a pattern All that advice. Was Madame Liu giving her a reading? The Chinese woman hadn't looked into her cup. Maybe just something she came up with on the spot for all of her customers.

"Actually I have been watching. The sheriff and the Harvey House matron, they sat over there the last time I was here. I wondered if they come to your tea room very often?"

Madame Liu sat back down. Josie continued, "I realize you might not want to trust me with the goings-on of your important customers. I also realize I'm a stranger and a female doing a man's job. That might be unsuitable in your culture. I've been told by everyone else that's the case." She felt a surge of frustration, hoping it didn't sound in her voice.

"I woman in a man's world," Madame Liu said. "You pay bill, then we talk." She stood again.

Reaching into her pocketbook, Josie removed several coins. "This is all I have. But I'll come back and pay the rest later." She opened her hand.

The Chinese woman stared at her palm. Then she pushed Josie's hand away. "You keep for rainy day. When case solved, you pay then."

Josie felt stunned. Had Madame Liu just said solved? Up until now, she hadn't considered that possible. Tears welled in her eyes. She brushed them away quickly. When she got more control over her emotions she nodded, still unable to speak.

Madame Liu sat down and poured another cup of tea, giving Josie a moment to collect herself. She began to speak, this time in a smoother voice. "Sheriff and Matron are very close. Kissie-pie close. But not respectable. They keep out of sight. The sheriff is engaged to Adelle DiWitt, but the rancher's daughter would never come to my shop. That's why the sheriff can safely meet with Miss Delgado here, so as not to arouse suspicion."

Josie's eyes opened wide. Madame Liu spoke in perfect English. She sounded just like a native speaker. If Josie closed her eyes, she'd mistake the Chinese woman for a tourist from the East Coast.

Madame Liu's steely gaze bored into hers. Josie held back a giggle. All that pidgin English had been put on. Part of her immigrant disguise. Madame Liu was no ordinary woman.

Josie picked up the conversation, knowing better than to comment on the change. "I won't tell Adelle, if that's what you're worried about. It's the investigation that matters to me."

Josie surprised herself. She trusted the Chinese woman instantly. So she told her everything she knew, hoping to get her perspective about the case.

"I have a list of suspects," she said, naming names.

Madame Liu nibbled on a cookie. By the time Josie stopped for a breath, Madame Liu had finished the rest.

It felt good to explain. She couldn't be expected to see it all for herself.

"This comes down to the entrance and the exit," Madame Liu concluded.

Josie felt perplexed. "What do you mean?"

Madam Liu gestured toward the front of the shop. "People come and go from the same door. The Chinese know how important this is when it comes to good luck. I never let anyone behind my beaded screen or out my back door. They would have to be someone I trusted entirely. Not a customer."

Madame Liu nodded toward the area behind the beaded curtain. "Old Chinese proverb. The teacher will open the door but then it's up to the student."

Madame Liu stood. She lifted the teapot along with the empty cookie plate and went to the back room.

CHAPTER FORTY-TWO

Josie stepped outside the front door of The Velvet Rose Tea Room and blinked at the bright sun. A voice called to her, but she didn't recognize who it was.

"Hey, Joe Mack."

She held her palm over her eyes. Daniel leaned against a familiar Ford truck. In the daylight, the DiWitt ranch insignia was clear on the side-door panel.

"Rio misses you," he said. "Want to go for a ride? I can drive you out to the barn."

Josie hesitated. She felt angry at Daniel, the way he and Adelle looked the evening before. But his offer... She couldn't refuse. "I'd love to see Rio." She didn't add his name, hoping he'd pick up that he wasn't the reason she'd agreed so readily.

She hoisted herself onto the passenger seat.

The truck bumped along the road. As he focused on his driving, she had a chance to get a good look at him—his profile, the firm chin. *He's different*, she realized. Daniel's hair had been shaped into a bun at the back of his head. His clear brown skin had been freshly shaved.

He caught her staring and smiled. "You've been busy. Investigating." Was Daniel making small talk? That, too, was new.

"I have," she sighed. "The sheriff has been, let's say, less than cooperative. Plus I had to get Lily out of dormitory arrest first. Fortunately she's no longer a suspect. Thanks, by the way, for the note about where they were holding her."

He nodded in response.

When he didn't pick up the conversation, she couldn't help herself. "I saw you with Adelle DiWitt. It was you in the truck, right?"

She knew she'd hit a nerve when he refused to look over. Finally he answered, "Yes. I picked her up."

"Do you work for the DiWitts now? I know you're in charge of the rodeo barn, but I didn't realize that included being a chauffeur." Josie deliberately left out the part about Adelle sitting so close.

"Fancy word," he commented dryly. "Chauffeur."

Daniel was rarely talkative, but now he shifted to sullen unresponsiveness. Which only made Josie more frustrated.

Once he pulled up to the barn, she was the first to step out of the truck. She didn't say thanks or see ya. The sound of Rio's sharp whinny distracted her from even pretending to be pleasant. *He knows I'm here*, she thought.

Daniel met her at the side of the truck. He smiled.

Josie hurried toward the barn. She found her horse with his head over the half wall. He nickered a greeting his large dark eyes bright with expectation.

She reached to scratch between his ears. "Hey there, fella. I missed you too."

The horse nudged her shoulder playfully with his nose.

"I didn't bring a carrot. But let's see what I can scrounge up." She turned around, but there was no sign of Daniel.

"In my office," came his voice from the other side of the barn.

Josie found him sitting at his desk, leaning over paperwork. "I've got to put in a few orders."

"Do you have any carrots? I didn't come prepared."

"Over there." He gestured to the corner where there was a crate filled with vegetables. "Our kitchen garden castoffs. Not good enough for the Hotel Castañeda," he explained.

Josie lifted the largest carrot from the pile. Her eyes lingered on the wall behind the container. *What do we have here?*

A photo of Adelle DiWitt standing next to Daniel. She stared into his eyes as he leaned back, his mouth open to laugh. The photographer had caught an intimate moment between them.

She took in the background of the photo. The barn and the distant view of the mountain range completed the image. "You and Adelle," she said, pointing to the photo.

He rose quickly. "I forgot to take that down." He shoved the photo into his pocket.

"You're friends," she added quietly.

He pulled it back out to stare at the photo, a slight smile playing on his lips. "Yes," he answered. "Friends." But the way he said it made Josie even more certain.

"You're more than friends. Oh Daniel, why didn't you say so before?"

"You didn't ask."

"Why do I have to ask you everything! Can't you just volunteer once in a while? Tell me. When did it happen?" Unable to suppress her jealousy, she blurted, "What are you thinking, being with a white woman? A rich one too!"

Her gut twisted with shame. After all, she was a white

woman just like Adelle. She, too, had strong feelings for Daniel despite their differences.

He shrugged. "You left without saying goodbye. I didn't think we were that close."

"You know that's not true!" Josie's face heated up. "You and Rio meant the world to me. I had to leave. They didn't give me time to pack, let alone explain. Please, Daniel." She stumbled over the last words, wondering if she'd ever be able to make up for that lack of goodbye.

He handed the photo to her. A peace offering of sorts. Something Josie was willing to take under the circumstances. "You both look very happy," she said.

"We are," he agreed. "But we aren't public. If her father found out, or little Frank..."

Josie knew full well that Native and white relationships were not acceptable. Although Adelle and Daniel wouldn't be the only mixed-race couple, Adelle's status would make it impossible for them to be welcomed by the Las Vegas society. Of course the sheriff wasn't a white man either. There's something more, Josie concluded. Power and influence for one. Perhaps Sheriff Cortez's status allowed Mr. DiWitt to dismiss his prejudice and misgivings.

"But she's engaged to Sheriff Cortez." Josie pinned the photo back on the wall.

"What can she do? Her father insisted," he said curtly.

"How's that? I can't image Adelle putting up with a marriage of convenience, if that's what you're calling it." *Do I tell him the obvious, that he's not rich and will never have a chance.*

"She did it for me," he explained. "She wanted to keep her father from looking in my direction."

Josie's stomach turned. Did Adelle tell Daniel that? She

could believe it. "Is that why she dates so many men? She had assignations with two before you picked her up. She's obviously friends with Elias McCall. Then Chef. Engaged to Cortez." Josie wanted him to see for himself that Adelle wasn't good enough. Her stomach twisted.

His eyes flashed with anger. "No," he said. "None of the others are with her. We're together." He turned back to his desk.

Josie gripped the carrot, aware that he'd shut down again.

"Thank you, Daniel," Josie said. "For telling me and for sharing about your personal life. I'll do my best to earn back your trust. I promise."

Daniel pulled the Ford alongside the front of the Castañeda Hotel. Josie was the first to break the silence. "Thank you for coming to get me. Just being with Rio makes me happy." She reached for the door handle.

"I'll explain to Dell that I told you." He stared straight ahead.

"She can talk to me any time," Josie replied. "You've helped me with my investigation. Now I realize all of that dating was a coverup. A distraction for her father and brother. I have a better idea of where to find my killer."

Josie stepped onto the walkway and headed toward the entrance to the Castañeda as Daniel drove away.

The doorman nodded. "Good day, miss." He tipped his hat. "Big party tonight. The Governor's Suite," he announced.

"Good day," she responded politely.

Making her way to the reception counter, Josie stopped. "Any messages for me?"

"I'll check, miss." The reception clerk returned with an envelope.

She slid her finger under the flap. The message was in a woman's open scrawl. 'My brother is accompanying me at tonight's party. Join us." It was signed: Adelle.

CHAPTER FORTY-THREE

Elias McCall stood outside the Governor's Suite. He stared at Josie. "Do you have an invitation?" One glance over her shoulder and then back to her face. "Any chance we can meet later?" His eyes sparkled with hope.

Josie unclasped her sequined clutch and showed him the note from Adelle. "I've been invited," she explained. "I'm working," she added under her breath.

"Where is your date?" He looked over her head into the hall.

"He's otherwise detained," she replied demurely.

A slight smile came to the corner of his mouth. "A good-looker like you shouldn't be left on her own."

Josie flushed pink under his gaze.

In his doorman's tuxedo, Elias looked bigger than life. He filled out the jacket to the point it seemed to be bursting. The black tie must have been made especially for his large neck.

She leaned closer. "If you're up for a dance later this week..."

Elias nodded and then opened the door to let her inside. Just as she swept past, he spoke in her ear. "Can't wait."

Josie stepped into the crowded foyer. When none of the assembled guests looked in her direction, she felt relieved. A waiter passed by, offering her a glass. She took the flute of champagne and pretended to sip. Then she made her way to the corner, between the end of the bar and a door leading outside.

A group of men stood nearby. "Napkin, miss?" A young man offered one from his tray. She wanted to shush him but smiled and took the napkin instead. She avoided his appraising glance and ducked behind a potted palm.

From her vantage point, she had a clear view of nearly everyone in the room. Adelle stood close by with her brother. Josie waited an acknowledgement but it didn't come. She watched Frankie DiWitt instead.

Frank Jr. left an empty glass on the waiter's tray and replaced it with one that overflowed. "Cheers, dear sister." He waved the glass in front of Adelle's nose and then took a long gulp. His words sounded slurred.

Adelle's brother nodded and then lifted the flute and drained it in one gulp. Josie looked away, feeling embarrassed for him and even for Adelle. *It's no fun having a drunken man as your chaperone.*

Josie's glance stopped on Chef Lansky. His date was a tiny blonde. She laughed and pulled at his sleeve. He didn't look at her; his gaze was focused on Adelle across the room.

Out of the corner of her eye, Josie caught sight of Sheriff Cortez. He had no one on his arm as he made his way toward Adelle and Frankie. Josie sighed. The sheriff looked quite spectacular in his Westen-style tuxedo. She watched as he leaned closer to kiss Adelle's cheek.

Frankie smiled his approval. Cortez gave him a polite nod. "DiWitt," he said. "Nice to see you again."

Frankie immediately left the couple to make his way toward the bar. "Whiskey. Neat," he told the server. While he waited, he turned to speak to the man next to him.

Josie wondered if now was the time to start a conversation with Frankie. He'd risen on her list of suspects. She leaned toward the plant and dumped her drink before sitting up straight to hold up the empty glass.

"Can I get ya somethin'?" Frankie slurred. He looked her over. "Do I know you?"

"I don't believe we've met." Josie offered him a hand. "I'm Josie MacFarland. And you?"

"Frankie DiWitt of the DiWitt family ranch. I'm the son." He held her hand a bit too long. "Get that lady another bubbly," he shouted to the server.

Josie did her best to hide her disdain. Frankie smelled of stale cigarettes and alcohol. That alone made her want to gag. She left her drink and excused herself. Frankie stared into his empty whiskey glass, oblivious to her goodbye.

Back behind the potted palm, Josie turned her attention to Adelle and the sheriff. Acting he perfect date, Adelle nodded politely as Mateo spoke. Her stilted laugh spoke volumes; she might be a bit bored with the sheriff, or at least had other things on her mind. Now that Josie knew about her relationship with Daniel, she wasn't surprised.

In fact, Josie felt sorry for Mateo Cortez. He obviously thought his engagement would assure him a certain amount of deference. He made every effort to keep her interest. Hadn't he dressed to look more like a politician, less like law enforcement? He continued to tell his stories, becoming more animated, like a child begging to be seen.

"Dinner is served," a waiter announced from the far

corner of the room. The delicious aroma of roasted meat and thyme spilled through the open doors that led to the dining room. Josie looked around. The custom was to take the arm of one's escort and walk together to be seated. Other than Frankie DiWitt, Elias was the only unaccompanied man.

Josie popped outside the door to speak with him. "I can't go into the dining room without a partner," she told him. "Can you leave for just a minute to escort me in?"

He smiled, obviously enjoying her request. "I wish I could, but I have to greet late arrivals. If they don't have the invitation, I have to bounce them. I'm sorry. I'm working." He sounded genuinely apologetic, she had to give him that. It didn't escape her notice that he used the "I'm working," just as she had earlier.

"Okey dokey. Not a problem. I'm going to take a moment to look around the rest of the Governor's Suite then. You can find me right down the hallway. I'll be snooping." She grinned and walked away as more guests approached, drawing his attention.

He has to work. I have to work. Neither of us is a guest at this shindig.

Josie found a hallway with a series of closed doors. She tried the knob on the first door, and it turned in her hand. The smell of musty books and cigar smoke met her nostrils. *The library*, she thought.

Sure enough, the walls were lined with dark wood bookshelves and bound editions of the classics. The bottom shelves were filled with old issues of *The Saturday Evening Post*.

A large rolltop desk stood to the right of the door. A key

had been left in the lock. A quick twist and she rolled back the front. Inside was a typewriter. One paper remained on the roller, a stack of documents and bills left on the side.

She glanced over the pages. Orders for food and liquor from various local vendors. Underneath, the orders were for alcohol and seafood. Illegally transported over state lines, Josie concluded. Definitely a punishable offense.

She slid the roll top closed right as the door opened. Adelle let herself inside with a cheeky grin. "Gawd, what a bore. I hoped to find you here." She closed the door softly and looked around. "I told Mateo I had to powder my nose. He was involved in some discussion about his campaign and run for sheriff. He won't notice that I'm gone." She glanced toward the desk. "Did you find anything important?"

"Orders for liquor," Josie said. "They're not even trying to hide their operation."

"That's it, darling," Adelle said. "Why do you suppose every important occupant of the Governor's Suite invites the sheriff to his party? He's in up to his eyeballs, turning a blind eye for years. Now that the war has been over for some time, the authorities don't even care about prohibition. They get a share of the profit paid under the table.

"I'm not interested in who drinks what and from where. In fact, every man in this town—the ones who matter—has focused their attention to something far more dodgy: the wayward behavior of women."

Josie felt confused. Hadn't the behavior of women always been the responsibility of decent men? It was their job to protect and defend the fairer sex.

"Social hygiene, it's called." Adelle looked stern. She brushed invisible crumbs from her satin brocade skirt.

"I don't know what you mean."

"Haven't you noticed? Now that money is being made,

our government is no longer interested in keeping people away from their booze. In fact, selling liquor has become not just fashionable but a mainstay.

"So now women are the problem. We spread venereal disease, apparently all by ourselves. Our independence undermines the very thread of 'American democracy.'" She rolled her eyes, using a deep voice to make her point. "We lured those soldiers during the war and now we fling ourselves at any man because of our depraved sexual needs."

Adelle's voice got more and more intense as her fingers twisted at the low neckline of her dress. "These are the big threat." She pointed to her cleavage. "Not to be seen by anyone other than my maid, my mother, and my husband. Otherwise men will give in to their natural instincts and have their way with me. When they come down with the clap, well, it's my fault."

"That's just ridiculous," Josie sputtered.

"You think so? They even have a name for what they're doing. 'The American Plan'." She frowned. "I heard there are fifteen hundred females incarcerated in camp cities! They were proven, in court, to be a menace to men. They were given internal examinations in search of disease. Even when no evidence of disease could be found, they were isolated and kept from returning home."

Adelle's specific numbers startled Josie. "Why haven't I heard about that before?" She felt her indignation keenly, her cheeks flushing with emotion.

"Most of the arrests are made behind the scenes. Women yanked off the street because they had a sway to their walk or didn't cover up enough. Maybe they were seen dining alone. No records are kept. Each state has its own jurisdiction, even New Mexico. You can't get anyone to talk about it."

Adelle's expression hardened. "But then someone I knew, it happened to her. My friend was pulled off the street by two government men. She's now living with her mother in disgrace. A virgin, Josie. No sexual experience whatsoever. Ahe's unemployable. The mother has to clean houses. That's why I know. Firsthand from her.

"And don't think for a minute you have to be anything but young and female. Even traveling unaccompanied makes any of us suspect. The men are in charge, darling. And we're the most convenient scapegoat for all of their woes."

Josie's stomach clenched. "I've eaten alone in public and traveled by myself just this past week. Do you think I'm in danger?"

"Darling, I have no idea. But I'm not going to let anything happen to you if I can help it. You can bet that's why Frankie the watchdog hangs around me all the time. What a drag. My father doesn't want me arrested, now does he." Adelle's face looked grim.

"I'm growing a bit mature to be that innocent. So Father has to step up and sell me off to the highest bidder. Trade me for a piece of land. Get some political clout. He's even looked the other way at Mateo's darker skin and Spanish heritage. I'm just another commodity."

Josie felt Adelle's resentment. She'd not heard of the American Plan, but now that she thought about it, hadn't she felt her freedom taken piece by piece, every time her mother talked about marriage and children?

Adelle and I have more in common than I ever imagined.

Josie knew now was the time to share. "Daniel told me. About you two."

Adelle's eyes grew wide. "He said he might, but I didn't

realize... So what do you think? Are you going to warn me off like my family?" Her friend's eyes blazed.

"I think you're a lucky woman," Josie replied "Daniel is an amazing and caring man. He was my first friend who wasn't in the Harvey company. You'll get nothing but support from me. I won't tell a soul either. Your secret is safe."

"That's all I needed to hear." Adelle pulled Josie into an embrace. "He said that would be your response. But I didn't know for sure." She kissed Josie's cheek. "I think we're like sisters, you and I. I've never had one before."

"Me neither." Josie smiled.

"So tell me quickly. What's next, Harvey House detective? How are we going to bring these men down?"

Now that she had Adelle, Josie felt less alone and more confident than ever. This new connection gave her hope. Maybe in time, Lily would come around too.

Adelle stood back as if she had something on her mind. "I have an idea. If I may..."

"What's that?"

"Why don't we mosey on over to Bobby Trask's room, take a peaky-boo?"

"I already did that," Josie insisted.

"Darling, you may have missed something. A small bit of evidence. Let's just take a gander, shall we?"

Josie thought for a moment. "My friend Lily can get us access. She's working tonight."

Adelle winked. "Brilliant. Let's go. Time's a-wastin'."

CHAPTER FORTY-FOUR

As Lily led the way to Bobby Trask's room, she hissed, "Who invited her?"

Josie arched an eyebrow. "Adelle's helping me with the investigation," she explained.

"I can be helpful," Adelle interrupted. "If you give me a chance."

Lily sighed. "Hurry up. I don't want Delgado to catch us." She used her key.

"Lily and I have never trusted Miss Delgado," Josie explained to Adelle. She closed the door to the hallway.

"She's an informant," Lily insisted. "But you wouldn't know anything about that, being a rich rancher's daughter." She slid the ring of keys into her apron pocket.

"Actually, Adelle knows quite a lot," Josie said. "About the vulnerability of women in the hands of the wrong man." She must have caught Adelle off guard. For a moment a cloud passed over her eyes.

Lily's lips pursed. She didn't even look in Adelle's direction.

"So this is just as he left it?" Adelle swept her hand over the room.

"The bloodstain is, at least." Josie bent her knees to have a closer look.

"What about that, did you look behind it?" Adelle pointed to a dressing screen in the corner.

"I don't think I did," Josie realized. She rose and stepped across the room. She ran her hand over the leather inlay. "Beautiful, don't you think, with the inlay and wood?"

"A fancy touch for special guests," Lily explained. "That screen—Bobby went on and on about it. Every time I stopped to freshen the room, he'd explain its uses and who designed it. Maybe that's why he insisted on staying here every visit."

Adelle nodded. "He was rather a bully when it came to knowing what he wanted."

Lily swung around. "I saw you go in and out of Bobby's room on several occasions. Odd hours. Late at night. All by yourself."

Adelle shrugged. "And you also saw me leave minutes afterward. I was there to look at his jewelry collection. I picked up several beautiful pieces. He had new ones whenever he came to Las Vegas. A few people on the pueblo worked for him."

Lily didn't look convinced.

Adelle continued. "I recently ordered turquoise inlay cuff links for Frankie for his birthday. I liked them so much, I got a pair for my father. You probably saw me then."

Josie felt impatient, done with the bickering between Adelle and Lily. *I have a murder to solve.* She stepped around Adelle to move one section of the trifold dressing screen. A full-length mirror hung on the wall. *Bobby must have been quite the dandy,* Josie surmised. *But what's this?*

Next to the mirror was another door. Lily pulled out her ring of keys and tried a few until finally there was a click. The knob turned in her hand. Lily opened the door and looked out. "Come see," she called over her shoulder.

Josie hurried closer. "So a vestibule and a stairway. I wonder where it leads..."

Lily gave her a shove back into the room. She quickly closed the door. "I bet the stairs lead to the main lobby. I can't believe I missed this area of the room. When I moved my sweeper toward the screen, Bobby always told me not to bother. I figured he was hiding something, but I never thought it was a door."

"No wonder Bobby insisted on the same room. He could come and go without being seen," Josie concluded.

"How convenient," Adelle drawled. "Even the matron can't watch two doors."

"Speak of the devil!" Lily's eyes flew open as they heard a key in the main door.

Josie gave Lily a quick shove. She unfolded the dressing screen to cover the corner. "Duck," she whispered. Unfortunately Adelle refused.

"Hello, Delores," came her voice from the other side of the screen. "Fancy meeting you here." Josie wondered if Adelle was acting as a decoy to give them time to slip out the back way.

To her surprise, Lily was having none of it. She rose to her full height and took Josie's hand. "I'm not afraid of her. Let's just face the music."

Inspired by Lily's change of attitude toward the matron, Josie smiled. They both stepped out from behind the screen together.

"Don't bother to explain." Matron held up her hand. "I

can see for myself. Three unauthorized women looking at a dead man's room. Breaking and entering. Wait until the sheriff hears about this!" A look of triumph came over her face.

"I have keys." Lily held up the ring. "It's my job to keep an eye on all the rooms. I invited Josie, she's the detective. That one came along for fun." She nodded at Adelle, who looked away with a smirk.

Delgado continued, "I will do the paperwork for disciplinary measures. Not for you, Miss DiWitt, but for these two."

Josie and Lily sat on the edge of the bed. Neither looked particularly contrite. Adelle walked around the room as if taking in the sights.

"I'll have you both packed and on your way home tomorrow," the matron announced.

"Your threats have no effect on me. I've been through far worse," Lily announced. Josie felt quite proud of her friend.

"We'll see about that." Delgado's eyes narrowed.

"I have every right to be here," Josie reminded her. "But I know you and the sheriff have a special arrangement. I wonder if Adelle is aware." When she looked over, Adelle had disappeared

"My relationship with Sheriff Cortez is none of your affair. And Miss Davenport, hand me those keys. I don't need to put up with your sass. I'm alerting the sheriff right this minute. As for you." She turned to Josie. "Stay out of my personal business. You're trying to derail the engagement of two people in love. Shame on you!"

The urge to explain caught in her throat. She ducked her head and bit her lip.

"Come with me." The matron took Lily by the hand. As

soon as the door closed, Josie sprang to her feet. Something had caught her eye as the matron lectured.

A small object was lodged between the floorboards. Josie hurried closer and picked it up. "A man's cuff link," she said softly.

It had been exquisitely designed with silver with turquoise inlay. The stone had been crafted in the shape of a steer head. The letter "D" had been etched inside.

She held it up to see more clearly. Then she turned it over. The initials "F.D. Jr." were engraved on the back. At that moment the door behind the dressing screen creaked open. Adelle walked around the screen, her face slightly flushed. "I wanted to confirm where the stairs led," she explained. "Is Matron gone yet?"

"To get the sheriff," Josie replied. She cupped the link in her hand, wondering how Adelle would react to her recent discovery. Even though the implication was obvious, Frankie was still her brother. Finally she gave out a sigh and held up the cuff link. "I found something," she explained.

Adelle came closer. She gently took the cuff link and stared. "Where did you find this? Look, there are his initials." She turned the cuff link over for Josie to see. Her voice dropped, then she inhaled deeply. When she looked up, tears had formed in her eyes.

In the same moment all the facts lined up for Josie.

Always in a hurry, she thought. Like a squirrel looking for the next nut, she'd focused on the blood on the floor and the body, not on any other clues.

Plus Delgado had deliberately misled her by saying two men went in and two men went out. She must have seen Frankie and known that he'd not left with the chef and Elias.

Even if she wasn't lying, Delgado knew there was a back

entrance. Anyone could have come and gone without being noticed.

"We need to get back to that party," Josie announced. "I want to have a talk with the sheriff before Matron gets to him first.

CHAPTER FORTY-FIVE

Elias McCall opened the door to the Governor's Suite. Josie caught a flicker of amusement in his eyes. "Shouldn't she be downstairs working?" Elias nodded toward Lily, dressed in her Harvey Girl uniform. She turned her head away.

Josie nudged her friend forward. "Consider her the answer to a last-minute employee request. She's here to help with the party. I don't have time to explain. My investigation has taken an important turn."

He raised an eyebrow but opened the door wider. "Suit yourself," he sighed.

But Josie could see right away that he had that look her brother got when he knew to resist would be futile.

She quickly assessed the empty foyer. No one lingered for a quick shot from the bar. Voices floated from the adjacent room. "Lily, go over there. Pretend to dust something. Look busy but invisible," Josie instructed.

Lily rolled her eyes but grabbed a nearby napkin. She immediately began to wipe the surface of a crystal decanter.

"Adelle," Josie said gently, "go fetch your fiancé. Don't tell him anything dramatic, just say that I need a word. I'll be sitting on that stool by the bar looking cool, calm, and collected." She knew she'd feel anything but.

"Mateo will be irritated."

Josie wondered if Adelle was having second thoughts. Now that her brother might be arrested.

Adelle kept talking in a low voice. "Mateo doesn't like being pulled away from important people. Maybe I should warn Frankie. He's my brother, don't forget." Her tone was pleading. "He could get away if I tell him. Father will send him somewhere safe until this all dies down."

"No, that's not true. This isn't just a scandal; crimes don't die down." Josie felt sorry for Adelle, but she knew what needed to be done. "It's time for your brother to admit that he killed Bobby. We all have to own up and pay the piper eventually. Once the sheriff makes his arrest, Frankie will be put in jail, where he won't get into any more trouble. Then it's up to your father to hire him a good lawyer. No more excuses, Adelle."

Lily glanced in her direction. She gave Josie a nod of approval and then returned to her task of wiping the decanter.

Adelle raised a trembling chin.

"Go get Mateo," Josie said. "Leave the rest to me."

With both women given an assignment, Josie perched on the last stool at the bar. She did her best impression of a woman enjoying a quiet moment. *I'll pretend that I ducked away from the party for a cigarette.*

Her heart beat rapidly. She reminded herself, *I've cracked the case and now it's time to see justice served.*

At that moment Frankie rushed into the room.

When he saw Josie, he stopped short. He adjusted his collar, still wobbly on his feet. Josie took quick note of his cuff links. Both glinted at his wrists. She felt a moment of misgiving. *Did he already replace the missing cuff link with a new pair?*

The double doors from the terrace swung open. A cool breeze announced the entrance of Adelle DiWitt on the arm of Sheriff Cortez. The sheriff's expression, his grim countenance, gave Josie the evidence she needed. *Adelle has already told him about Frankie.*

"What's this about?" Cortez confronted Frankie.

"I have no idea." Frankie ran his hand through his hair. "I was just looking for another drink." His voice sounded thick, as if covered with dust.

"Mr. DiWitt dropped something at the crime scene, something you missed." Josie held out her hand. Nestled in her palm was the silver cuff link. The sheriff had a closer look, then returned it to Josie's palm.

Frankie's lips parted, face turning beet red. "That's not mine!"

"Odd. The link has the ranch logo. Like the pair you're wearing now," remarked the sheriff. He removed Adelle's hand from the crook of his elbow. His hand shot out to steady Frankie. "How did Miss MacFarland come by one of your cuff links?"

Frankie's tinny laugh made Josie shiver.

"Is this a joke? Misplacing a cuff link isn't exactly a hanging offense. I don't know how she found it, do I? I just met her tonight."

"I found that cuff link as a part of my investigation. In the room where Bobby Trask was found dead."

The seriousness of the situation finally seemed to dawn on Frankie DiWitt. He removed both cuff links from his shirt and handed them to the sheriff. "Have a look. A matching set. The DiWitt logo. The one she found doesn't belong to me. A cheap imitation. Those Natives. Always out to make a buck."

Cortez took the cuff links. He looked at the front, then the back. "These look like a matching pair," he told Josie.

Did I make a mistake? Josie wondered. *I was so certain that it was Frankie.* Her stomach tightened into a knot. She was ready to apologize but then stopped. Holding out her hand she said, "Why don't you see for yourself?"

Cortez took it between his thumb and forefinger to inspect both sides. He shook his head. "This one is different." He scowled at Frankie. "All three are the finest quality, not imitations. I know the artist, from the Naranjo family. You see here. Two have your initials. But one does not." He held it up for Frankie's inspection.

Adelle stepped in front of Mateo. "I bought that pair—the ones without the initials—for my father. I stored them in my jewelry box to wait for his birthday." She spun around to confront her brother. "Did you take them behind my back?"

Frankie's mouth hung open. He had a right to be shocked. It seemed Adelle was no longer going to be bullied into making excuses for his behavior.

Sheriff Cortez let out a low breath. "Mr. DiWitt, I think it's time for you and I to have a private word back at the police station. I have many questions."

Frankie's eyes darted to the doors leading to the terrace. In two strides, Elias McCall had him by the collar. He turned Frankie around and held his hands behind his back.

Frankie cleared his throat as if to protest. "At least let me grab another drink. I have the feeling this might be a long night."

The sheriff half pushed and half shoved him toward the door. "None of that. We're going to the station. Say adios to the ladies."

Then he turned to Josie. "Please come by my office early tomorrow morning. I'd like to discuss just how you got access to Trask's room and how you found the evidence. Every detail."

He slipped the cuff link into the pocket of his pants. The door shut behind Frankie and him with a heavy finality.

Josie exhaled, her shoulders finally releasing. "I'm parched. How about a glass of lemonade?"

But before she could even sit down, Lily was across the room with her arms outstretched, her eyes shining with tears. She pulled Josie into a fierce embrace.

"Thank you," Lily whispered into her ear, her voice trembling. "Thank you, friend. You saved me."

For the first time, Josie allowed herself to believe it. She'd done something right. She'd kept Lily safe and brought the killer to justice.

CHAPTER FORTY-SIX

"Miss MacFarland," the courthouse policeman greeted her. "Sheriff Cortez is waiting in his office. Come this way."

Now that's more like it. Ushered right in without an excuse. Josie found him sitting behind his desk.

"Good morning," Cortez greeted her. "Thank you for making time in your schedule." Before she could respond he asked, "Coffee?"

"I've already had mine," she replied demurely.

He shoved a paper toward her. "Down to business, then. I was able to interview Mr. DiWitt last night. He didn't confess to killing Bobby Trask. In fact, he was adamant that he was being framed. But I'm not surprised. The cuff links and his access through the back door of the room. Then his previous connection with the victim, including the bootlegging. Everything points to him.

"I spoke to Matron Delgado early this morning. She acknowledged that she saw two men leave Trask's room but that Frankie was not one of them. 'Three went in but only two came out' were her exact words."

Josie nodded. "So she lied to me..."

"The matron did say that she deliberately misled you. It must have been difficult for her. One must realize that finding a dead body at her hotel must have been such a shock. I can tell you that over the years, I've found Miss Delgado to be a reliable Harvey Company employee. She often shares her keen observations with me. Perhaps in time she will extend you the same courtesy."

Josie turned her head and bit her tongue. Once she regained her composure she explained, "The matron and I have a history that will never make her a reliable witness. Was she the one who suggested that you arrest Lily Davenport?"

"She was," he admitted. "Another mistake. I was prepared to accept her suggestion at the time. There was the matter of the murder weapon in her room. But then you kept insisting that Lily couldn't be the killer. After a while I had to agree. Even without Adelle's insistence, I could see for myself that Miss Davenport is a Harvey Girl through and through. Then, as you said, she had no experience with guns, and her temperament was not one of a killer." Now he looked grim.

"Good thing we sorted all this out." Josie smiled. She watched his expression when she used the word "we."

"We have our killer," he agreed reluctantly. "There's one more thing that may interest you. Frankie DiWitt confessed that he wrote that letter, pretending your services would no longer be needed. He claimed it was a prank." The sheriff cleared his throat. "A sad business."

"That makes sense," Josie said. "Such an unsuitable job... for a woman."

The sheriff nodded. "I have not changed my mind. But the Harvey Company hired you, so I must bow to their wishes."

And to their considerable influence on your election campaign, Josie thought.

"So we have the cuff link, the time of death, and the weapon," she said. "Plenty of evidence to convict Frankie in court, wouldn't you say?" When he didn't add his agreement, Josie kept talking. "The distinct pattern on the butt of the Smith and Wesson will convince a jury. Did the gun belong to Frankie?"

"Yes, he had one in his possession." Cortez looked away, unable to give her eye contact. *Probably embarrassed that he'd not seen that sooner,* Josie thought.

"Did Frankie tell you why he killed Trask?"

The sheriff looked surprised.

"Oh right. He didn't confess. How silly of me," Josie said. But she did have lingering doubts. Why wouldn't he just tell the sheriff everything? It would go better for him in the long run.

"This is not important, señorita," Cortez said dismissively. "Frankie doesn't have to confess. We have enough evidence." Josie knew this was her cue to leave.

But he had something more to add. "Quien se acuesta con perros amanece con pulgas," he replied.

Josie picked up one familiar word. Perros meant dogs. She quirked her eyebrow.

"Whoever lies down with dogs wakes up with fleas," the sheriff translated.

"That includes Bobby and Frankie." Josie deliberately left out Lansky's name. She watched his expression, wondering if he was willing to arrest the chef, a Harvey employee.

"My job is to arrest killers and keep my town safe, not to round up every man who knew Bobby Trask or Frankie DiWitt. There's no need for you to worry about any of this.

You kept the murder out of the papers. That's what you were hired to do."

Josie knew better than to press further. She stood to go. "Looks like we've completed this investigation then. I'll be reporting to my employer and packing my bags."

A huge smile overtook his face. "It's been a pleasure, Miss MacFarland. You solved your first case." He shrugged.

Josie couldn't quite put her finger on it, but something was missing in his praise. But it was time to get going. So she reached for the door.

"Adios, Señorita MacFarland."

"Adios, Sheriff." She closed the door, his low chuckle following her down the hall.

CHAPTER FORTY-SEVEN

After the short walk from the courthouse, Josie strolled inside the bustling Castañeda lobby. Two porters loaded bags onto rolling carts. Guests stood in clusters, train tickets in hand.

"Miss MacFarland," a voice called from the reception desk. "There's a phone call for you. Come around the desk."

Josie's curiosity flared. *Likely Adelle*, she thought.

"Hello, Josie MacFarland speaking." She spoke briskly into the receiver.

"So happy I caught you. The place must be a zoo this time of the morning," came a breezy female voice, not Adelle's.

Josie hesitated. "May I ask who's calling?"

"Your employer," came the crisp reply. "We haven't spoken before, but I wanted to thank you personally. You've done a remarkable job protecting my family's name and I couldn't be more pleased."

"Your family?"

"Oh, sorry I'm Katherine—Kitty Harvey. Granddaughter of Fred Harvey. Ford is my father. Perhaps you've heard of me?"

Josie blinked. She recalled that Fred Harvey had several children. That his son Ford had taken over the company after his father's death. "Hello, Miss Harvey," she said, feeling ill at ease.

"That's me, sweetie. I'm staying out in Abiquiu. I just love the desert air. And the company. I won't be coming to meet you. Too busy. I'm acquiring some art pieces for my collection. You can imagine the bickering. Anything to save a few bucks. Then I'll head back to California. Always something, isn't it?"

Josie wasn't sure how to respond. Miss Harvey's tone felt like gossip with a friend. But Kitty clearly operated in an entirely different world. Maybe her friendly tone was how she spoke to all of the Harvey Company employees.

Before Josie could gather a response, Kitty continued. "I've doubled your salary and hope you'll be available when I need you next."

Scratching came over the line. Then it went dead.

Josie set down the receiver, the conversation echoing in her ears. She waited, but no one called back. So she hung up the phone and stepped into the lobby, her mind whirling. *Double the pay. Another job...*

"Josie, darling!" Adelle's voice rang out over the din of people talking.

Just who I want to see, Josie thought. She turned, hoping to share her news.

It seemed by her appearance that Adelle had fully recovered from the previous evening's ordeal. Freshly powdered and primped, her plum-colored skirt looked spotless with her smooth silk blouse.

"I've just finished a late breakfast. Why don't you join

me for a cup of coffee? My treat. We'll share a slice of that piñon nut torte. A little celebration. You did such a marvelous job last night. Really I had no idea what a great detective you'd be."

Josie felt a little bowled over my Adelle's infectious energy.

"I'm off to California on the next train," Adelle said. "I heard from Kitty earlier. We're going to meet and then travel together.'

So they are friends, Josie remembered. "I'd love to have coffee," she responded.

"Just a moment." Adelle opened her purse. "Just checking to see if I have my itinerary. I don't want to miss my departure time."

Josie peeked inside Adelle's bag. Her cheeks flushed hot at what she saw. Tucked into the side pocket of Adelle's bag was a small Smith and Wesson handgun. One with a leather grip that included a crisscross pattern on the butt.

"Is that yours?" she asked, her voice low.

Adelle snapped the bag shut. "Of course, darling. My Smith and Wesson, made for me, a gift for my sixteenth birthday. Women who live in Las Vegas require a gun to protect their virtue. I thought I explained last night. The American Plan. You'd best get your own gun if you're going to stay longer."

Josie felt a rush in her ears. Before she could object, Adelle offered her elbow. "Come along now, Josie. No hard feelings. Let's have that coffee and I'll explain."

They walked toward the dining room in silence.

"It will take a minute to ready your table, Miss Diwitt," the Harvey hostess said. "Why don't you sit over here? I'll be right back when the table's ready to seat you."

An alcove with two chairs and a small table served as a makeshift waiting area.

Josie wanted an explanation about the gun. *Are there two identical ones? Maybe that would explain it.*

"Did your father give your brother the same kind of gun on his sixteenth birthday?" She hoped that was the case. Though Frankie hadn't said anything to the sheriff, if she remembered correctly.

When Adelle smiled, she noted a hint of apology. Why would she do such a thing?

The truth hit her, just like a thunder loud and overhead.

She wanted to duck and run, just as she had in the past. Taking a minute, she paused, feeling her nerves tingle. She stared at Adelle's face and swallowed. *I can't go now. I want to hear every detail.*

CHAPTER FORTY-EIGHT

Josie perched on the edge of her seat, her eyes fixed on Adelle's purse. "Did your father give your brother the same kind of gun on his sixteenth birthday?" she asked again.

She wanted, maybe needed, for Adelle to have one more chance to explain.

Adelle's low laugh felt like a scolding. "Oh, sweetheart. Boys in New Mexico get their guns long before girls do. Knee-high to a grasshopper. This is the Old West." She draped her skirt across her knees. "My gun? One of a kind. Unique. And I'm ever so glad to have it back in my possession."

Adelle's voice dipped into a more confidential tone. "Delgado found my monogrammed hankie on the floor next to Bobby's body. She knew I was in trouble right away. At first she planned on bribing me for money or influence.

"She withheld the hankie from Mateo. When he hurried to Bobby's room, he found my gun under the bed. Due to his quick thinking, he was able to remove the gun before anyone saw. Then he sent the body to storage."

Josie's breath hitched. "But I saw Delgado with your

handkerchief—the one with the C monogram—that first day. She acted as if it was hers. What was her plan?"

"He told me later that he was in such a hurry to cover up my involvement that he left my hankie. Then he remembered you were already in the storage room looking at the body. He didn't want to admit to Delgado he'd made a mistake. So he returned to the Castañeda to bargain with her to get it back.

"She was upset of course. Cried and cried when she learned of his plan to marry me. He convinced her that he'd keep seeing her after the wedding, so she handed over the hankie."

"That's the one he showed your father during dinner that night," Josie mused.

"Such a show." Adelle frowned. "But Father fell for it and gave me up. Just like that. Mother got the handkerchief back.

"After that Mateo got Elias to plant the gun and a Harvey House hankie in Lily's room. You were so insistent, kept following him—he had to move quickly. It all would've worked just fine, if only you'd given up and gone home.

"Miss Harvey House Detective," she said mockingly. "You wouldn't let Lily take the rap. Like a dog with a bone, you insisted she was innocent." She gave a theatrical sigh and crossed her arms. "You ruined everything."

Josie's jaw tightened. "So you decided to frame Frankie instead."

Adelle shrugged. "Mateo and I figured your curiosity might serve our purpose. I needed Frankie off my tail; he's so clingy, it's pathetic. With a bit of finagling, we came up with another plan."

Josie could barely take a breath.

Adelle continued. "With Elias's help—it took a little arm

twisting—he finally agreed to a blind date setup. He managed to lead you to the sheriff's office and steer you toward the ledger."

Josie remembered the exact moment. How Elias made everything so easy. Breaking into the sheriff's office. Finding the exact evidence folder. Pointing to the ledger with Frankie's initials.

"Elias planted that idea in my head," Josie whispered, more to herself than to Adelle. "That Frankie was also a suspect."

"After that, it was easy. I invited you to the Governor's Suite. I knew you'd poke around. When I suggested checking Bobby's room again, you jumped."

Adelle glanced at her nails. "You arranged for Lily to let us into Bobby's room. Quite convenient. I was prepared to ask Matron. But she exacts a price. Lily showed up for you because you're friends.' She looked at Josie in disbelief.

"Naturally Matron interrupted us. She's always there, Johnny-on-the-spot, the little know-it-all. While she was lording it over you and Lily, I slipped behind the screen and dropped the cuff link.

"I told you earlier, I bought a pair for Father and one for Frankie. The only difference was that I had Frankie's initials already engraved on the back. That turned out to work in my favor. So I took one of Frankie's—he'd never notice—and swapped one with Father's. A mismatched set which convinced Mateo, and even you, that he was guilty."

Josie's mind reeled. "Jeepers, Adelle. Your own brother." She remembered how sorrowful Adelle was when he got arrested. Tears in her eyes. What an act!

"Oh, who cares about him! Frankie gets everything he wants. He's free to go where he wants and do what he wants. I knew you'd jump to conclusions that it was his cuff link because you were already suspicious of him."

Josie saw now how she'd underestimated Adelle—her vanity, her cunning. The way she roped in Mateo and Elias to do her bidding. With the entire story explained, she didn't doubt for a second that the DiWitt debutante was capable of deceit and murder.

Adelle continued. "Mateo was waiting at the party for our return. He played shocked. I confirmed the cuff link, and just like that, Frankie was in the clink. I finally had a night to myself."

"Did a night to yourself include Mateo?" Josie wanted to know if Adelle had genuine feelings for the sheriff.

"My engagement was a means to an end, darling," Adelle said lightly. "Of course Mateo thinks it's real. But I only agreed to marry him because he blackmailed my father with my handkerchief. He said he'd arrest me otherwise. So, naturally, Father made a deal."

Her brittle smile sent a chill down Josie's spine.

"I'm the prize filly, remember. In answer to your question, I did not spend the night with Mateo. Daniel and I were together. What a man."

"Daniel..." Josie whispered. "Mateo will be crushed."

"No skin off my nose. I never intended to actually marry that man. A few months from now, after he's re-elected, I'll stage a very dramatic breakup." She raised the back of her hand to her forehead like a silent movie heroine. "I'll cry buckets. He'll act wounded. The public will eat it up."

She leaned closer, her voice laced with acid. "I've seen the way you look at him. You're not immune to his charms. But Mateo will still get what he wants in the end. Sympathy, standing in the community, and plenty of votes. A small price for my freedom."

The words hit Josie like a punch to the gut. Adelle DiWitt had used everyone, including her, to get her way. What price freedom? But there was something left unsaid, something in Adelle's tone, a hint of sadness.

"Adelle..." Josie hesitated. "You never said. What was the real reason for all of this? The gun. The lies. The cover-up. Why did you kill Bobby Trask?"

CHAPTER FORTY-NINE

Adelle's gaze dropped, her confidence faltering for the first time. Josie watched as she gathered herself, smoothing her skirt with the palms of both hands. When she finally spoke, her voice was stripped of its usual spirit.

"Bobby had been trying to trap me for over a year," she said quietly. "He'd grab me, corner me, force himself on me. I told him no. Repeatedly. He offered jewelry and favors. When he realized I didn't want my father finding out about my—how do I say it without making you blush...extracurriculars—he knew he had something on me.

"Suddenly I couldn't meet him at the church. He insisted that I come to his room. Always had a drink waiting. And if I got tipsy..." Her jaw clenched. "He wasn't a gentleman. That last night, I left my hankie on purpose. As an excuse to come back through the other door. I was ready to end it. One way or another."

Adelle's voice turned sharp. "He yanked me by the hair. Pushed me onto the bed. Unzipped his pants and said I could have the hankie, for a price. I kneed him hard. He went down, groaning."

She drew a shaky breath.

"My hand was on my purse. The gun was inside. I couldn't fire it. But I could swing. So I did. The butt hit his temple. He dropped. And I ran."

Silence hung between them, thick and bitter. Josie's skin crawled.

"My only regret?" Adelle's voice hardened. "Leaving the gun and the handkerchief behind. So unlike me. I'm Miss Cool, Calm, and Collected. But at least I was free of Bobby. The next problem will be Mateo. Not as bad, but in the end he wants the same thing." Josie swallowed hard. "What a terrible ordeal," she said softly. "But flaming Lily? Framing Frankie? You could've told the truth." Adelle's eyes flared. "What do you take me for? Don't you remember what I told you about the American Plan?" Her cheeks flushed. "Besides, I don't owe you, a priest, or anyone else a confession. If there's a God, he can punish me later." A waitress appeared. "Right this way, ladies. Your table is ready." Josie rose slowly, her mind spinning. No wonder Cortez had been distant when she arrived. He'd known about Adelle's secret. He was using it. *He thought he'd caught himself the perfect wife, someone who would bring status and, let's face it, beauty to his home.* The waitress seated them at a table for two. Josie's mind continued to whirl. Though Adelle's story brought her heartache, it didn't take away from the fact that she'd killed a man. Finally she found her words. "So you killed Bobby Trask. You covered it up and blamed Lily, then Frankie. You used me to make that happen. And I fell for every bit of your lie."

CHAPTER FIFTY

Adelle closed her menu. Her voice dripped, honey-smooth. "Oh, darling. Don't take it so personally. You know I'm not some butterfly to be pinned under glass. Not some man's pretty possession either. Bobby thought he could own me.

"You'll soon learn. Women in the West know the score. We aim to kill. It's them or us." Her gaze locked on Josie's, daring her to disagree.

Josie's thoughts spun out of control. She didn't argue. Didn't tell Adelle she was wrong. Instead, an image flashed in her mind of herself frozen in the middle of the tracks, the low *chugga-chugga* of the train growing louder as it rounded the bend. The whistle cut through the air, sharp and clear, and her whole body trembled.

Her legs shook beneath the table. Every part of her screamed, *Run!*

But then the moment passed and a quick thought came to mind about her fear. *I'm afraid...of failure.*

How I'll look to others—all of those people who paint women's success in certain terms: wife, mother, good Catholic. And don't forget the Harvey Company with their own set of rules. And after them, the sharp-eyed townspeople whispering in corners. For so long, I chased everyone's approval, let their expectations twist me into shapes that never quite fit.

Once she composed herself, her legs stopped shaking. She met Adelle's gaze. "I have learned," Josie said softly. Her voice didn't waver. "Just not the lesson you think. Maybe the real criminal won't get convicted." She paused to let that sink in.

I have learned that justice doesn't always prevail. That people are complex. That they believe their own story until it fails to serve them. And that your way of looking at the world doesn't have to be mine.

CHAPTER FIFTY-ONE

"Sit," Madame Liu said, gesturing to the small table by the door.

Josie obeyed. She felt numb, still having trouble summoning the right words. By the time the older woman returned with a pot of hot tea, Josie could barely lift her eyes.

"Bad day," Madame Liu said simply, setting the pot down. Without waiting for an invitation, she took the seat across from Josie and poured two cups. "Drink."

The fragrant steam rose, jasmine and something else Josie couldn't name. She took a cautious sip, then drained the cup. It was the first thing that had tasted right since the lemonade the night before. The memory of her thinking she'd solved the case only made it worse.

"I've been duped," she muttered.

Madame Liu didn't blink. She refilled her cup. "Have another cup of tea," she said lightly. Her tone melted into gentle laughter.

Josie managed a faint smile. "My employer said more work is coming." A trace of pride crept into her voice.

"She liked that I kept the Harvey name out of the papers."

Madame Liu nodded. "Good. Now you can at least afford to pay for my cookies."

"I didn't get the killer though. They arrested the wrong person."

"Ah." Madame Liu nodded. "The sheriff made his arrest. His job, not yours.

She doesn't seem too worried about my role in all of this, Josie realized. *Should I tell Madame Liu that Las Vegas's shining jewel, Miss Adelle DiWitt, is a cold-blooded killer?*

She looked across the table, hoping for some hint of what the older woman was thinking. Nothing. Then it dawned on her that of all the people, including Daniel, Lily, even the sheriff, it was this quiet shopkeeper who'd made her feel accepted.

"Madame Liu, have you ever heard of Sherlock Holmes? I need to tell you what happened. Will you be my Watson?"

"I have read Conan Doyle," she replied crisply. "And I refuse to be your Watson. Madame Liu stood abruptly. "I'll get fresh tea and cookies and be right back. Now that you're done with that investigation, I want to hire you to help me.

"Your discretion is of the utmost importance."

Josie couldn't believe her ears. "Is this a favor?"

The corner of Madame Liu's mouth quirked.

"That depends. If you pay your tab, then I ll negotiate a monetary reimbursement. But only if you get the job done to my satisfaction."

Josie felt relief bubble up from her chest. She watched Madame Liu disappear behind the beaded curtain, her mind a whirl with anticipation.

"Another case."

Maybe this means I'm a real detective now...

AUTHOR'S NOTE

Author's Note

One step into the lobby of the Castañeda Hotel in Las Vegas and you know you're somewhere special.

Maybe it's the old train depot nearby. Maybe it's the Southwest architecture and the scent of mesquite drifting on a dry desert breeze. Or maybe it's the life-sized poster of Judy Garland dressed in a crisp Harvey Girl uniform, clean, efficient, and ready to take your order.

I was instantly transported back to childhood: my mom and me on the sofa, a bowl of popcorn between us, watching *The Harvey Girls* on TV. We'd sing along, "On the Atchison, Topeka, and the Santa Fe," with loud, joyful voices. It was more than a film; it was a moment of connection.

That memory stayed with me. So did the stories passed down from my mom, my grandmother Josephine, and her sister Adelle. Three women shaped by the Great Depression. None were Harvey Girls, but they carried the strength and seriousness of women who had weathered hard times.

AUTHOR'S NOTE

Their stories, their resilience, and their love inspired this series.

I selected 1929-1930 time frame for this story to capture the years between the world wars. The soldiers had returned from "over there," reclaiming their lives—at least until history called so many back decades later. In the meantime, the world changed. Prohibition, the stock market crash, and the rise of youth culture opened up something unexpected: possibility. Especially for women who dared to leave home in search of independence and purpose.

Josie MacFarland is not a Harvey Girl, at least not anymore. She was fired during her first year for not quite fitting in. When we meet her, she's returned to the scene of her greatest failure, only this time, she's someone entirely different. In this reimagined story, Josie is a detective hired by the Harvey Company to solve a murder at the Hotel Castañeda.

You might wonder: Why not make her a current Harvey Girl? The answer, in part, comes from historian Lesley Poling-Kempes's excellent book *The Harvey Girls: Women Who Opened the West*.

When Poling-Kempes began her research, she asked a Southwestern newspaperman what he thought of the Harvey Girls. His reply? "They weren't important. After all, they were only waitresses."

But the Harvey Girls were so much more.

Something rarely discussed but addressed in *An Unsuitable Job* is the suspicion many Harvey Girls faced in the very towns where they lived. Some were branded as immoral or worse. That perception was fueled, in part, by a government program known as the American Plan.

Initially created to combat venereal disease in US troops during World War I, the American Plan often became a tool to police and persecute women especially those seen alone in public or who didn't meet arbitrary standards of "respectability." As Adelle tells Josie, women could be pulled off the street, forced to undergo invasive exams, and held indefinitely, without trial and without cause.

The long shadow of that era meant that many Harvey Girls kept their stories quiet. Even decades later, the stigma lingered. Their uniforms may have been clean and pressed, but their reputations had been soiled by suspicion.

And yet, so many of these women became community leaders, business owners, educators, and trailblazers. They helped settle the Southwest with grit, grace, and hard work. That's why I had no trouble imagining a different story: What if the Harvey Company had its own detective in the 1930s? Josie MacFarland came to mind immediately, named after my grandmother, Josephine.

For more about the real women who inspired this story, I highly recommend Poling-Kempes's book. And if you're curious about the American Plan, I suggest *The Trials of Nina McCall: Sex, Surveillance, and the Decades-Long Government Plan to Imprison "Promiscuous" Women* by Scott W. Stern.

In the meantime, go ahead and pop some popcorn. Settle into your favorite chair. And join Josie MacFarland as she steps back into the Castañeda. Not as a waitress but as a woman determined to find the truth.

I hope you all enjoy Josie's adventure into the Southwest and that you, too, will always remember to "Think for self."

Bonnie Hardy
January, 2026

PIÑON NUT TORTE WITH HONEY-LAVENDER CREAM

Inspired by the flavors of the
American South West

Ingredients:
For the Torte Crust:
1 ½ cups all-purpose flour
½ cup unsalted butter, chilled and cubed
¼ cup granulated sugar
1 large egg yolk
2–3 tablespoons ice water

For the Filling:
1 cup piñon nuts (pine nuts), lightly toasted
¾ cup light brown sugar
½ cup heavy cream
3 large eggs
1 teaspoon pure vanilla extract
½ teaspoon ground cinnamon
¼ teaspoon salt

PIÑON NUT TORTE WITH HONEY-LAVENDER CREAM

Honey-Lavender Cream

Ingredients:
1 cup heavy cream
2 tablespoons honey
½ teaspoon dried culinary lavender
(optional: finely ground)

Instructions
Torte Crust:

1. In a large mixing bowl, combine flour and sugar. Cut in the butter using a pastry cutter or fork until the mixture resembles coarse crumbs.

2. Add the egg yolk and ice water, 1 tablespoon at a time, until the dough holds together when pressed.

3. Shape the dough into a disk, wrap in plastic wrap, and refrigerate for 30 minutes.

4. Roll out the dough on a lightly floured surface and press it into a 9-inch tart pan. Trim the edges, prick the bottom with a fork, and chill for another 15 minutes.

5. Preheat oven to 375°F (190°C). Blind bake the crust by lining it with parchment paper, filling it with pie weights or dried beans, and baking for 15 minutes. Remove weights and bake for an additional 5 minutes until lightly golden. Set aside.

Filling

1. Reduce the oven to 350°F (175°C).
2. In a mixing bowl, whisk together brown sugar, heavy cream, eggs, vanilla, cinnamon, and salt until smooth.

3. Stir in the toasted piñon nuts.

4. Pour the filling into the prepared tart crust and bake for 25–30 minutes, or until the filling is set and golden brown. Cool completely before serving.

Honey-Lavender Cream

1. In a small saucepan, gently heat the heavy cream with honey and lavender until it just begins to simmer. Remove from heat and let steep for 10 minutes.

2. Strain the lavender (if used) and chill the cream in the refrigerator.

3. Whip the chilled cream until soft peaks form.

To Serve

Slice the torte and serve with a generous dollop of the honey-lavender cream. Drizzle a bit of honey on top for extra sweetness and garnish with a sprig of lavender or a few piñon nuts for an elegant touch.

BOOK GROUP DISCUSSION GUIDE

Welcome to the discussion guide for *An Unsuitable Job*, the first Harvey House Mystery featuring Josie MacFarland. This guide includes discussion questions and a historical sidebar to spark conversation. Whether you're meeting in person or online, we hope it adds depth—and a dash of vintage intrigue—to your book group.

Josie's Independence

Josie chooses a profession—and a life—that defies expectations for a young woman in 1929. Where do you see her longing for independence intersecting with fear or doubt? Did you relate to her desire to be seen and valued?

"Unsuitable"—According to Whom?

Throughout the story, Josie hears that detective work isn't a "suitable" job for a woman. What does "unsuitable" mean in Josie's world? In your own life, have you ever been told you were "unsuitable" for something?

Historical Realities: The Great Depression

Economic instability shapes everyone's decisions in the novel. How did financial insecurity influence the characters' choices? Did you see echoes of today's challenges in their struggles?

Found Family vs. Blood Family

Josie finds unexpected allies at the Castañeda. How does this "found family" compare with the family she left behind? Which relationship resonated most with you, and why?

Setting as Character

The Castañeda Hotel and Harvey House culture are deeply rooted in history. How did the setting influence your experience of the story? Did it feel like a character in its own right?

Justice vs. Reputation

Some characters would rather protect their standing than reveal the truth. Have you ever witnessed a situation where protecting appearances mattered more than doing what was right?

Josie and Sheriff Cortez

Their relationship is layered—tension, respect, suspicion. How did their dynamic evolve? Do you trust him? Why or why not?

Courage in Small Acts

Josie's most courageous moments are often quiet and intentional. What moment demonstrated her deepest courage?

Women's Work

Harvey Girls were expected to be compliant, polished, and proper. How does Josie disrupt that expectation? What expectations about "women's work" still linger today?

The Cost of the Truth

Who paid the highest price for the truth to come out? Did the ending satisfy your sense of justice?

Power of Belonging

Josie longs for a life where she can be fully seen. How does this longing shape her choices? What gives you a sense of belonging?

Historical Sidebar for Book Clubs

The American Plan (1917–1930s): Under this U.S. policy, women could be detained without evidence if authorities suspected them of being "promiscuous," "immoral," or believed they might carry a sexually transmitted infection. They could be held in institutions, examined, and denied due process—simply for being in public without a man or for working in certain professions. The policy disproportionately targeted young, single, and working-class women.

A woman could be arrested not for what she did, but for how she appeared.

The American Plan

The American Plan—a real U.S. policy targeting women under the guise of "public health"—appears in the novel. How did learning about it affect your reading experience? Did it change how you viewed the constraints imposed on Josie and other women of the era?

Bonus Question — For Fun

Cast the Film: Who would you cast as Josie? Lily? Sheriff Cortez? Bobby Trask?

ABOUT THE AUTHOR

Bonnie Hardy, a retired professional turned author, is celebrated for her expanding mystery universe set in California's mountain and desert landscapes. Her cozy Lily Rock Mysteries follow amateur sleuth Olivia Greer, known for her uncanny ability to draw out confessions from the most unlikely people, while her Redondo & Rose: Neighbors in Crime series transports readers to Palm Desert, where mentalist Rex Redondo and his grounded next-door neighbor, doula Vivienne Rose, uncover secrets in the sunbaked desert. Bonnie's newest historical mystery series begins with "An Unsuitable Job," introducing Josie MacFarland, a former Harvey Girl turned private investigator in 1929 New Mexico. Against the backdrop of the elegant Castaneda Hotel, Josie becomes the first-ever "Harvey House Detective," navigating a world that doesn't welcome women in charge. Inspired by Agatha Christie, Bonnie's tales of mystery and community masterfully blend fast-paced whodunits with clever sleuthing, rich emotional undercurrents, and the enduring spirit of women who won't be underestimated.

- facebook.com/bonniehardywrites.com
- instagram.com/bonniehardywrites
- bookbub.com/authors/bonnie-hardy
- goodreads.com/bonniehardy

www.ingramcontent.com/pod-product-compliance
Lightning Source LLC
LaVergne TN
LVHW040043080526
838202LV00045B/3460